ON THE LAM

BY CLABE TAYLOR

ON THE LAM

Copyright © 2013 by Clabe Taylor

A Spymasters Literary Guild Series Book

Clabe Taylor Enterprises

www.clabetaylor.com

www.spymastersguild.com

ISBN 978-0615930312

Printed and Bound in the United States of America

"We have met the enemy, and he is us."

Pogo the Possum, 1971.

Prologue

I never expected to be on the lam at my age. Certainly not with a degenerate Mexican ex-con riding shotgun and a flatulent Blue Heeler in the back seat. They say the truth is sometimes stranger than fiction, and now I believe it. Fiction, after all, is what got me into this mess in the first place.

You see, I write spy novels for a living. Classic good guy versus bad guy stuff. Black and white, no nuances or shades of gray. If I had lived in the nineteenth century, I would have written those western dime novels starring ruggedly handsome cowboys and stunningly beautiful women with plunging necklines and enormous boobs.

My novels have never made *The New York Times* Bestseller list, but I do have a small cult following of loyal readers, who eagerly await each and every bit of new drivel I put to paper. My publicist happens to be one of them. Of course, her loyalty is suspect. She might not be such an avid fan if I didn't visit twice a month to have sex with her. Call me a whore if you want, but I consider it marketing. It's just part of the job.

Writing hasn't made me rich and famous. Far from it, actually. Some months I spend more on my publicist than I make from book royalties. But somehow I manage to make the monthly payments on my used Ford pickup, and I'm usually able to maintain a minimal stash of chronic and Nicaraguan rum to keep my creative juices flowing.

I trace my current dilemma back to the phone call I received from my libidinous publicist last October. At the time I was listening to the Texas Tornados and sucking on my new vaporizer, a gift from a former CIA colleague of mine, who decided he'd rather spend his time surfing and smoking weed in Central America than playing shuffleboard and writing his memoirs for his grandkids. When my smart phone's custom ringtone exploded with the shrill Mexican *grito* of Pedro Infante's *"He Nacido Mexicano"*, I almost pissed my pants. I was that stoned.

"Clabe, is that you?" I recognized the sultry voice of my Cuban-American publicist and imagined her sitting in a lounge chair on the balcony of her South Beach condo, pleasuring herself as she spoke to me. Not that I consider myself such a sex symbol that the mere thought of me would lubricate her private parts, mind you. She's just that horny. Come next tax season, I'm going to write off my Viagra purchases as a business expense. It's either that or use a splint on my member to satisfy her insatiable appetite for sex. At her age, not to mention my own, such behavior is unseemly.

"*Hola*, Carmen," I answered. "*¿Cómo estás, mi amor?*" She loved it when I spoke Spanish to her. My accent made everything sound dirty, she always said. I took that as a compliment.

"Clabe, I have something for you."

Oh no, I thought. She's going to make me have phone sex with her. In my current state of elevated consciousness I didn't know whether I could come up with the proper vocabulary. I walked over to the kitchen sink, ran some cold water into one hand, and splashed it on my face. I desperately needed to concentrate.

"I finally got what you've been waiting for," she said.

"Hmmm," I said, stalling for time. I was mystified and took a sip of my Cuba Libre and reached down for the vaporizer mouthpiece.

"Clabe, are you there?" she asked. "You're not smoking pot, are you? You promised."

"*No, mi amor...para nada*[1]," I reassured her. "Just thinking about you."

---

[1] No, my love...no way.

"I hope not," she said. Carmen was always trying to make me stop smoking weed and drinking. She was afraid it affected my sex drive.

"You're killing me with the suspense," I said. "What are you talking about?"

"Listen, I've got you a spot on 'Fox & Friends'. They want to talk with you about your spy novels and the Mexican drug cartels," she said, already breathing heavily, probably from the thought of me in my designer Ralph Lauren boxers, paring down my yellowed toe nails with a dull Swiss Army knife.

"Are you serious?" I asked. "What happened to those lame internet blogcasts you normally book me on?"

"What can I say, *amorcito*? You're moving up in the world. Your last book obviously caught someone's eye besides your usual pothead fans."

Now that WAS hard to believe. I had written my second novel about the War on Drugs during a brief period in my life when I took myself seriously and had reduced my intake of both cannabis and alcohol, a mistake I later recognized and corrected. I cited my brief stint as a CIA officer, hired Carmen as my publicist, and brazenly touted myself as an expert on border security issues and the drug war. The results were unexpected. The book sold. First a hundred copies, then a thousand, then ten. Before

I knew it, I had earned enough money in royalties to afford a veterinarian for my gassy Blue Heeler. A psychiatrist for my own maladies would have to wait.

"They have a sister station in Dallas. Can you make it to their studios tomorrow morning?" she asked.

I was vaguely disappointed that there was to be no phone sex, but the thought of finally appearing on television as a major-league talking head had its appeal. Maybe this was the break I had been waiting for.

"Yeah, I'll be there," I answered.

Chapter 1

"Sweet Jesus!" I exclaimed as I opened my eyes at 5:30 the next morning to the jangling of one of the last mechanical alarm clocks on the planet. Two things came to mind immediately. First, I must have been more sober the previous evening than I thought if I was able to set the alarm clock. But secondly, I realized that sobriety is a relative concept because I had a raging hangover the likes of which I hadn't experienced since at least the previous Saturday.

Some things mellow with age, but hangovers aren't one of them. They become even more beastly, and that was exactly how I felt. A quick shower and shave only partially restored my humanity, and I grabbed a Shiner Blonde from the fridge as I took my Blue Heeler out for his morning rounds. Over the years my rule for the timing of the first drink of the day had become more and more flexible. Ten years ago I would never have considered a drink before 5:00 P.M. Then it was 4:00, then 3:00, and before you knew it, noon somehow had a righteous ring to it. Not long after that, I decided that my artificial time constraints were nothing but a cowardly adherence to bourgeois conformity, and I began having my first drink with breakfast.

That bold decision took a lot of pressure off me. My health improved, and my cheeks took on a rosy glow that I hadn't seen in a mirror since I was a toddler, waddling around the house in diapers. There was a kind of natural harmony and balance to that realization since I knew that in a few years I would be back in diapers, waddling around the house again and dribbling like a leaky faucet.

The cold beer hit the spot, and I belched. My cow dog cocked his head at the sound and glanced at me, but he wasn't one to let anything interfere with his enthusiastic search for fresh animal droppings. That Blue Heeler ate shit with a relish that warmed my heart. The year before, I had been horseback with him running at my side on a 10,000 acre ranch in northern Wyoming. The country was wild, and I knew the land was crawling with animal life. The dog knew it too. When he ran across some bear droppings in the trail, I didn't have time to call him off. He scarfed up the berry-sweet hors d'oeuvres with alacrity and a deep appreciation for the finer things in life. For him that wilderness trail was a five-star Parisian restaurant.

I didn't expect Carmen to trust me to make it on my own to the studio in Dallas, and sure enough my cell phone rang as I was loading the dog into the back of the pickup truck.

"Clabe, I hope you're out of bed and on your way to Dallas," said my publicist in her thickly accented English. It was an hour later in South Beach, and I knew she'd be standing in front of the full-length mirror on her eighth-floor balcony, admiring herself in her satin nightgown as the sun streamed in through the cascading red and white bougainvillea.

"*Buenos dias*, Carmen." I did my best imitation of a seductive "good morning" as I drove down the driveway of the Texas ranch where I rented a tiny guesthouse. Lush pastures of green Coastal Bermuda lined the gravel driveway, and purebred black Brangus cattle grazed serenely on either side of the fence. "I'm on my way. Don't worry, I'd never let you down."

I said that hoping she wouldn't remember my last visit to South Beach. She had insisted we go salsa dancing, and I don't know whether it was the late hour, or the ungodly number of mojitos we had drunk, but by the time we got back to her condo, and she had dug out her favorite sex toys for an evening romp, there was no chance of coaxing any excitement out of my insubordinate whacker. It looked like a dangling piece of limp rope. That's one thing you can't fake. I pleaded a headache, but Carmen knew the truth and never let me forget it.

There's a fine line between consuming enough alcohol to be able to overlook her sagging flesh and vague halitosis and imbibing too much and humiliating oneself with the specter of early-onset impotence. In my case it actually wouldn't be that early. I seem to miscalculate and upset that delicate balancing act more and more as time goes on. Soon I'm going to have to choose between the consumption of alcohol and fornication, and it's going to be a close call.

I drove through Fort Worth on I-30 and then the mid-cities on Highway 121. My cow dog rode in back of the pickup and glared threateningly at the passengers and drivers of vehicles we passed. I hope nobody looked at him askance. That mean sonofabitch had bitten more people than I'd been able to count, and he was known to jump out of moving trucks just to give chase to an errant cow or a vagrant Mexican. He had developed an unhealthy obsession with Latinos that was hard to explain. He hated them. I had an unapologetic racist for a dog. I'm glad he wasn't able to discern my own anarchic political leanings. He was a control freak and would not have appreciated my relativism. I probably should have tied him in back before I left, but my head was pounding too much for rational thought.

I managed to open a jar of generic ibuprofen with one hand and threw a handful of the little orange pills into my mouth and washed them down with a couple of greedy gulps from my second Shiner Blonde. They'd be kicking in by the time I got to Dallas, and a gentle beer buzz would mellow my adolescent urge to outrage the television audience, something I knew would be sure to cross my mind at precisely the wrong moment.

I peered out into the maw of existential suburban despair that stretches without interruption for over 9,000 square miles around the Dallas-Fort Worth metroplex. I felt the jackboot of middle class conformism exerting pressure on my medulla oblongata. Judging by the churning in my stomach, though, it appeared more likely that the vomiting center of my lower brainstem would be activated soon. I swigged more of my cold after-breakfast beer to calm my queasiness. Mercifully, we approached the Dallas skyline and the nausea subsided. Big cities make me nervous and claustrophobic, but at least when I'm in Dallas I don't want to puke from the sheer futility of life like I do when I drive through Euless and Bedford.

I slowed down in Dallas and took an exit towards the looming skyscrapers wondering what the topic of the day would be. I was already a minor talking head, a frequent guest on neo-conservative talk shows although rarely invited back for repeat performances after voicing some very non-neoconservative views on foreign policy and the War on Drugs. It was my resume that secured the invitations, though. The letters "C-I-A" in this day and age aroused intense curiosity even in the least sympathetic scenario and often awe and respect. Now I was finally going to be on national TV. I hoped I didn't blow it.

I left my pickup in one of the many parking garages in downtown Dallas and made my way along a busy sidewalk towards the high-rise where the studios were located. My Blue Heeler walked at my side, his head almost touching my knee and growling incessantly at passersby. People saw the odd-looking beast from a distance and gave him a wide berth. A Blue Heeler is a feral breed of dog, part Dingo and part English sheepdog, or so the story goes. In reality, the breed is a study in misplaced aggression, stubbornness, and loyalty so intense that the dogs should be registered as deadly weapons, and convicted felons should not be allowed to own one.

I entered the high-rise that matched the address Carmen gave me, and I heard my name called.

"Mr. Taylor?" A dreamy feminine Texas drawl pronounced my name with more sex appeal than I thought humanly possible. I turned to my right expecting to see a vision of Texas loveliness, but was disappointed to encounter a stocky, crew-cut lesbian with a clip board under her arm. She walked up to me and shook my hand in a vice grip worthy of an NFL linebacker.

"Have you been drinking, Mr. Taylor?" she asked suspiciously, sniffing the air in front of me with an expression of unfeigned disdain on her manly features. "Isn't that a violation of the terms of your probation?"

Damn, I thought. I hate the internet. Big Brother is always watching, and you cannot escape the nosy motherfucker. She had obviously run my name through some data base and learned my deepest darkest secret. So I had a record. Big deal! Ours is an Orwellian world populated by willing snitches and cyber stalkers. And we think it's normal.

"Just behave yourself now," she said. "Follow me and don't let your dog piss on the carpet."

I meekly followed her to a bank of elevators. The doors opened, and we stepped in. My dog promptly farted out loud.

"Mr. Taylor!" she exclaimed.

"It was the dog," I insisted.

She rolled her eyes.

"Please, I've heard that before," she said as she covered her nose with her hand and turned away from us.

I looked down at my dog and wanted to kick his sorry ass. He looked at me and wagged his tail. It wasn't a promising way to launch my new career as a nationally known author and television personality.

Chapter 2

I was on the air for no more than two minutes although I'm told that this is normal for a "talking head" television appearance. That was more than enough time to establish several truths. The "Friends" obviously were a bunch of serial douchebags with the possible exception of the blonde, who I'm positive had spent a fortune on plastic surgery and breast implants.

"Mr. Taylor, you've acquired what can only be described as a cult following of readers, but your books have yet to go mainstream. They have not been received well by the critics, and the government is threatening to prosecute you for the unauthorized disclosure of classified material. How do you respond to that?"

Half of that was news to me, but I couldn't let on that the "Friends" knew more about me than I did. I wasn't even sure which one had asked the question. I was too busy checking out the blonde's legs on the video monitor. That was a complex juggling act that required a lot of multi-tasking concentration. I wished I had brought one of the cold Shiners into the studio. The ibuprofen was kicking in and my headache was receding, but the early morning beer buzz was fading fast. I've often thought that sobriety is an evil that needs to be confronted with boldness and courage. Both of those qualities were rapidly evaporating in the hot glare of the studio lights.

I reached down and caressed the ears of my Blue Heeler while desperately thinking of an appropriate response. The government is threatening to prosecute me? What the heck for? That whole book was a figment of my imagination. The inspiration for the plot probably came from the synergistic effect of the testosterone supplements I washed down every day with copious volumes of Shiner and Dos Equis. I hadn't had access to classified material for over twenty years. Did this asshole know something I didn't?

"Listen, fuck the critics and the federal government," I blurted out and immediately regretted my choice of words. I could imagine the loud bleep in the five second delay, and I saw the "Friends" cringe.

"The government prosecutors must be smoking some of the ganja they've confiscated from the medical marijuana dispensaries in California if they think my books contain any classified material," I continued. "I wrote a novel. Last time I checked, that means fiction."

The blonde chimed in.

"The Department of Justice claims you might have revealed classified information regarding sources and methods. How do you respond to that accusation?" she asked and peered into the monitor with what I perceived to be an overtly sexual interest. Of course, that's how I interpret any glance from a female, no matter how casual and no matter the age, race, or shape of the subject. I was corrupt and debased. I knew it but had no remedy for the malaise.

"Gretel," I responded and hoped I had gotten her name right. "If I revealed classified information in my last book by claiming the vice president of the United States was in cahoots with the Sinaloa drug cartel, then I'm guilty. Prosecute me, convict me, and sentence me."

"From what I understand, it may come to that," she said mysteriously and leaned forward in her chair ostensibly to adjust the sheaf of papers in her hands. But I swear she did it on purpose to show me some cleavage. I hope the television viewers at home appreciated it as much as I did. This was an area of my undisputed expertise. She must have been aware of my reputation. A brief examination of that cleavage was all I needed. I visualized those gazongas and liked what I saw. Don't ask me how I can do that. It's a gift. Divine omniscience, if you will, and I'm never wrong.

"What are you working on now, Mr. Taylor?" she asked.

Here we go. Just what I was waiting for. My chance to plug my new book deal.

"*The Ganja Times* has agreed to publish my next novel in serial format," I responded. "I'll be sending them an episode every other week."

"Can you give us a hint of what the book is about?" she asked.

"Let's just say that in my new novel the Russians get cozy with the Mexican drug cartels and form an alliance of convenience," I responded, giving just enough information to tantalize any potential readers out there.

Holy shit! I saw the disaster unfolding in slow motion a few seconds before it actually happened, but I was distracted by Gretel's cleavage. If my reactions had been quicker, I probably could have stopped it.

A Mexican studio technician with a light meter had caught my Blue Heeler's attention. The poor trusting fool kept pointing that light meter at us and inching forward, closer and closer to where we sat. My dog began to whine softly and growl. I instinctively sensed what was going to happen. It was a law of nature. Like a child who's just learned to walk, and who invariably totters into the only mud puddle for miles around, the only Mexican in the studio blithely moved in our direction, unaware of his proximity to a vicious canine racist. The result was predictable, and the incident took place as if the scene had been carefully scripted for a Hollywood movie.

The dog sprang at the technician, who had approached to within six feet of my chair, and attached himself to the Mexican's Achilles tendon, shaking his head back and forth and snarling like the Hound of the Baskervilles.

"*Chinga tu madre!*" the Mexican screamed in terror, throwing his light meter into the air and trying desperately to get away from my Blue Heeler. Women screamed from behind the set. Producers shouted in anger. The Mexican staggered into view of the video camera, dragging one leg behind him with the dog's teeth embedded deeply into the back of an expensive designer cowboy boot. I saw his horrified face on the TV monitor and the shocked faces of the "Friends". Then the screen mercifully went black.

Chapter 3

A uniformed security guard with a shaved head and goatee grabbed me roughly by the elbow.

"Sir, you need to leave now," he said.

"Is the interview over?" I asked innocently. I felt someone take hold of my other elbow, and two storm troopers began to frog-march me towards the bank of elevators. My Blue Heeler growled threateningly and advanced on the two meatheads with the hair on his back bristling. The guards let go of me in a panic and drew their handguns.

"Call off your dog or we'll shoot him!"

The situation was rapidly careening out of control, and only fast thinking and some serious diplomacy could diffuse the crisis and prevent a case of cold-blooded murder. I knew that a plea of self-defense would never work for a Blue Heeler.

"Anyone got a beer?" I asked hopefully.

"Get out!" screamed a producer from behind the enclosed control room. The sound was distorted and the PA speakers screeched with feedback. The entire studio staff stared at us with condemnation in their eyes. My dog and I had morphed from the exalted status of talking-head stars into pariahs of the worst sort. I felt dirty and morally unclean. I tried to maintain as much dignity as possible as I walked with my Blue Heeler at my side into a waiting elevator, cursing Mexicans, lesbians, and the slings and arrows of outrageous fortune.

As the elevator doors closed, the last thing I saw was the lesbian giving me the finger, her face twisted in anger. On the elevator ride to the lobby I had time to think about my life, and how I had probably screwed up my one and only opportunity to break out of the bonds of literary obscurity.

Something stank about the interview, though, and what the "Friends" said about the government planning to prosecute me. How could they know I was under investigation if I didn't? What dastardly conspiracy was afoot? But even more importantly, what was my crime?

Firing up the occasional blunt was barely considered a crime even in Texas, and certainly my habitual use of Nicaraguan rum did not even rise to the level of a misdemeanor. Disclosure of classified information? That simply wasn't possible. I was writing fiction. My books were the product of an overactive and possibly deranged imagination, but I hadn't seen a classified CIA cable in several decades. I read the news, extrapolated, and put it to paper. That's all there was to it.

I was so shaken by that piece of information that I didn't pay much attention to the two suits on either side of the lobby sitting nonchalantly in faux-leather couches and pretending to read copies of the *Dallas Morning News.* My Blue Heeler did, though. He hated cops and could spot them a mile away. Actually, he hated anything that didn't fit into his vision of the world, and these two looked about as out-of-place as Rush Limbaugh in Speedos at the Iron Man World Championship in Hawaii. The dog growled, and I called him to my side.

From the parking garage I drove to the nearest convenience store and bought a six-pack of Shiner. As the Sri Lankan manager cashed me out at the counter and watched in surprise, I opened the twist-cap top of one of the bottles and chugged the contents without coming up for air.

"Sir, you cannot drink here," said the Sri Lankan in his lilting accent.

"Obviously I can, sir," I responded, matching his politeness with my own version of civility. "I just did."

I tossed the empty bottle in the trash can on the sidewalk in front of the convenience store and surveyed the street. It had been a lifetime since the CIA trained me in countersurveillance techniques, but it was all coming back to me in a rush of long-dead memories and beer-saturated adrenaline. The beer helped me to relax and focus. I saw a generic white Ford sedan parked about fifty yards down the street, and I swear two heads ducked out of sight when I glanced their way. The two suits from the studio lobby? Jesus! Maybe the "Friends" were right and I really was a person of interest in a federal investigation.

I drove at high speed away from Dallas and the scene of my latest debacle and flew through the mid-cities in a blur. When I got back to my house west of Fort Worth and took a walk in the north pasture of the ranch, I swear to God I saw the same white Ford sedan parked in front of a doublewide trailer on the adjacent property. This was getting out-of-hand. Had the feds set up an observation post on my neighbor's land? Did they have my house bugged, and were they using that trailer to receive burst transmissions of the recordings?

I returned to my house and hit the Shiner with a vengeance. When the beer alone failed to calm my paranoia, I took out what was left from a half-gallon of Flor de Caña rum and mixed a Cuba Libre to enhance the numbing effect of the beer. I've found over the years that beer chased with rum (or is it the other way around?) has a profoundly calming effect on my psyche and can actually nip a panic attack in the bud. And speaking of bud, I filled my vaporizer with what was left of my rapidly dwindling stash and fired up the latest scientific advance in cannabis consumption.

Soon my thinking had crystallized into a series of possible exit scenarios, and I focused on my dilemma. I realized what I had to do. There really was no choice except to flee. Despite my certainty that I had broken no laws, I knew the feds didn't care about nuances. The absence of a crime? That was completely irrelevant if they had a hard-on for their target. As the Russians used to joke, "Just give me a body to arrest, and we'll invent the crime."

Those bastards! I couldn't leave without letting them know they were dealing with a formidable adversary. I refused to bend over and take this Big Brother intrusion into my private life without a fight. I needed to send them a message.

My Blue Heeler followed me with his eyes, tracing my every step. If I left one room and went to another, he was by my side. I was grateful for his loyalty and knew I would need his companionship if we were to survive the next few days together. The ordeal was going to be intense.

I rummaged through my kitchen and garage, looking for components that would make a loud bang and produce a lot of smoke. I rejected out of hand the possibility of using my shotgun and SKS assault rifle. The SKS was for scaring off stray dogs, nothing more. I would usually fire it into the ground at their feet just to scare them. I couldn't kill anything, not even a pesky armadillo. When I was a kid, I used to ply the Guadalupe River in a motor boat shooting water moccasins. Even that made me feel guilty. The feds didn't have much to worry about, I realized, but I did know how to create a distraction.

I would set their car on fire. That would be the plan. Eliminate the possibility of pursuit! The simplicity of the plan was brilliant. I first packed my truck with essential supplies including all the hard copies and digital files of my work. It made sense to remove the evidence. Then I measured a cup of powdered swimming pool chlorine into one side of a large envelope and measured an ounce of Brylcreem into the other side. I grabbed an armful of newspapers and headed towards my target.

I couldn't remember if I had learned about the combustible mixture in the paramilitary course I took at the Farm, or if I had stumbled upon it while researching explosives on the internet for one of my novels. At any rate, I was armed with the highly flammable mixture, and all I had to do was mix the ingredients, wad up the newspapers, and stuff them into the top of the gas tank. It was a pyromaniac's dream. The newspapers would spontaneously burst into flame and ignite the gasoline fumes producing a massive explosion. Or so I hoped. I would haul ass back to my house, innocently get in my truck with my dog, and hightail it for parts still unknown. The plan was the essence of distilled operational genius. I felt as if I were back in Moscow during the Cold War, meeting agents and putting down dead drops. I popped another Shiner and drained half of it for inspiration.

I low-crawled to the fence separating the two properties, picking up a fair number of grass burrs and cactus thorns in the process but intent on reaching my objective without being seen. My heart pounded with excitement, and I flinched every time a twig popped or a branch broke. I needn't have worried, though. The watchers were in a festive mood. I heard muffled laughter and the discordant sounds of music. The feds were partying and not likely to notice my surreptitious approach.

My plan went off without a hitch. I reached the car, unscrewed the gas cap, and inserted the newspaper like a bulky fuse and stuffed it in as far as I could. Then I crushed the envelope, mixing the synergistic ingredients. I ran back towards my house, all thoughts of stealth far from my mind. I wanted out of there before the surveillance car blew sky high.

As I raced down the long driveway in my truck to the Farm-to-Market road that passed in front of the ranch, the FBI surveillance sedan exploded in a red and orange ball of fire. As I turned right and accelerated towards Fort Worth, I looked back and saw the eerie silhouette of my house, backlit by the flames engulfing the FBI car. I mashed on the accelerator to put some distance between me and the towering fire. I knew I had to ditch the truck. It probably already had a homing device on it, but even if it didn't, every police car in the state would be looking for it within the hour. I had blown up a government surveillance vehicle and was allegedly the subject of a federal investigation for other unspecified and possibly more serious crimes. The day that had begun with such promise had gone to hell. I was on the run.

Chapter 4

There was only one man in the entire country I could turn to for help. A man who hated the United States government with the same passion as he loved the Dallas Cowboys and old reruns of *The Lone Ranger*. He identified with "Tonto", and the reruns fed his deep animosity towards America, which he viewed as racist and reactionary.

Gustavo "Goose" Rivera was a former Mexico City lawyer who used to handle corporate law issues for the Sinaloa Federation. He did five years in the medium-security federal prison at El Reno, Oklahoma for laundering money on behalf of the drug traffickers. Now he mowed lawns, mucked out horse stalls, and drank way too much tequila and Tecate, usually in that order. He was my closest neighbor, and we played chess every Thursday night. Goose had won the El Reno chess championship during his stint in the slammer and loved to humiliate me. The way he announced "check" and then "mate" was pompous, and the all-knowing look in his dark, basilisk eyes was condescending. But Goose was also the owner of an old rusty Chevy Silverado pickup that I desperately needed.

"You did what, you stupid *culero²*?" he shouted when I told him what had happened. "*¿Estás loco³?*"

"I had no choice," I explained. "They were closing in on me."

"So now what?" asked Goose. He had been cleaning stalls all afternoon and smelled like manure. I put my hand to my nose in disgust.

"You smell like horseshit, Goose!" I said accusingly. "Why don't you go take a bath, and I'll put my things in your truck."

"Horseshit?" he asked. "No, take a deep breath. That's what life smells like, bro. Nothing wrong with Mother Nature."

I couldn't argue that fact. Goose took off his reeking clothes and headed for the bathroom. I heard him turn on the water in the shower, and I went to the kitchen and reached in the fridge for a bottle of Tecate. I used a spoon to leverage off the cap and took a deep draught. Mexicans had learned how to brew beer from the Germans, and most of their brands put *gringo* beer to shame. I emptied the bottle and started unloading my pickup.

---

² Asshole
³ Are you crazy?

My Blue Heeler was waiting for me in the truck. I had to tie him up to keep him from going after Goose. I was afraid Goose one day would tire of his antics and shoot him. Besides, today I didn't want to offend my Mexican friend. I needed his Chevy.

"Rigo," I said, addressing the dog by his name, short for Rigoberto. "You stay away from Goose today, will you? He's my friend and your behavior embarrasses me."

Rigo wagged his tail and whined. I couldn't trust him, though. He was known for acting friendly towards an unsuspecting Mexican and then biting him on the heels when the Mexican turned his back. If I hadn't seen Rigo attack dogs twice his size, I would think he was a coward. But he was just stealthy. Like a predator stalking game.

"What's the plan?" asked Goose as he emerged naked and dripping from the shower. That was a sight I certainly didn't need to see. I closed my eyes tightly and tried to exorcize the vision from my brain. Goose had more Spaniard in him than Indian, and he was one hairy motherfucker. Naked, he looked more like Sasquatch than a human being. He also had the unnerving habit of stroking his uncircumcised penis as he strutted around naked in front of me. It must have been a habit he acquired in the prison showers at El Reno. He was proud of the fact that he was uncircumcised. He claimed it gave him almost an extra inch in length. I promised to fill Goose in on the plan after we hit the road and finally convinced him to put on some clothes and to pack a small suitcase.

We stashed my truck in his barn and headed towards Fort Worth in his Silverado with Rigo growling in the back seat. Goose kept glancing at him out of the corner of his eye. The dog made him nervous and I didn't blame him. Rigo was demented, deceitful, and he had no morals.

"Why are the feds after you?" demanded Goose as we drove east on I-30 towards Fort Worth.

I was at the wheel. In Texas a Mexican is five times more likely to be pulled over by the police than an Anglo. Of course, he's at least five times more likely to have committed a crime, but let's not split hairs. Profiling is a bad thing, right?

Goose knew all that, and he didn't mind the implication of my driving. He knew I loved him like a brother. When I called him a "Greaser", I said the word with *cariño*, with love and tenderness. Same as when he called me a "*pinche gringo*[4]". No, you had to see beyond Goose's occasionally crude verbiage to ascertain the depth

---

[4] Damned gringo

of his affection and loyalty. His deeds spoke volumes. Like the time he held my head as I vomited up my dinner of *enchiladas verdes* and tequila on the dance floor at Billy Bob's when even the two Mexican hookers we hired left in revulsion. That was love and devotion.

"Why are they after me?" I repeated his question. "You mean besides me blowing up their surveillance car?"

"Yeah, why were they following you to begin with?" asked Goose in Spanish. His English was pretty basic and generously sprinkled with prison jargon and colorful obscenities, which he didn't even understand. After I explained to him one day that "punk ass bitch" was not an acceptable form of address in English, he spoke mostly Spanish with me.

"Something about me revealing government secrets in my novels," I said. "It's ridiculous!"

"If it's not true, why are you running?" asked Goose. His grandmother had been a schoolteacher in an impoverished village in the Sierra Madre, and Goose had inherited her propensity for logical thought.

"Ha, that's a good one, Goose," I said. "Since when do the *federales* need a reason to put the screws to someone? You should know that better than most people. Maybe they just need a fall guy for some reason."

"But why pick you? No, something's going on." Goose had more street sense than anyone I knew, and when the conversation turned to crime and punishment, I listened to him like an acolyte listens to a Catholic priest; in awe of his knowledge, but on guard and conscious of the danger of being sodomized.

"What kind of crap are you writing now?" he asked. "More fairy tales about the drug cartels?"

"I'd describe my novel in somewhat different terms," I answered defensively. I knew Goose hadn't read any of my books, and so I didn't take offense. "I'm writing about a fictional alliance between the Sinaloa Federation and the Russians."

Goose did a double-take and his jaw dropped. I didn't like the look on his face, and I pulled off the interstate into the RV camp on I-30 just west of Weatherford. I got out of the truck, reached into the cooler in the pickup bed, and opened two beers. I gave one to Goose.

"What gives?" I asked.

"Where did you hear about the alliance?" he asked.

"What are you talking about? I made it up," I said.

"Like hell you did," said Goose. He shook his head, locks of thick black hair falling into his face and covering his eyes. He brushed his hair back with his hand. "*¡Ay, caray!*" he moaned.

Pieces of the puzzle started falling into place. I looked at Goose's face and the truth hit me like a sledge hammer.

"Jesus! You don't mean...?" I couldn't even finish the question.

"Yes, I do," said Goose.

"But how?" I asked. "How could it be true?"

"Antonio Salcido is ambitious," he said as if that simple statement contained the answers to the myriad of questions that flooded my mind. Salcido was the head of the Sinaloa Federation, and his megalomania was legendary.

"But I'm writing fiction," I insisted. "I haven't had access to classified information for thirty years."

"Then you are one clairvoyant sonofabitch," Goose said. "We're fucked!"

Chapter 5

That was powerful language even coming from Goose, who usually couldn't express a single thought without using a string of obscenities for punctuation. "Fucked" is an emotive word. It evokes images of Armageddon and the Apocalypse, but it has to be used sparingly, or it loses its punch. I knew what Goose meant, but I figured he was employing a bit of artistic license, engaging in hyperbole, or maybe just trying to frighten me. But when I looked in his eyes, I knew he was spooked. I could even smell fear in his perspiration.

A shadow passed over his face, and I looked up to see a turkey vulture flying low just over our heads. Was this an omen? I normally wasn't superstitious, but when I heard the hollow flapping of the buzzard's wings, a chill ran down my spine. Maybe we WERE fucked.

"Since when have you been scared of the U.S. government?" I asked. "You handled your five years in the Big House pretty well, I'd say."

That was an understatement. The federal prosecutors and the FBI had put pressure on Goose to testify against his co-conspirators. He told them to bugger off; in Spanish, of course. They threatened him with twenty years and even put him in solitary confinement for six months to intimidate him. In protest, Goose stripped naked in his cell and refused to eat. The feds weren't used to a nude Mexican inmate on a hunger strike. The hacks complained about the sight, and the FBI eventually relented and put him back with the general prison population. In the end the judge refused to go along with the prosecutor's demands for a life-ending sentence, and Goose did his five years with dignity and had been a law-abiding citizen ever since.

"Law abiding" is a relative concept, of course. I always suspected Goose had regular sex with the ewe he kept penned near the barn, but I couldn't prove it. The ewe always glanced at him with fear and loathing in her eyes. But I always figured a man's sex life was his own private business. Who was I to criticize Goose? Indelible images of Carmen in one of her many kinky sex outfits riding me like a deranged Muppet were etched forever in my memory. I had contemplated filing sex abuse charges against her, but I wasn't underage, and I knew she would argue that the sex had been consensual. Besides, she was my publicist, and there are some things you just have to do to make it in this world.

"I'm not scared, you moron," answered Goose. "The U.S. government is the least of our worries now."

Goose drained his beer and looked at me as if I were a slow student and he a teacher at the end of his patience.

"You mean....?" I started to ask.

"No shit, Sherlock," he said acerbically, switching to English and using a colloquial expression correctly for once. "Let's hope Antonio Salcido doesn't watch Fox and Friends."

"¡Puta Madre[5]!" I exclaimed.

Of all the luck. I happen upon a clever plot idea for a thriller, and it turns out to be the truth. I understood why the drug traffickers would be pissed that I let the cat out of the bag, but I wasn't sure why the USG would want to keep the news under wraps. How were they involved anyway? The government was protective of its secrets, but very selective about prosecuting for unauthorized disclosure. If it suited their plans, they would go after the bean-spiller with a vengeance. But only if their target couldn't fight back. The feds pick their fights carefully. Maybe that's why they had chosen me to pick on. I laughed out loud. I had no illusions of being a tough guy.

"What's so funny?" asked Goose.

"Oh, nothing. I'm just day dreaming," I answered.

---

[5] Spanish equivalent of "Holy Shit!"

"Day dreaming?" Goose asked. "At a time like this?"

He drained his beer and took another. He screwed off the top and tilted his head back and drank with purpose. I felt guilty that I had burdened Goose with my problems. Like a brown recluse spider luring a juicy insect into her web, I had taken an unsuspecting and innocent ex-con trying to live a righteous life and turned him into an unwitting accomplice, an accessory to serious crimes. When Goose cast his lot with me, he exposed himself to "aiding and abetting" charges at the very least. In a worst case scenario, he might join me on the hit list of the Sinaloa Federation. He was right. We were buggered.

"So, I'm afraid to ask. What happens in your book?"

"Well, it's going to be published in serial format. I've only got the first couple of chapters written," I answered.

"And what the *chingada* [6] is going to happen?" Goose raised his voice. He was losing his patience with me, and I don't blame him. He had probably planned to spend a quiet day drinking and staring at the wall, and I had barged in and dragged him off to become a wanted

---

[6] In this context: "What the fuck?"

man; pursued by both the USG and the most powerful drug cartel in Mexico.

"So far I've got the Russians providing the cartel with a small attack submarine," I confessed. "I'm not sure where I'm going to take it from there."

"¡A la verga[7]!" cursed Goose. He threw the beer can as far as he could. I knew he was angry because he hadn't even bothered to empty its contents. Foam spewed in all directions as the can flew through the air and then rattled across the gravel lot where we had parked his truck. He turned towards me, and I swear I thought he was going to throw a punch. I steeled myself for the blow, but it never came.

"What possessed you to write about a Russian submarine?" he asked.

"Why not?" I asked. "It's a catchy idea for a thriller. The cartel has been using little submergibles for years. They park them in little coves and rivers and bring them out when they need them to deliver a load of coke. Having the Russians custom-build one for them would just be a logical progression. Geometric extrapolation. It was a good idea."

---

[7] Oh shit!

"We're dead men!" Goose screamed at me, his eyeballs threatening to pop out of their sockets.

"What the hell are you talking about?" Now I was getting riled, and I shouted right back at Goose.

"You know damn well what I'm saying," he said and looked at me ominously. "You *gringos* can put a man on the moon, but you can't add two and two and get four."

At times I could be a little slow on the uptake, but the truth eventually began to sink in with the finality of a case of herpes.

"No!" I choked, and for once my glib tongue failed me miserably.

"Yes!" he shouted and ripped open his shirt revealing a chest so hairy I wondered if Goose was really human.

"Go ahead and shoot me," he screamed. "Pierce my heart with a silver bullet, you fucker. I curse the day I ever met you!"

Mexicans can get melodramatic, but I had never seen Goose so wound up. I slapped him hard across the face to get his attention. He fell silent and sheepishly buttoned his shirt with the one button that still hung precariously by a single thread.

"Sorry," he muttered. "It's just that I was beginning to enjoy life."

We climbed silently back into the truck and continued on our way. I knew that if Goose was right, our chances of survival in the long term were slim to none. But how could I possibly have known that the Sinaloa Federation had really acquired an attack submarine from the Russians? The coincidence strained credulity. It was uncanny.

"Goose," I started to ask, breaking the silence as we kept to the speed limit traveling east on I-20, skirting Dallas to the south.

"Don't talk to me," he answered still pouting.

I glanced over at Goose and couldn't believe my eyes. That tough old Mexican had tears streaming down his face. He was sobbing like a baby.

"Goose," I said, trying again to smooth his ruffled feathers. "Tell me you're joking."

"*Qué pendejo eres[8]*," he muttered again and again under his breath.

Before long we left the DFW metroplex behind us and continued east. I figured that keeping to the interstate was probably the wiser strategy. We'd run into

---

[8] What an asshole you are

fewer police cruisers on the back roads, but in the Texas hinterlands a weeping Mexican ex-con riding in an old beat-up pickup truck with an intoxicated, crazed Anglo at the wheel was likely to attract attention. About eighty miles east of Dallas we passed the "Billy the Kid" museum on the right. I read the sign that sat precariously on top of the dilapidated building.

"WHO SHOT KENNEDY?" the sign asked. Ah, yes. Conspiracy theories. The world loved them. Especially the kind where the government was scheming against the people, and the wealthy and powerful from different continents conspired to control the world. Had I accidentally stumbled on one of those conspiratorial scenarios? Could this really be happening? I looked at Goose's tear-stained face and began to whimper softly.

Chapter 6

I don't know why, but I began to breathe easier when we crossed the Texas border into Louisiana just west of Shreveport. As if leaving Texas afforded us some degree of anonymity or made us harder to locate. That was delusional, I knew. The feds could find us no matter where we were, and I suspected they were already looking for me. Still, it was a relief to cross the state line.

The Mexican radio stations had begun to thin out, and the absence of shrill Mariachi trumpets and Mexican voices yammering and wailing out of tune was foreign to me. When the fundamentalist ravings of on-the-air evangelical ministers replaced the soothing sounds of *Los Tigres del Norte*[9], something profound happened to me. I crossed some ethereal boundary of sanity and descended into a hellish redneck nightmare out of a Faulkner novel. I missed Texas already.

Still, we had to go on. Home had become a dangerous place, and the more distance we put between ourselves and Texas, the better. Or so I thought. We drove silently through the night, and in the wee hours of the morning as we approached Monroe, Louisiana, I heard

---

[9] Popular norteño band

an insane preacher on FM radio. He howled in ritualistic cadence and worked himself into a frenzy about hell and damnation and the consequences of not accepting Jesus as one's Savior.

I could just see the crazy bastard frothing at the mouth in the studio. What an act! I sat at the wheel of the truck transfixed and in awe of his genius. I listened for a half hour and only turned off the radio when the greedy preacher began to ask for money. I was disappointed. He was just another entrepreneur, a salvation huckster. He peddled Fire and Brimstone to an audience that needed his dire warnings and prophetic admonitions to keep them from crossing the line into moral depravity. In this part of the country I figured that just meant incest.

"Why'd you turn that off?" asked Goose.

"It makes me sick to hear preachers sell Jesus for money," I answered. I thought Goose was asleep, and I was surprised he had been listening to the preacher.

"Nothing's free in this country," he said. "The preacher needs money to broadcast his message."

"He's a fake," I insisted.

Goose sat up in the passenger seat. A passing car illuminated his face with its headlights, and I could see he was angry.

"Have you no soul?" he asked. "That man spoke from his heart."

"It's a put-on," I said calmly. "He spoke from his wallet. He knows what his audience wants to hear, and he gives it to them. Just like what I give my readers."

"Oh yeah? All twenty of them?" Goose was an insensitive bastard. That was a low blow.

"There'll be more for this book," I told him. "A national magazine is going to publish one chapter every other week. It'll be like the old-time serial novels. I'll be giving out autographs in malls soon."

"You won't live long enough to enjoy your fame," he claimed. "The drug cartel will decapitate you with a chainsaw. Maybe during a book-signing in one of your malls."

Goose had a point. Maybe I should welch on the contract with *The Ganja Times* and put this all behind me and write children's stories about Golden Retriever puppies that grow up and protect their owners from speeding ice cream trucks. I would make a public announcement. Let the government and the cartel know I had changed my mind.

"So if I don't write the story, you think they'd leave us alone?" I asked.

Goose looked at me indulgently. Like an older brother or a kind uncle.

"And you're supposed to be an expert on the drug cartels," he scoffed.

"Come on, Goose. I got to make a living somehow. I know a few facts."

Yeah, I read Borderland Beat and *El Blog del Narco* and had memorized some statistics. I was aware of the general trends, but Goose had lived it and had been in contact with some major players; even in the Big House.

"If you don't write the book, they'll still kill you. Because you ratted them out. You mentioned the alliance and the submarine. If it was me, I'd kill you too. "

"So why not go ahead and write? It might make life interesting. The little bit I have left, that is."

"Because if you don't write the story, they might leave your family alone. Otherwise, they'll kill them too."

I laughed out loud, and Goose looked at me again like I was crazy. He was doing that more and more as the trip went on.

"What family?" I asked. I had never spoken to Goose about my private life, and he didn't know I was divorced and had no children.

"You're all alone?" he asked, sympathy creeping into his normally acerbic tone. I glanced at him, and I swear his eyes were all teary.

"It's okay, Clabe, we have each other." He patted me on the shoulder and began to massage my neck with his huge hand.

"Hey, cut that out!" I cried and leaned towards the door to get away from his caress.

"Ha, you're not only an imposter, you're a homophobe," he declared. "Or maybe you're just afraid to show your emotions. You really should see a therapist."

"Someone should," I said.

Goose just shook his head in pity. He thought all Anglos were emotionally stunted.

"Go ahead and write the story," he said. "Like I said before, we're screwed no matter what we do. We'll go out in a blaze of glory. Like Bonnie and Clyde."

I figured Goose had seen the movie at El Reno. Occasionally his knowledge of American pop culture surprised me, but lately he preferred Spanish-language films and had a soft spot for the dark, perverted themes of Pedro Almodóvar. They were more in character, I guess.

Goose was a morose motherfucker in the best of times. Now, with the U.S. government and possibly a

Mexican drug cartel after him, he fell into a deep funk and didn't say a word to me for the next several hours. Several times I heard him mutter in Spanish, and once I thought I heard him cry for his mother. I empathized with the ugly brute. Sometimes late at night when ghoulish thoughts invade my inner peace, I just long for a full belly and a warm place to sleep. But when a Mexican ex-con who resembles a werewolf starts sniveling in the passenger seat next to me, I realize how tenuous life is and how we all just hang from a thread. It was unnerving.

Rigo must have sensed my unease, and he jumped into the front seat between Goose and me, growling at his nemesis, and laying his head in my lap. He gave a contented fart and went to sleep. Goose grumbled, and cracked the window, but Rigo's proximity made me feel more secure, and I drove on through the dark Louisiana night knowing I had at least one friend in the world who wouldn't abandon me.

Sometime after midnight I pulled into a rest area outside of Vicksburg, Mississippi. I couldn't keep my eyes open any longer. The beer, weed, and the stress of learning that my life was careening to a bad end had taken their toll. I needed to sleep for a few minutes.

I slipped the automatic transmission into "P" and got out and stretched. Rigo jumped out after me and promptly cocked his leg on the tire of a Lexus sedan that was parked next to us.

"Sir, could you control your dog, please?" An irate middle-aged woman in the Lexus rolled down her car window and icily voiced her request in pseudo-polite terms.

"Sure, sorry about that," I replied and whistled for Rigo, who promptly ran to my side and sat. I forgot all about the woman and was trying to loosen up my hamstrings. They were tight after so many hours in the truck and my ass hurt.

"Sir, you're supposed to have your dog on a leash. It's the law."

The same voice. Her tone slightly more exasperated than before. I ignored her and walked around to the back of the pickup and rummaged through the cooler in search of a Shiner. Goose had begun to stir and slid out of the truck. He cursed loudly in Spanish and groaned. Rigo followed me and sat obediently, watching Goose with concern. I knew Rigo wouldn't tolerate him approaching me, and Goose had the good sense to stay away.

"Sir, are you drinking and driving? That's not allowed in Mississippi," the woman volunteered. "If you won't put your dog on the leash, I'm going to call security and report you."

At two o'clock in the morning with a head full of zombie and stale beer on my breath, my patience with the woman was wearing thin. But I didn't want her to call security.

"Sorry, Ma'am, it's been a very long and difficult day. Are you a believer, by the way?" I asked suddenly.

The woman perked up.

"Yessir, I am. I found Jesus 50 years ago when I turned seven," she promptly responded.

"Then maybe you'll understand my plight," I said. I took a deep breath and wondered what pious claptrap was coming out of my mouth next.

"I'm the lead singer of a Praise Band," I began. "We call ourselves 'Rock n' Roll Hosannah'. Today we played a gig at the First Methodist Church in Shreveport, and we were heckled by a bunch of atheists. I'm pretty sure they were Democrats."

"You poor boy!" the woman exclaimed.

"I bore witness in front of the congregation, and we drove the heathens from the House of God!"

"Amen!" she said. "The Lord was with you." She raised both arms with her palms up. I knew I had struck the right note with her.

"Praise the Lord," I responded. "My drummer lost consciousness and fell to the floor, his whole body twitching like a dying catfish. It must have been the Holy Spirit." I nodded my head in Goose's direction. He was walking around the front of the truck, and his silhouette appeared suddenly out of the dark. The woman gasped.

"Don't feel sorry for him. He bears his physical affliction with grace," I said.

The woman stared at Goose and then looked to me for reassurance.

"But it's been a stressful day, and I've succumbed to temptations of the flesh. I've sinned. I drank beer to relieve the stress of seeing those godless liberals blasphemy and ridicule my faith. Can you ever forgive me?"

The woman approached me and embraced me enthusiastically.

"I already have. Bless you," she said. "You are doing the Lord's work."

I felt the woman's breasts press against my abdomen, and I felt a stirring in my loins. This could get awkward, I thought.

The woman felt it too, and she pulled away from me suddenly. She looked at me curiously but then smiled and got back into her car and drove away. I breathed a sigh of relief. We had dodged a bullet. Carmen would have been proud.

Chapter 7

All three of us got a couple of hours of fitful sleep at the rest area despite Rigo's incessant farting and Goose's snoring. Next time I have to make a run from the feds, I'll be more discerning about the traveling companions I choose. So far all the vet's remedies for Rigo's severe flatulence had proved ineffectual. An invisible yet potent cloud of rancid stink enveloped that dog most of the time. Goose himself was a walking time-bomb. It was only a matter of time before he lost it and went off on a drunken rampage leaving destruction and mayhem in his path. I'd seen it happen too many times before.

"What state are we in?" asked Goose as he woke up and stifled a yawn.

"Mississippi," I answered and headed toward the restroom with Rigo at my side.

"Is that near Alabama?" asked Goose as he slammed the pickup door and hustled after me.

"Sure it is. Don't you know U.S. geography?"

"I know where Texas and Oklahoma are," Goose replied. "Where's Alabama?"

"Right next door to Mississippi. We'll be there in a couple of hours. Why?" I asked.

"I know a place in Alabama where we can lie low for a few days if we need to," he replied.

Goose wasn't joking, and I perked up. We needed a place to stay other than a motel. We couldn't use credit cards on this trip for security reasons, and very few motels would take cash and ask no questions these days. I was wary, though. If Goose was suggesting a place to crash, there must be strings attached.

"I won't stay in a whorehouse," I warned.

"Not a bad idea," he said. "Too bad we're not in Mexico. Whorehouses everywhere."

Goose was untrammeled by the conventions of society and was partial to whorehouses. I knew why. He had married a 16-year old prostitute in Durango right before he got arrested and extradited to the United States. He always was proud of the fact that she chose him to marry. He used to brag that she was just a neophyte prostitute and had been with fewer than one hundred men. In his eyes that made her almost a virgin. He was devastated when she remarried even before he was sentenced.

"You have friends in Alabama?" I asked.

"Not really. My mother lives there," said Goose.

"Your mother?" I asked. Now that was news. Somehow it had never crossed my mind that Goose even had a mother. My mind wasn't capable of making that great leap in evolutionary logic to picture Goose as a suckling human baby caressed and adored by a loving mother. Somehow I couldn't give up the image of a baby with Goose's leering eyes, thick moustache, and week-old growth of heavy beard. Not exactly the kind of baby that politicians would stop to kiss. They'd be more likely to stuff him, put him in the Smithsonian, and claim they'd found the missing link.

"Yeah, she's a cook at a trailer park for migrant workers," Goose explained.

"Does she look like you?" I asked, trying to hide a smirk.

"No, I got all the looks in the family," Goose responded with a straight face. I think he was being serious.

I had forgotten it was Sunday morning, and the rest area was filling up rapidly with middle-aged Southerners; the menfolk in cheap polyester suits and the women in flowery cotton dresses. I assumed they had just gotten out of church and were on the way to Luby's for chicken fried steak and mashed potatoes smothered in milk gravy. At least that's what they would have been doing in Texas, but I didn't think the Luby's franchise extended all the way to Mississippi. Judging by the waistlines of the locals, though, they definitely had a source of super-sized meals and high-fat food somewhere nearby.

Everyone gave us a wide berth in the men's room and on the sidewalk back to the truck. Maybe word had gotten around about the hard-luck Praise Band, but the looks we got did not seem entirely sympathetic. One enormous woman with calves the size of redwood trees gave us a self-righteous "Hmmmmph!" and turned away as she passed us. We weren't looking for any more confrontations, and I decided to continue our trek east towards Alabama. I reached in the cooler in the bed of the pickup truck and was grateful to see that our supply of Shiner would probably last till the liquor stores opened Monday. I didn't think our chances of scoring cold beer on a Sunday in the Deep South were very good unless we went to a NASCAR race. We unscrewed the bottle caps and each guzzled a half-bottle to jumpstart the day under the disapproving gazes of several matronly women and their docile husbands. I swear those poor sons o' bitches looked at us with envy.

Most Southern men, I'd always observed, were cowed by their women and forced into a pathetic form of psychological bondage that gradually emasculated them. I had noticed the same phenomenon back home in Texas and always wondered how the badass hell-raisers that settled Texas back in the early 1800s evolved into the church-going, pious eunuchs of today. I thought about that as we pulled out of the rest area and eased into the Sunday morning traffic on the interstate. The subject could make intriguing material for a future book or at least an internet blog entry.

"Do you have an address for your mother?" I asked Goose.

"Yeah, I've got her phone number too. She's expecting us," he said. "We're going to have *cabrito* [10] tonight!" Goose licked his fingers and smiled in anticipation.

"You called her?" I asked.

"Yeah, I borrowed your cell phone while you were asleep," he admitted sheepishly and handed it back to me. "Sorry, I won't do it again."

I looked at the scrap of paper he showed me and saw the address of the trailer park located near Auburn, Alabama not far from the Georgia border. It sounded good to me. I needed some time to finish the first chapter of the new book and email it to *The Ganja Times* before the

---

[10] Baby goat meat

rapidly approaching deadline. I had less than twenty-four hours to submit the final version of Episode One.

We crossed the Alabama state line about fifteen miles east of Meridian, Mississippi. I was on my third beer since the rest area, and Goose wasn't far behind. We were both hungry, and we searched the billboards and green interstate signs for a suitable eating establishment.

"I want some chicken," Goose declared.

"Fried?" I asked

"Yeah, and some mashed potatoes and gravy," he added.

"No tacos or enchiladas?" I asked.

"There you go with your racial profiling again," admonished Goose.

Goose was a scoundrel with a set of truly eclectic views on life. He thought it was perfectly normal for the Sinaloa Federation to put me on a hit list, but he looked down on me when I refused to knuckle under to the anti-free speech PC agenda. Profiling was one of his pet peeves.

"Where were you born, Goose?" I asked, trying once again to insert reason into the conversation.

"Durango, Mexico."

"So you're Mexican," I said.

"And?"

"And Mexicans eat enchiladas and tacos," I reasoned. "That's why they call it Mexican food."

Goose vehemently shook his head.

"No, you're a racist," he declared. "No doubt about it."

I saw a sign for a Chick-Fil-A restaurant and took the next exit off the interstate. Maybe Goose would mellow a little with a full belly. I didn't even catch the name of the little town we entered. It didn't matter. Chain restaurants and stores had gobbled up the character and soul of small-town America. Each town looked the same, no matter where you were. Except for the predominance of enormous waistlines and bloated faces in this little town, which narrowed our geographical choices, we could have been anywhere in the country. Wherever you looked, you saw familiar names: McDonald's, Burger King, Home Depot, Office Max, Best Buy, Sonic, and the list went on and on. Small town America was dead. Hell, it was even getting hard to find a "Beer, Bait, and Ammo" store, even in the South. I pulled into the Chick-Fil-A parking lot, aware that I was a shameful co-conspirator and accomplice in America's rush towards its own destruction.

"You stay in the car with Rigo," I said to Goose. I didn't want to attract any more attention than necessary, and I preferred that my Mexican sidekick stay out of sight.

"No way," Goose objected. "That schizophrenic bastard will bite me in the ass as soon as he loses sight of you."

Goose slid off the passenger seat and followed me into the restaurant. I felt every eye in the place glued to us. Mothers gathered their children to their skirts while I translated the menu into Spanish for Goose who was oblivious to the attention he attracted. We took our bagged food out to the truck and ate while Rigo whined and begged for a piece of chicken. Fifteen minutes later we were on the interstate again, heading for an Alabama trailer park inhabited by migrant workers and a rendezvous with Goose's mother. I looked forward to meeting the lovely woman.

Chapter 8

As we approached Montgomery, Alabama I was scanning the available FM radio stations and ran across the "Rick & Bubba Show". At first I thought it was a spoof. Like something in a Saturday Night Live skit or a clever bit from an improv comedy club act. The name itself made me laugh out loud, and I temporarily forgot about our rapidly deteriorating chances for survival.

I could just picture two fat-assed southern rednecks behind the microphones, dressed in stained white t-shirts eating Moon Pies and swilling RC Cola. They weren't serious political commentators, but as I listened, I realized these guys were making sense. If you took away their over-the-top southern accents and their "good ol' boy" delivery, Rick and Bubba's arguments were reasonable and well thought-out. Especially when you consider the mélange of conservative views they were obligated to espouse, most of which are damned difficult for a judicious person to defend. Bubba and Rick weren't hemmed in by their own ideology or narrow-mindedness, and that was a rarity in political discourse nowadays; on both sides of the aisle.

Goose tried to listen as well. He had no problem understanding their accents. He had rubbed shoulders with white rednecks in the slammer and was used to their drawls, but these two yahoos were not talking about drugs or pussy which initially threw Goose off. His English vocabulary had been stunted by his exposure to prison society.

"I don't get it," he suddenly announced in Spanish.

"Get what?" I asked. I was almost afraid to hear what was coming next.

"Bubba says if the government restricts his right to buy a gun, they're taking away his freedom, right?" I figured this was a rhetorical question, but for once Goose had intrigued me with his understated powers of reason.

"Yeah," I answered. "That's what I heard him say."

"But Rick says women shouldn't be allowed to have abortions because it's immoral, right?"

"Correct," I replied.

"Well, that's fucked up," said Goose.

"What do you mean?" I asked. I think Goose had reached an epiphany in his understanding of American politics.

"If the government doesn't have the right to tell somebody he can't have a gun, how can it tell a woman she can't have an abortion?"

"Welcome to America, Goose," I said. "You should run for office."

I handed him my cell phone.

"Turn on the GPS in this thing, and let's see how close the trailer park is now," I suggested.

"Are you crazy?" he asked.

"What?"

"That's how they found that computer guy in Guatemala," said Goose. "The *federales* can find us if you use your GPS."

"You mean McAffee?" I asked. How the hell did Goose know anything about that nutcase?

"Yeah, that's him," replied Goose. "I saw it on *CNN en Español*."

"No, that's different," I said, but I wasn't sure. "That was geographic metadata on photos or something, wasn't it?"

"Who knows? Let's not take any chances," suggested Goose. "We can find the trailer park using the map."

We followed the interstate into Montgomery and turned on I-80 heading towards the Georgia border. As we approached Auburn, traffic picked up on the freeway. We stopped to gas up at a Love's Travel Stop near Tuskegee. This time I made Goose stay with the truck, and I went in to pay cash for the gas and to buy some ice for the cooler.

No use tempting fate twice by unleashing Goose on the unsuspecting Alabamians.

Ice had become a dire necessity. The beer was getting warm. Few things are worse than guzzling warm beer as you barrel down the interstate on the down slope of life racing towards a rendezvous with your own fate. Cold beer dulls the pain in your soul, and makes you consider the loftier things in life truly worthy of a man's consideration.

We passed Auburn and turned off on a state highway going south. Rigo opened his eyes and sat up in the seat next to me and Goose, and all of a sudden it hit me. What the hell were we thinking? I was taking a vicious Mexican-hating Blue Heeler into a migrant worker trailer park, into the bosom of the enemy. It would be like letting a fox loose in the chicken coop. Goose saw the worry etched on my face. He read my mind.

"What are you going to do with that dog?" he asked. "If he bites anyone, my mother will kill him and make tacos out of him."

"It'd be a tough fight," I said.

"Not really. You haven't seen my mother," Goose stated quietly. We looked at each other and then Goose guffawed. I had never heard him laugh like that. It was demonic.

"Ha, ha! It's going to be like the Alamo," he grinned. "Mexicans as far as the eye can see."

"Anyone likely to have a gun there?" I asked.

Goose shook his head.

"No, they don't want to give the police an excuse to turn them over to *La Migra*. My mother has a big knife, though. She used it on my father once. She'll kill that dog with it."

An armed Mexican wouldn't slow down a Blue Heeler, of course. But Rigo and I would have to watch our P's and Q's at the park. On the positive side, I knew that even if Rigo bit one of the Mexicans, nobody was likely to call Animal Control or the police. They'd rather take the law into their own hands than call the police and risk deportation. No, it would be vigilante justice. I snapped the leash on Rigo just in case as we approached the rendezvous.

We were close now, and both Goose and I looked for signs pointing to the Iglesia Cristo Rey. The trailer park was supposedly located in back of the church. Goose called his mother on the phone, and she promised to come out to the highway and flag us down. Goose said we couldn't miss her. I wondered what he meant.

Sure enough. Three minutes later I spotted a figure standing under a large blue and white sign with the name of the church in large Gothic letters. As we got closer, I thought Goose must have misunderstood his mother. I saw a tall man with long hair dressed in a t-shirt, army fatigue pants, and combat boots. A black beret sat jauntily on his head. Maybe she sent someone else to meet us, I thought. We slowed down and turned into the dirt road where the man stood waving at us. As we slowed down and pulled alongside, he stuck his head in Goose's window. I almost screamed, and Rigo lunged at the intruder, growling ferociously before retreating and cowering on my side of the seat.

Goose exchanged a sloppy kiss with the man while I looked on in dumb amazement.

"Don't be afraid. It's only my mother," said Goose. "Mamá, this is Clabe, a famous writer from Texas. He speaks Spanish. Clabe, this is Doña Luz." Goose's sudden display of etiquette was unexpected.

I stared but couldn't say a word. I mouthed a greeting, but no sound came out. In retrospect, I don't think I behaved badly. In fact, I believe I kept my composure in view of what I saw looking into the truck. Now I understood what Goose meant when he said he got all the good looks in the family.

Goose's mother had almost as much facial hair as her son. Her face was deeply pockmarked, and I wondered if she had suffered from smallpox as a child. Her nose was bluish red, veined, and bulbous; the kind hopeless alcoholics have after decades of drinking. She was a large woman, easily six feet tall, unusual for a Mexican female, and she was stout. Her arms were thickly muscled and well defined. Her large breasts were incongruent with her abundant facial hair and muscular arms, and there was something completely asexual about her. I didn't know whether to give her a manly handshake in greeting or a polite peck on the cheek. I opted for a wave of the hand and tried not to stare.

Rigo cringed in the seat beside me, almost crawling into my lap. He whined like a little puppy. So this was Goose's mother. After the initial shock had passed, and we had time to get acquainted in her trailer, I began to feel safe and protected in the presence of this woman, or whatever she was. At least I was glad she was on my side. She brought us cold beer and laid out a spread of corn tortillas with chipotle bean sauce.

"The *cabrito* will be ready in a half hour," she said.

I got out my laptop, hooked up my "hotspot" internet source, and checked my emails. There were several messages from my publicist Carmen, each one more hysterical than the last.

I read the first one. "Where ARE you, *mi amor*?" she asked. "What have you done? Call me right away."

I didn't think that would be a good idea. I needed to concentrate. I downed the cold beer, and Goose's mother immediately placed another in front of me. The way she looked at me made me uneasy, but I didn't give it a second thought. I opened the file for my new book and started to edit chapter one.

Chapter 9

Sometime around midnight I curled up in a surplus army cot that Goose's mother had borrowed from some friends. Rigo lay under the cot, wary and alert. I had never seen him so subdued in the presence of Mexicans. He was terrified of Goose's mother even though the woman paid him no attention whatsoever.

I was satisfied with the rough draft of my first chapter. I had introduced the protagonist in an exotic setting and revealed his identify in a surprise ending. I also hinted that unnamed people were looking for him. In a serialized story it's important to insert a hook at the end of each chapter to keep the reader engaged and looking forward to the next installment. I felt I had accomplished that. I planned to edit the chapter in the morning and then email it to the magazine. I would also contact Carmen, my publicist, and see what she knew about my predicament. I lay down in the cot and dozed off almost immediately.

Rigo and I both have crazy, wacked-out dreams. At least I assume his are wacked-out based on his antics while sleeping. My dreams usually involve foreign countries, strange women giving me blow jobs, and bizarre international intrigue, usually with a tenuous connection to my previous life. I'm not sure what Rigo dreams about, but he growls, barks, and whimpers as if all hell were breaking loose. He thrashes around with his legs; his tail wags, and his lips and eye lids twitch convulsively. I wish I could hook up some electrodes to his brain and view his dream in color on a video monitor. Maybe in his dreams Rigo has testicles and runs around humping all the female dogs in the neighborhood. He might chase squirrels or deer or run with a pack of feral Blue Heelers, terrorizing West Highland Terriers and Labrodoodles.

In the wee hours of the morning I began to dream. The dream was creepy and sexual in a perverted way. It was sketchy as most dreams are, but I remember some important details. I was lying in a sleeping bag in a tent and was part of a Sandinista commando unit camped in the Nicaraguan jungle during the Contra War. Some of the guerilla fighters were women. Che Guevara was there too despite the fact that he had been dead for decades. It was dark, and someone began kissing me and sliding a hand down my Ralph Lauren camouflage boxers. I was aroused and returned the kiss, but something wasn't right. I felt the wispy hairs of a scraggly mustache and the bristly scratchiness of a three or four-day old beard. I reached up with my hand to feel the face of my lover, and I touched a beret. In that instant I knew I was kissing Che Guevara, and I pushed him off in disgust and sat up in the sleeping bag. That's when I woke up. I was in the cot, and in the dim light surrounding me I saw the silhouette of Goose's mother on the floor beside me. She picked herself up with as much dignity as she could muster and left the room without saying a word. I was left wondering if that had been part of the dream too, or if she really had been fondling me. I wanted to throw up or take a shower, maybe both.

The next morning we breakfasted on steaming *chilaquiles* and leftover *cabrito*. I was embarrassed about what had happened during the night and kept glancing at Doña Luz. She gave no indication that anything was amiss. When I looked at her face and allowed for the possibility that I had touched those lips with my own, my appetite evaporated. I knew we couldn't stay in the trailer park. I couldn't risk spending another night and having Goose's mother attempt to make love to me. Maybe next time she would do it at knife point. I suspected it had been years or decades since some drunken sot had discarded what remained of his self-respect and had sex with that woman. She might not be dissuaded so easily next time.

"Goose," I called out as we walked through the trailer park after breakfast with Rigo on a leash beside us.

"*¿Qué pasó?*" he asked.

"We've got to keep moving," I said.

"But why? We're safe here with my mother," he said.

I knew I couldn't tell him the truth. He'd think I made it up, or that I was the one who tried to have sex with his mother. I would have to concoct a story.

"My publicist says the feds know where we are," I lied. "They've sent someone from their Atlanta office. We've got to keep moving."

"*¡Hijole!*" he exclaimed, genuinely alarmed. "Why didn't you say something earlier? Let's get out of here now." That was just what I'd hoped he would say.

Goose wasn't afraid of many things, but he respected the power and long arm of federal law enforcement. The law itself meant nothing to the feds, and Goose knew it. He had lived through it and didn't want to repeat the experience.

Rigo understood immediately that we were packing to leave. He jumped into the back seat of the pickup and wouldn't leave the truck. He didn't want to be left behind with Goose's mother. Maybe he sensed that she would indeed carve him up with that long knife and make tacos out of him, but you couldn't have pried him from that seat with a front end loader.

Goose and his mother had a teary farewell. It would have been almost touching if it hadn't been for that frightening physiognomy. As we drove away I waved to her and damned if she didn't blow me a kiss. That was when I knew it hadn't been a dream. I shuddered and stomped on the accelerator pedal.

We headed south on Alabama State Highway 431 toward Columbus. We were intending to skirt Atlanta and make our way to the South Carolina coast where I hoped to scout out potential safe houses; a place where we could stay anonymously, and where I could continue writing my serialized novel. Goose said he had a friend on John's Island in a Mexican community south of Charleston. That sounded good to me. As long as his horny, hirsute mother was not there.

An hour later I pulled off into a picnic area and called Carmen in South Beach. I didn't understand smart phone technology and wasn't sure whether the feds could track me by the GPS function in the phone or not. I had to risk the call, though, and decided to keep it short just in case. In the old days at least, the police usually needed a certain amount of time to pinpoint your location if they were bugging your phone.

"Carmen?"

"Clabe, thank God you called!" she said. That already sounded ominous.

"Where are you?" she asked. I was paranoid. Was there an FBI agent standing next to her with a pistol stuck to her temple forcing her to ask me that particular question, or had she been recruited to help them find me? Maybe she was just worried about me. I had no way of knowing.

"I'm safe. That's all you need to know," I replied cryptically. Goose cracked open the last six-pack of Shiner and handed me a bottle. He sensed my tension and knew I needed the beer.

"The FBI came to see me," she said and lowered her voice when she pronounced those three infamous letters. "They wanted to talk about you."

"Oh?" I replied. I tried to sound nonchalant even though my heart pounded and my bowels gurgled.

"They wanted to see a copy of your latest novel. They said something about classified information," she said. "I told them to fuck off."

Now that was a lie if I ever heard one. Carmen thought of herself as a rebel and a non-conformist, but she was delusional. The only thing unordinary and non-conformist about my publicist was her jacked-up sex drive and her perverted positional preferences. If the FBI said "jump", Carmen would ask, "how high?" I pitied the poor agent who had drawn Carmen as an assignment. There was no doubt that he would end up with her in the sack, thinking he could pry more information from her that way. He later would lose all self-respect because of what he had done. He might resort to binge drinking and serial thrill seeking to forget the loathsome depths to which he had sunk. He would never be able to wash off the smell of her perfume. I had experienced it myself.

"They want me to let them know if I hear from you," she confessed. "What should I tell them?"

"Tell them there's no classified information in my book. Tell them it's a damned coincidence. God Bless America!" I screamed almost incoherently and signed off before the feds could get a fix on our location.

Carmen called back several times over the next couple of hours, but I refused to answer the phone. I couldn't trust her anymore. Maybe they had threatened to deport a few of her cousins back to Cuba. I knew some of her relatives in Miami were there illegally. One was a known drug dealer, and two were pimps. Carmen herself had admitted that to me. The feds weren't above using that kind of extortion, and Carmen would be more than happy to oblige. No, my break with Carmen had to be definitive. I had to sever the umbilical cord.

From now on my only communication with the literary world would be an occasional email to *The Ganja Times*. It was only a matter of time before they chimed in on the topic too. I suspected they would welcome the scandal and the media attention if it came to that. My predicament would only increase interest in my story and sell more copies of the magazine and advertising. I might become a cult hero in the marijuana legalization movement and then perhaps Mainstream America might clasp me to its bosom. Maybe I could ask for a raise.

Chapter 10

We crossed the Georgia state line and continued our reckless dash towards the Carolina coast where I hoped we might find safe refuge. As far as I was concerned, my only crime had been the minor destruction of government property, hardly the type of misdeed that should occasion an FBI manhunt. Anything else they had against me was a fabrication or pure misunderstanding, but try telling that to a government prosecutor eager to make a name for himself, much less to a Mexican drug cartel assassin with a third-grade education. I assumed the Russians would make their appearance sooner or later.

Goose was a different story altogether. He had paid his debt to society long ago, and I dragged him into this mess out of pure selfishness. I was an egotist, and I was using a true friend to save my own ass. I felt like a back-stabbing bastard.

"Goose," I said. "Are you asleep?"

"No. *¿Qué quieres*[11]*?*" he asked.

"I want to apologize," I said.

"For what?" he asked.

---

[11] What do you want?

"For involving you in this goat-fuck," I replied. "I'm sorry."

"Oh that," he said, shrugging off my role in ruining his life. Goose rummaged in the bottom of the cooler and managed to find one more bottle of Shiner, which he handed to me. "Are we out of *mota*[12]?" he asked.

I liked that about Goose. He lived for the moment and didn't hold grudges. Twenty-four hours ago he had been suicidal. Now he just wanted to smoke some weed. I handed him my traveling vaporizer.

We had driven almost a thousand miles across the Deep South, and it had been an education for both of us. The South was supposedly a bastion of individual freedom, or at least that had always been my impression. But wherever you turned here, somebody was trying to tell you how to think. Politics were deeply immersed in religion and religion was everywhere. You couldn't escape it even driving down the highway.

I turned on the radio for some relief and found a country music station. Here it was again. A singer crooned about wanting to have a beer with Jesus. Then came Ronnie Dun with his own nostalgic tune about a mystical place where he had both drunk his first beer AND found

---

[12] Spanish slang for marijuana

Jesus. Was there some preternatural connection between beer and Jesus that I was missing? I was drinking plenty of beer but had yet to experience my own spiritual rebirth.

"Hey, slow down!" said Goose. "There's *chota* [13] everywhere along this road."

I looked at the speedometer and realized I was doing 80 in a 55 mph zone. I eased off the accelerator. All we needed was to get stopped by an eager George state trooper and tossed in the hoosegow for a whole litany of substance abuse violations. The local cops would run my name through the data base, and my lie to Goose about an FBI agent showing up from the Atlanta office would come true.

"Sorry," I mumbled. I eased off on the accelerator, and the truck slowed down to the speed limit.

We drove into South Carolina early in the afternoon and pulled into the visitor center on the interstate just across the state line. A large chartered bus had just disgorged a crowd of hefty teenagers all wearing identical blue t-shirts emblazoned with a white cross and an inscription below proclaiming "Aiken Second Baptist Church: God's Mission to Mexico".

---

[13] Police

I walked to the restroom and stood at the urinals with several of the kids from the bus.

"I can't believe I missed two weeks of American Idol," said one.

"No kidding! We couldn't even find any weed down there," said the second youngster.

"I'm glad we went," said another voice. "I felt up one of the Mexican girls on the last day. She showed me her tits."

"Really, which one?" asked the first teenager.

"You know, the Mexican preacher's daughter."

"Cool," said the first teenager.

"Hey, she showed me her tits too," said another of the teenagers.

"Maybe it's part of their culture," said the first voice.

I gave myself a couple of half-hearted shakes and zipped up my jeans. On the way to wash my hands, I heard a loud commotion outside and immediately had a sinking feeling in my gut. I had left the car without giving Goose any guidance on how to behave himself. That was like giving carte blanche to the Mongol Horde to rape and pillage. Never a good idea. I heard Rigo barking, and I sprinted out of the men's room. As I exited the service area, I heard Goose's loud voice and heavy Spanish accent in English.

"Baptize me, you skinny motherfucker!" he shouted.

I turned the corner and saw Goose holding a slight man by his clerical collar and shaking him.

"I wanna be saved!" Goose screamed. Rigo barked and tried to jump through the window, but fortunately I had remembered to leave both windows cracked only about six inches. I immediately calculated that Rigo was out of the equation and not a problem.

"I can't! You have to attend baptismal classes first," protested the Baptist preacher, turning his head to avoid the spray of Goose's spittle. "Let me go!"

"Call 911!" screamed one of the women chaperones.

"That Mexican is going to kill Preacher John!" shouted another.

I rushed to the scene and promptly slapped Goose in the face, once on either cheek. That brought him out of his trance, and he let go of the little preacher. I tried to straighten the man's white collar and began to apologize. The poor man was trembling.

"I'm so sorry," I said, knowing I had to come up with a believable story to garner some sympathy or have one of the chaperones call the state police. "I hope you can understand. My friend got some bad news last week. He has a malignant brain tumor. It's terminal, and he hasn't been himself since."

"I should say not," said the preacher, brushing himself off and fixing his clerical collar. "He tried to strangle me."

"Try to understand his dilemma. The man could die any day, and he hasn't been baptized yet," I explained. "By the way, don't you recognize him?" I added in a whisper.

"No, I don't," said the preacher. "Should I?"

A small crowd had gathered around us, and a ring of zaftig women formed a protective half-circle around Preacher John.

"I don't recognize him either," said one of the women. "Who is he?"

"Didn't you ever watch "Zorro" on television?" I asked.

"Sure, when I was a kid," answered the preacher.

"I did too," said the one of the women. The fall air was getting crisp, and she shivered in a sleeveless summer dress, which she had likely worn during the church mission in Mexico. Everyone was beginning to calm down, and I began to breathe easier.

"Well, don't you recognize Sergeant Garcia?" I asked. "This poor man used to be a famous Hollywood actor. He's lived a life of sin. Fornicating and drinking and raising hell."

At the mention of the word "fornicating", the women raised their eyebrows and began to look at both me and Goose with undisguised interest.

"He has repented and wants nothing more than to be baptized in the church before he dies," I claimed. Goose, meanwhile, stood meekly by my side with his head bowed. He mumbled under his breath, and I was grateful that nobody in the church group spoke Spanish. His utterances were not very Christian-like.

"*Que se vayan todos a la chingada*[14]," muttered Goose. I elbowed him in the side, and he fell silent.

I hope no one would google "Zorro" on a smart phone and call me on my lie. The real actor who played Sergeant Garcia died about 40 years ago, and he wasn't even Hispanic. But everyone stared at Goose with a new respect and sympathetic eyes.

"I suppose I could make an exception," said Preacher John. "I think the Lord understands when one of

---

[14] They can all go fuck themselves.

his children is in pain. These are extenuating circumstances."

"Praise God!" cried out another one of the women. "This 'Messican' is about to be Born Again!"

"Jason," the preacher called to the boy who had copped a feel in Mexico.

"Yessir?" said Jason.

"Go to the vending machines and bring us a few bottles of water for the baptism," requested Preacher John. He handed the boy a fistful of one-dollar bills.

The boy was back in less than two minutes with five bottles full of clear water. Goose was already on his knees, praying with Preacher John and the overweight women in their summer dresses.

"The vending machines were out of order, and the faucets in the lavatories weren't working, so I found these bottles in the trash and filled them up with water from a commode," said Jason as he handed the bottles to the preacher.

"The Lord will always find a way," the preacher said and began to unscrew the bottle caps and pour the water into a plastic bucket one of the women had brought him from the bus.

"Wait a minute," I said. "You can't baptize my friend with toilet water!"

The preacher raised his hand and smiled condescendingly at me as if I were a small child incapable of understanding the mysteries of the Faith.

"It's purely symbolic," he said. "I will bless the water in Jesus' name. It will be as pure as the driven snow."

"It doesn't snow in Aiken, South Carolina," I protested.

Goose apparently didn't quite understand what was happening. He looked up at me questioningly.

"Did he bring the water?" he asked in Spanish.

I nodded my head.

"Preacher John will bless the water for the baptism." I said it without conviction, and I knew later I would feel guilty if I let this lurid charade continue. I moved forward to stop the proceedings, but one of the Baptist women took a step to her left and intentionally blocked my path. I could see the righteous challenge in her eye. She was a large woman with significant muscle tone in her arms despite the loose flesh in her triceps which flapped in the stiff breeze. The Aiken natives seemed determined to baptize my friend with toilet water by force, if necessary, and I finally acquiesced. Who's to say it wasn't the right thing to do? It would have required violence and brute force on my part to stop the ceremony.

I dislike street brawls, especially with women who look like they can kick my ass.

I watched with morbid fascination as Preacher John gripped a handful of hair on the back of Goose's head and dunked him in the bucket of toilet water. Goose came up spitting and spewing water, and his greasy hair hung down and covered his eyes and ears. He bowed his head with the others as Preacher John began to pray.

"In the name of the Father, the Son….."

I tuned out the familiar words and thought how surreal it was that Goose was kneeling here at an interstate rest stop in South Carolina, receiving the sacrament of baptism with his head drenched in toilet water.

I kept my distance, though, lest one of the women grab me for baptism as well. They were on a roll, and as I walked back to the car I heard Preacher John shout for the hymnals to be passed around. Soon the Baptists were singing "Take Me to the River", and Goose was unabashedly weeping while several of the women dried his head with a towel and tried to comfort him. He reached out and grabbed one woman's buttocks with his hand but she gently removed it and sang even louder. As if Goose had inspired her.

I couldn't imagine what had gotten into this hardened criminal from Durango, Mexico. It must have been his two-day beer binge. Goose tended to get sentimental when he stayed drunk for more than twenty-four hours. In the end, I don't know who was happier; the Baptists or Goose. They had saved another Mexican and now could add Goose to their list of mission converts. Goose, for his part, had been baptized and reborn and swore to go forward and sin no more. I had never understood religious fervor, and certainly didn't trust the sincerity of Goose's conversion. Frankly, I just wanted to get the hell of there. Rigo, I think, shared my sentiments.

Chapter 11

Ninety minutes later we exited off I-95 onto South Carolina State Highway 17 and drove north. We had run out of beer earlier in the afternoon, something which had to be remedied soon. I was hungry, my head ached, and my ass was numb from the long drive. South of Charleston we turned right on Main Road, crossed the Intracoastal Waterway, and drove to the intersection with Maybank Highway on John's Island. Despite the cool temperature, the air was heavy with moisture, and we could sense the proximity of the Atlantic Ocean. Rigo was anxious and sniffed the air repeatedly and whined.

We parked in a strip mall next to a Piggly Wiggly grocery store and went in, hoping to buy some Shiner even though it was Sunday evening. I doubted a store in South Carolina would sell us alcohol on the Sabbath, but it was worth a try. Piggly Wiggly, as it turned out, didn't carry Shiner, but we filled up a shopping cart with cases Dos Equis and feigned innocence as we approached the cashier.

"Can't sell you beer on Sunday," said the cashier apologetically. She smiled at us, and there was something about her manner that told me this transaction might be negotiable. I would have laid even money she was a graduate of some cut-rate local rehab center. She stared at the beer with a longing that was almost lustful. I looked around the store. At this hour the Piggly Wiggly was almost deserted.

"Nobody's watching," I said. "Cash us out and take a 12-pack for yourself."

She only hesitated a second.

"Now that's what I'm talkin' about," she said and hurriedly bagged our beer and placed her own 12-pack under the counter. She smiled and nodded to us as we left but avoided direct eye contact.

Goose and I opened our bottles of beer in the truck and drank gratefully, moaning softly with our eyes closed and spilling cold beer down the front of our filthy t-shirts. I put Rigo in the back of the pickup and dished out a cup of dog food into his bowl. He eyed our beer jealously. I swore he would rather have sat in the cab and drunk with us. You can call it anthropomorphism if you like, but that dog and I were in cerebral sync.

A half hour later we tracked down Goose's friend in a double-wide trailer along a dirt road lined by tall pine trees just off Maybank Highway. There were nine Mexicans living in a three-bedroom trailer. They all had jobs, and they all pitched in to pay the rent. The house was filthy and smelled of burnt corn tortillas and dirty laundry. The Mexicans didn't seem to mind the stench, but they sure didn't appreciate our sudden appearance in their neck of the woods. Our reception was cool and reserved.

The beer I brought into the trailer went a long way towards breaking the ice, though. I gathered the Mexicans had run out of beer the day before and had no hopes of buying any more until payday, still four days off. That explained their foul mood. The frowns and cold stares were soon replaced by grins and an occasional *grito*. Within a half hour they were pounding me on the back, calling me "*carnal*[15]" and promising to introduce me to their sisters.

Someone hauled out a cooler full of beef tamales that were probably meant for tomorrow's lunch on the job. Most of the men were illegally in the country, and they worked for several landscaping companies in Charleston County that weren't overly scrupulous about examining their fake social security cards and driver's licenses.

Goose sat down with his compatriots and proceeded to get beastly drunk. Within fifteen minutes he had told them everything about us. He spilled his guts. I

---

[15] Brother

wasn't worried, though. The other Mexicans were just as drunk, and nobody believed a word of what Goose was saying. Certainly no one would remember anything the next day.

"This *gringo* is one bad *vato* [16]," Goose kept repeating partly in English and partly in Spanish. "The FBI was after him, and he blew up their car. Antonio Salcido and the Sinaloa Cartel have a contract out on his life. But the *gringo's* gonna cut off Salcido's head. With a chainsaw in a shopping mall in Dallas. I heard him say so."

The Mexicans laughed so hard they spit up their beer, and one of them finally ran outside to throw up. I heard him retching, and then I heard Rigo barking and snarling. The Mexican burst through the front door, wide-eyed and pale with fresh vomit still dripping from his chin. The front of his trousers was wet from his crotch to his left knee. He had pissed himself, and the vertical pee puddle was still spreading.

"Get the gun," he shouted. "A dog tried to kill me out there. It might be the *chupacabra!*[17]"

"We ain't got a gun," one of his friends replied. "Sit down and shut up."

---

[16] Dude

[17] Literally "goatsucker". A legendary dog-like creature in Mexican folklore that kills livestock and drinks their blood.

"Well, get me a machete. We can't go outside until we kill that dog," the first one insisted. "We'll be prisoners in this *gringo* trailer until that dog dies!"

I knew if I wanted to get any sleep, I was going to have to do it in the truck. I picked up a six-pack and grabbed a couple of tamales. I said *buenas noches* to everyone and excused myself. They were still arguing about what to do with Rigo when I walked out the door. I unrolled a sleeping bag in the front seat and crawled inside, but I couldn't sleep. Rigo, on the other hand, had no such problem. He lay down in the back seat and was snoring within thirty seconds.

I finally sat up and got out my laptop and turned on the internet hotspot. I knew we couldn't stay here with Goose's friend, or I'd miss the submission deadline for my next episode. It would be impossible to write in that chaotic environment. I searched Wadmalaw Island on Craig's List, looking for cheap houses to rent. I jotted down several phones numbers to call in the morning. I ended up falling asleep with the laptop on my chest and woke up with a crick in my neck.

The next morning the line for the bathroom was long, and the hot water had turned cold a half hour before we staggered into the house. Six forlorn, hung-over Mexican laborers in baggy white boxers with towels slung over their shoulders stood in the narrow hallway waiting to take a shower. They scratched their balls self-consciously and offered a subdued, *"Buenos dias."*

Goose and I cleaned up the best we could without braving the long line. We rinsed ourselves off with the hose outside and applied copious amounts of Old Spice High Endurance deodorant to cover what the soapless rinse had missed. We ate what remained of the tamales and washed them down with cold beer. Goose sat and chatted with his friend while I made a few phone calls and lined up a couple of houses to view.

An hour later we drove east on Maybank Highway towards Rockville, through the forgotten South Carolina of "Gone with the Wind". It was a nostalgic journey into an idyllic era of antebellum fantasy. Towering live oaks formed a canopy above the highway, and long wispy strands of grey Spanish moss hung from the branches and shimmied snake-like in the early morning breeze. I expected to see "darkies" on the side of the road, smiling and waving to us and singing a song by Stephen Foster; maybe "Old Black Joe" or "Old Folks at Home".

I did see plenty of black folks, but they weren't lining the road, and they weren't waving at us or singing. They stood in small sullen groups in front of a public housing project just south of Main Road. A few bedraggled drunks made their way from the gas station convenience store back home with brown paper bags in their hands shaped suspiciously like wine bottles. I saw more young black men wearing headphones and walking along Maybank Highway on their way to poor ramshackle houses and single-wide trailers further to the east. A few were hitchhiking. We passed a commercial establishment on the left with the sparky name of "Johnson Baby Grand". A middle-aged black man stood in the doorway with a broom and watched us go by. I was surprised that there was a market for baby grand pianos in this community.

I began to wonder if the house I had called about was in a black neighborhood. So much the better, I reasoned. Nobody would ever find me in that part of town. The thought cheered me up considerably, and I hoped a black landlord wouldn't mind renting to a white tenant in this part of the country. Goose stared in silence at the blacks we passed. He had an affinity with racial minorities and looked upon them as brothers in persecution. I don't think he had ever spoken to a black man outside of the wire, though.

"Goose, I want you to let me do all the talking this morning," I proposed.

"Fine with me," he mumbled in response. "Talk all you want. Just don't fuck it up." I glanced over at Goose and realized he was barely alive, suffering from a monumental hangover. He sipped his cold beer peevishly and closed his eyes. I figured the bright sun filtering through the Spanish moss was drilling a hole through his eye sockets.

The closer we got to Rockville, the more certain I became that the house I had called about was not in a poor black neighborhood after all. Quite the contrary. Maybank Highway had suddenly morphed from an area of low-income housing into a vacation enclave for Charleston's Townie Aristocracy. The houses were old, but majestic, and they reeked of money and the glory days before modernity sucked dry America's soul. Tiny dirt roads intersected Maybank Highway from either side and ran like perpendicular capillaries through neighborhoods of widely spaced, multi-storied white houses with huge front porches and neoclassical wooden pillars. Some of them were in need of repair, but most were well-maintained despite their age and came with carefully manicured lawns and gardens. I knew all of them had lurid stories of their own to spill; depraved tales of forbidden sex between the young aristocratic white sons of the South and their black female servants. I figured if it had been good enough for

Strom Thurmond, a goodly number of like-minded young preppies must have followed in his footsteps. The place reeked of illicit sex and closet carnal appetites. Where was Carmen when I needed her?

Chapter 12

We turned right on Sea Island Yacht Club Road and snaked slowly around two bends in the dirt road before we saw the Rockville Presbyterian Church. A sign on an exterior wall dated the church back to 1850. I glanced at the written directions to make sure we were still headed in the right direction. We turned left with the old Church on our right and followed a narrow dirt alley past an immense oak tree that must have been several hundred years old. Its trunk was gargantuan. A cactus grew out of a thick branch high in the tree about twenty feet off the ground. Squirrels capered along its branches and clouds of gnats hovered in the beams of sunlight that fought their way through the foliage. I glanced to the left and saw a body of water in the distance. That must be Bohicket Creek, I thought. Some creek. It must have been almost two hundred yards across. We were a mere stone's throw from the ocean, I realized.

A Mercedes SUV was parked in front of the house, and I assumed it belonged to the landlord. I glanced at Goose and hoped I hadn't made a mistake by bringing him along. Jesus, he looked disreputable. Rigo stayed with the truck, and Goose and I straightened our clothes, brushed back our hair with spit on the palms of our hands, and went inside to speak with the owner.

Two minutes later we sat with the landlord on the screened-in, second-story porch overlooking Bohicket Creek. The house had twenty-foot ceilings, rustic wood floors and was spacious and perfect in every way. It would be a writer's paradise, especially for one on the lam. No one would ever find me here unless Goose got drunk again and started running his mouth.

But I sensed tension in the air and reluctance on the part of the landlord. I wondered whether he had reservations about Goose living in his house. As I answered his questions about my background and intentions, Goose sat quietly and stared at the landlord with his malevolent beady eyes. The poor man began to squirm uncomfortably in his chair.

"We were actually hoping to rent to a family," he finally said. Beads of perspiration had appeared on his forehead. I kicked Goose under the table, but the crazy Mexican was oblivious to the blows, and he continued to stare.

The landlord had introduced himself as Rivers Pickney. He was about thirty-five years old with a receding hairline and was already turning to fat. He was wearing a pink Polo shirt with the collar turned up, shorts, and a pair of flip flops. His designer sun glasses for some reason were placed backwards on top of a University of South Carolina baseball cap, which he removed and placed on the table in front of us. I later came to understand that this was the mandatory uniform for Charleston men of Pickney's social class and age. He wouldn't change his shorts for khaki trousers until it snowed, or until he saw someone else do it first.

Pickney was jovial and good-natured, but obviously suspicious of outsiders. He said he had a law practice in Charleston, as did his father and grandfather before him. He claimed with pride that he had never been to Europe or even the West Coast. He was a South Carolinian, and more importantly, he said, a Charlestonian. I wanted to tell him he was a glorified townie with an inherited bank account, but I kept quiet.

"I'm not sure a pair of bachelors would be acceptable to the neighbors," he added. "Everyone knows each other here, and most of us are distantly related. We have to think of our neighbors' concerns."

That was getting close to a turn-down, and I scrambled, trying to think of a counter argument, anything to sway Pickney in our favor.

Goose suddenly sat up with a start. I made a discreet hand signal for him to keep his mouth shut and kicked him again, but he ignored me.

"What's the problem, Mr. Pickney?" asked Goose in a polite tone of voice and in good, grammatical English that I had never heard from him. "Could it be you're reluctant to rent to homosexuals?"

I'm not sure who was more surprised: Rivers Pickney or me. I felt the color rise to my face, and the landlord coughed and stuttered in response.

"N-n-n-no," he replied. "Of course not. You must have the wrong impression of us here in Charleston. We're not like the rest of South Carolina. We're actually rather liberal, at least in comparison," he said, trying to regain his composure after Goose's bombshell. "Some of my good friends at the law firm are homosexual...'er, I mean g-g-g-gay."

"Because if you are, Mr. Pickney, there would be certain legal remedies available to us. I have a law practice myself in Mexico City. Even there we are sensitive to the rights of the gay community."

My mouth fell open. Where had Goose been hiding this knowledge of English? Where was his usual obscenity-laced street-wise jargon? I started to object, but then realized that Goose's line of reasoning was working. Pickney was scared to death of a law suit.

"Mr. Pickney," I said, interrupting and winking surreptitiously at Goose. "If it would help our transaction, I'm prepared to give you six months' rent in advance...in cash." I took a thick envelope stuffed with one hundred dollar bills out of my shirt pocket and laid it on the table in front of our prospective landlord.

He stared at the envelope, deep in thought. "And the security deposit?" he asked.

I took out my wallet and dealt another twenty one-hundred dollar bills on the table. Pickney took one more long look at Goose and then pocketed the money.

"I'll have a copy of the lease to you tomorrow morning. Can you take possession of the house today?" he asked.

As the landlord drove away, I looked at Goose and broke out laughing.

"Homosexual, uh?" I asked.

"It worked," Goose said and left it at that.

I knew I'd just have to get used to the neighbors thinking Goose and I were a gay couple. I didn't mind the "gay" part, but I didn't like people thinking that Goose and I slept in one bed and might be buggering each other at night. That gave me the shivers. He just wasn't my type.

Rigo loved the place as much as Goose and I did. The first he thing he did was to cock his leg in the neighbor's lawn. He was marking his territory, and I wanted to do the same.

The place was a veritable paradise. The house itself was freakishly out of place. Its modernistic 1970s architecture clashed horribly with the traditional antebellum-style houses on either side. Once you got inside, however, it would have been difficult to improve on the layout and use of space. I set up my "office" in front of the floor-to-ceiling windows in the living room leading out to the screened-in porch. When I sat at my desk, I looked out across Bohicket Creek to desolate, uninhabited marshes on the other side. It was beautiful, even if it was the East Coast. Goose sat on the porch and inhaled six beers before coming up for air. He pointed to a pod of dolphin and muttered in English.

"Big fucking fish."

I would have explained that the big fish were dolphin, but that would have necessitated more of a lesson in marine mammalian biology than I was prepared to give. It was heaven, and the tranquil atmosphere had a synergistic effect on my writing. Over the next two days, I wrote four chapters and was ready to email my next submission to *The Ganja Times*. We were back in business, and the only challenge we faced was to locate a source of high-quality chronic.

Goose solved that problem on the third day when he made the acquaintance of the gardener next door. Nacho was a twenty-five year old wetback from Guanajuato, who mowed lawns and trimmed hedges for most of the homeowners on this section of Bohicket Creek. That night we packed some of Nacho's sweet home-grown *mota* into the vaporizer and washed it down with Flor de Caña rum and ice cold Dos Equis. I booted up the computer, and we streamed some Mexican *ranchera* music from the internet.

Nacho went ape-shit when he realized he could speak Spanish with his new neighbors. He lived rent-free in a little shack in back of the house next door with his eighteen-year old black girlfriend from the Dominican Republic and passed the time fishing and shooting squirrels when he wasn't too stoned to get out of bed. I couldn't figure out what his girlfriend did. She didn't appear to have a job, and she spent a lot of time on the dock talking on her cell phone although I was pretty sure she wasn't working on her tan.

This time of year the houses on Bohicket Creek were deserted for the most part. Their owners drove down from Charleston on holidays and weekends if the weather was bearable. That didn't happen often. I got into the habit of fishing in the morning. It was trout season, and I found a fishing rod and tackle box in the storage room on the first level of the house. Because of the threat of hurricanes, all the houses near the water had their first story of living quarters on the second floor of the house.

Goose would smoke a joint when he got up, wash it down with a beer, and dive off the dock into the chilly waters of Bohicket Creek. He refused to wear a swimming suit. I realized that could become a problem when the neighbors appeared for Thanksgiving, but for the time being nobody seemed to mind.

After a week in our new home, the editor of *The Ganja Times* called. He was hyped up and excited, and I immediately suspected he had just got off the phone with the FBI.

"Clabe, where are you?" he asked. "Great stuff you're giving us, by the way."

"Good to hear from you, Joel," I said.

Nacho chose that moment to come in unannounced through the back porch and started yammering in Spanish, shouting for Goose. I motioned for him to shut up, but he ignored me. Goose answered him at the same decibel level, and it suddenly occurred to me that a little white lie might be appropriate.

"I'm in Cabo," I said.

"Mexico?" he asked. "Sounds like all hell is breaking loose down there."

"Can you think of a better place for me to be?" I answered his question with one of my own..

"Maybe not. They're looking for you, Clabe," he said. "Keep moving."

So my employer knew I was a wanted man. I guess it was bound to happen. I just hoped it wouldn't change our deal. I needed the money.

"So they called you," I said. "Is that going to be a problem for us?"

"Hell no," he responded quickly. "We've never sold this many copies of the magazine, and advertising revenue has doubled in the last two weeks. It's all because of you."

That's exactly what I wanted to hear.

"I'll have the next episode to you right on time," I promised. That was the truth. I had already written the chapter and backed it up on an external hard drive and emailed it to several close friends. I wasn't taking any chances.

We all sat around that night, smoking Nacho's weed and drinking my Nicaraguan rum. We talked about America and Mexico and love and hate. Somehow the two topics blended into one, and then we gave politics a stab. We laughed when Nacho said none of it meant shit to a tree. He was right, of course.

I couldn't take my eyes off Nacho's girlfriend. I couldn't even remember her name, but those springy puppies of hers pointed towards the stars with a clarity and optimism that normally I would have found inspiring. But for some reason that day, those little twins were disconcerting to me. I became distracted and felt rootless and ungrounded and adrift. Thoughts of tits and sex do that to me now and then.

Chapter 13

I woke up the next morning with an erection. That hadn't happened in a while, and I interpreted it as a positive sign although I hated to waste the woody. I had a vague recollection of a dream with sexual content, maybe something to do with Nacho's girlfriend, but the only warm body near me was Rigo. He was licking my face and begging for breakfast. I was pretty sure he hadn't been in the dream; at least I hoped not.

I fed Rigo, placed a packet of Earl Grey tea in the Keurig, and sat down at my computer to scan the news feeds from around the world. It was an old habit from my days as a "talking head". I checked my Twitter account and was amazed to see that I had gained fifteen more followers overnight. I wondered how many of them were FBI snitches or hired guns from the Sinaloa Cartel, or maybe I was just suffering from delusions of grandeur. The new followers were probably nothing more than my usual menopausal groupies, who had nothing better to do than read my books and internet blog entries while they sat around in their bathrobes and slippers, smoking cigarettes and drinking coffee. I needed to post a couple of provocative political opinions to keep the buzz going, but it was too early in the morning to stretch the intellectual envelope. I hadn't even had my first beer of the day.

Goose had, though. I saw him crawling naked out of Bohicket Creek onto the dock and reaching for a bottle of Dos Equis after his morning dip. He was naked and so hairy he could have passed at a distance for a black Lab or a Newfoundland retrieving a bottle of beer except that he was standing on two legs.

There were several emails from Carmen asking me to call. She had sent her last message at 3:30 A.M., and she sounded desperate. In the old days I would have known she just couldn't sleep and wanted to have phone sex, but today I suspected she was frightened about what the FBI would do to her relatives if she wasn't able to answer questions about my whereabouts. Nobody wanted to be deported back to Cuba even with the Castros on their way out.

Carmen was a duplicitous old slut, and I couldn't trust her as far as I could spit. I blocked her email address, so I wouldn't have to read any more of her messages. She had turned into a common snitch. I needed inspiration and positive vibes, not a continuous guilt trip from an oversexed Cuban émigré who was prepared to dish me up to the FBI like a sacrificial lamb.

I looked out on the dock and saw Goose kneeling in prayer. That had become part of his morning ritual. Ever since the Aiken preacher baptized him with toilet water at the interstate rest area, Goose had taken his new identity as a born-again Christian to heart. He had even become arrogant about it and bragged about having been baptized with water from a toilet bowl. He claimed it made his conversion that much stronger. He prayed several times a day and spoke of redemption and salvation almost as much as he talked about alcohol, marijuana, and sex. He didn't seem to view the two categories as mutually exclusive. That's what I liked about Goose. He wasn't troubled by his own inner contradictions. I knew he would make a good Christian. He might even become a deacon in the Aiken Second Baptist Church.

"So what are you writing about now, *gringo*?" asked Goose as he opened the sliding glass door on the porch and walked into the living room, half of Bohicket Creek dripping and puddling on the six-inch wide floor boards.

"At least wrap a towel around yourself, Goose," I suggested. "I can't think with you standing there naked. You look like Sasquatch or something that escaped from a fucking zoo."

"You're just jealous, *gringo*. Personally, I'd rather die than have a hairless-Chihuahua body like yours. That's why you never get laid."

"Oh, and you do?" I asked sarcastically.

"I will soon," he said. "Nacho's going to lend me his girlfriend. He promised."

"Get dressed and go fix us some *huevos rancheros*," I said. I didn't even acknowledge Goose's claim about the girl. I hoped Nacho had been drunk when he made that promise. Nothing good could come of two Mexicans sharing the same girl in a house on Bohicket Creek in Rockville, South Carolina.

I heard Goose thumping around in his second-story bedroom and whistling "*De Qué Manera Te Olvido*", an old Vicente Fernandez song. Then I heard him come barreling down the stairs. The front door slammed, and I knew he had gone to get the newspaper. Goose had already gotten in the habit of drinking his second beer of the morning over the local paper although I doubted he understood much of what he read.

"*¡Hijo de su puta madre* [18]*!*" I heard Goose's muffled shout and heard the front door slam again and the unmistakable sound of Goose running up the stairs.

---

[18] Sonofabitch!

"You made the front page!" he shouted as he waved a copy of *The Post & Courier,* Charleston's daily newspaper.

"What?" I answered incredulously. "Gimme that." I ripped the paper from Goose's hands and looked at the headlines.

"CIA: MEXICAN DRUG CARTEL LINKS UP WITH RUSSIA," the headlines shouted.

"What the hell?" I asked out loud.

"See?" said Goose triumphantly. "What did I tell you?"

I hurriedly read through the article which was a reprint of a *Washington Post* piece from the day before.

"Jesus!" I exclaimed. "It's like reading my own novel! But where's the submarine?"

Goose grumbled and walked towards the kitchen.

"We're fucked," he said under his breath. That line was starting to get old.

"Just shut up and cook the eggs, will you?" I said. Goose's smug demeanor was getting on my nerves.

I grabbed the newspaper and read the article, paying closer attention this time. The author was a prominent foreign affairs correspondent in Washington, and he quoted a CIA report and anonymous sources in the intelligence community. The article, however, contained no specific information. It was a clever amalgam of hearsay and speculation. It shared no details about the kind of assistance the Russians allegedly were providing to the Mexican drug cartel or what they were getting in return. Except for the headline, it was empty verbiage.

I felt my pulse racing. This is what Goose had been talking about back in Texas. But it was one thing to hear it from my intoxicated, half-crazed sidekick and another thing entirely to read it in a reputable newspaper. I wondered if the CIA leaked the report after reading the first episode of my serial novel. But why? That made no sense.

The article in the Charleston newspaper and later Goose's *huevos rancheros* left me in a bilious state of mind and stomach. I was in no mood to write, and I suggested to Goose that we go fishing. The house came with a jon boat complete with a 25-hp Evinrude outboard motor and a half tank of gas. We even had a registration for the boat, and I had bought an out-of-state fishing license online. No need to call attention to ourselves by petty violations of local regulations, I reasoned.

I hadn't operated a motor boat since I was a kid in Texas, but it only took a few minutes of tinkering to fire up the engine and head out against the incoming tide. Goose was all for the idea. He had never been fishing with a rod and reel. His experience with fishing expeditions had been limited to dynamiting schools of fish in the Sea of Cortez with his narco buddies. He looked at my fishing rod with open derision.

"That's not how you fish," he said, nodding at the fishing tackle. "We need some explosives, bro."

"Not today, Goose. "This is the way people fish around here," I said, pointing to my rod and reel. I could just imagine the reaction of the South Carolina Department of Natural Resources to reports of a couple of yahoos dynamiting fish on Bohicket Creek. I tried to explain this to Goose.

"Come on, man," he complained. "You blew up an FBI car, and now you're afraid to blow up some fish?"

There was a perverted logic to most things Goose said, but I refused to even grace his protestations with a reply. I revved the Evinrude up to almost full throttle, and the jon boat raised its nose obediently and leaped across the chop that had suddenly appeared as Bohicket Creek emptied into the broader North Edisto River about one-half mile from the Atlantic Ocean.

"Slow down you sonofabitch!" shouted Goose, but I pretended I couldn't hear him over the rush of cool air in my face and the roar of the motor. He clasped either side of the boat with his hands in a death grip, and I could see his knuckles turning white. This should keep him quiet for a while, I thought, and coaxed a few more RPMs out of those 25 horsepower as we raced passed Horse Island on our left and turned southeast towards Seabrook Island and the Atlantic Ocean.

I heard the "wop-wop-wop" of the helicopter blades over the shriek of the outboard motor a few seconds before I saw the police helicopter pass over us at a height of about one hundred feet. Someone in uniform peered down at us through binoculars, and the helicopter made a slow circle around the jon boat even as we plied the river at full throttle, bouncing high over the increasingly rough chop and smacking the waves with a wrenching "whack" that sounded like the boat was coming apart at its welded seams. The helicopter stayed with us for about a minute before veering suddenly north and flying back towards Charleston.

"They found us!" screamed Goose.

I eased off the throttle and made a wide loop, pointing the boat in the direction the helicopter had disappeared. Goose was beside himself. I think he was more pissed off than frightened. It would take more than the appearance of a police helicopter to scare that unrepentant criminal.

"I told you to stay off the damn cell phone," he shouted. "But no, you're too fucking smart, right? Always know better than 'ol Goose."

That was the first time I had heard Goose refer to himself in the third person. It must have been that damned baptism. Becoming a Christian had completely gone to his head and made him insufferable. I was worried about the helicopter too, but I tried not to show it. There were any number of explanations for the presence of a police helicopter flying over the North Edisto River and their apparent interest in us. But I had been trained by the CIA not to believe in coincidences, and as much as I hoped it had been just a case of mistaken identity, I fully expected there to be a welcoming committee for us back at the house.

The boat bounced high across the choppy waves of the river and then hit smoother water as we got into Bohicket Creek. I maneuvered the boat along the dock, adjusting engine speed until the boat stood still against the tide. Goose jumped onto the dock and tied the boat with a rope. Rigo came running down to meet us. That was a good sign. It meant nobody was in the house waiting on us. They would have had to kill Rigo before he would allow strangers onto the premises. Maybe we were still in the clear.

Chapter 14

The day was shot. Completely laid to waste. At least for working on the next episode of my serial spy novel. There's something about waiting for the police to arrive that sucks the creativity right out of your brain and then makes your intestines cramp; usually in that order. I sat staring out the window at the pelicans flying low over Bohicket Creek in bomber formation but wasn't able to appreciate the idyllic scene. In my mind, I was already in a federal prison cell back in Texas, marking off the days left on my sentence with a piece of chalk on a concrete-block wall.

Goose, on the other hand, seemed calm, at least on the surface. He was more experienced than I was with defiance of the judicial system. He had a long history of breaking the law with impunity. Even when captured, convicted, sentenced, and completely at the mercy of sadistic hacks and prison wardens, he had exhibited a pugnacious, kiss-my-ass attitude that must have been inspirational to the first-timers at El Reno. But despite his calm, outward demeanor, I could see Goose wasn't himself. When a man throws down six bottles of Dos Equis in thirty minutes, I know he's battling demons.

"Go easy, Goose," I suggested. "The day's still young."

"I need to get laid," he said. "I'm going over to Nacho's house." He hadn't mentioned the police helicopter since we got back to the house, but it had to be on his mind.

Goose went upstairs to his bedroom to change clothes and appeared a few minutes later in boxer shorts decorated with red fire engines. He looked like a forty-year-old toddler or maybe a pedophile.

"At least put on a shirt," I suggested.

He nodded his head and clambered back up the stairs. When he came back down, he was wearing a pair of wrap-around sunglasses in addition to a sleeveless t-shirt and a pair of huarache sandals. The door to the back porch slammed, and soon the sounds of Calle 13's badass reggaeton beat drifted over from Nacho's shack. The floor to the old house vibrated with the staccato beat of "*Querido* FBI". How appropriate, I thought. Every now and then I heard the crash of breaking glass and the shrill laughter of Nacho's girlfriend. I wondered if Goose was actually getting laid. I tried not to picture that two-backed beast.

Rigo began barking at the front door and woke me up from my voyeuristic daydreams. I walked across the living room to look out the window and froze. A Charleston County Sheriff Department's white SUV drove slowly across the yard and parked next to Goose's truck. A jet-black deputy sheriff, well over six feet tall with a massive beer belly, rolled out of the SUV and jotted down Goose's Texas license plate number before walking purposefully towards the front door.

I locked Rigo in the storage room on the first floor and opened the door.

"Can I help you?" I asked, trying to keep my voice under control. I looked up at the smiling deputy sheriff who looked vaguely familiar to me.

"I sure hope so," he said.

I waited, but he just stood there smiling.

"Can I come in?" he asked.

That was a little odd, I thought, but I didn't want to piss off a local lawman on my fifth day in South Carolina.

"Sure, come on up," I said. I could hear Rigo whining in the storage room, but I didn't dare let him out.

"You got a dog in there?" he asked.

"Yep, he's not too friendly to strangers, though," I responded.

"You mean black strangers?" the deputy asked, still smiling.

"Something like that," I replied.

"That's alright. I've got a Pit Bull bitch that hates you white folks," said the deputy.

I'm glad we settled that. The cat was out of the bag. The deputy was black, and I was white, and both our dogs were racists. That wasn't a crime, I thought, especially in South Carolina, but it was an odd way to strike up a conversation.

The deputy followed me up to the second floor. I could hear the *clump-clump-clump* of his boots behind me, and I half expected to feel his billy club on the back of my head. Music still blared from Nacho's house, but the day had taken an ominous turn.

"I hate to bother you like this," began the deputy.

"What can I do for you?" I asked curtly.

The deputy looked around the house and then out to Bohicket Creek.

"You got a cup of coffee?" he asked.

I thought that was border-line impertinent, so I decided to test the deputy.

"No coffee," I said. "How about a cold beer?"

"Hell yeah," he answered. "That's even better!"

My eyebrows arched in surprise, but I got up and went to the kitchen and retrieved two bottles of Dos Equis from the fridge. When I walked back into the living room, the deputy had his feet up on the coffee table. He took them down when he saw me.

"Nice place," he said.

I handed him the beer, the bottle icy and glistening in the sunlight that poured through the sliding glass doors. He emptied half of it before coming up for air.

"Yeah, we like it," I said. We've only been here five days. We're renting."

"We?" he asked.

"Yeah, I've got a roommate," I said.

"He's not Mexican by chance, is he?" asked the deputy.

Oh, shit. Here it comes, I thought.

"Why would you think he's Mexican?" I asked, stalling for time.

The deputy laughed and finished the Dos Equis.

"Got another?" he asked.

"Sure," I replied and walked over to the kitchen to get another beer for the thirsty deputy sheriff. This was already the oddest conversation I'd ever had with a cop. The music next door was still reverberating, and it sounded like the party was in full swing. I hoped it would continue. This would be a bad time for Goose to show up, I thought.

"Do me a favor, will you?" asked the deputy.

I handed him the beer and opened another for myself as well.

"What's that?"

"Just tell your roommate to wear a swimming suit, okay?" The deputy slapped his knee and chuckled. "Miss Myrtle down the way complained. Said there was a naked man swimming in the creek this morning."

"Really?" I replied.

"Yeah," the deputy answered. "She's pretty sure about it. She was watching him with a pair of binoculars, she said. These old white ladies get kind of horny this time of year, you know." He smiled broadly and winked.

I breathed a sigh of relief. If that was all there was to this visit, there might yet be hope for the day.

"Are you a homosexual?" he asked.

I almost choked on my beer.

"Now what kind of a question is that?" I replied. I heard stomping on the outside side stairs coming up to the porch and loud voices in Spanish. Oh no, I thought. Here it comes.

"Clabe, this little girl is hot!" yelled Goose in Spanish. Nacho and the black Dominican girl were right behind.

They burst through the door onto the porch and staggered through the sliding door that I left open. I caught my breath. Goose had shed his t-shirt and was sporting only his boxers and huaraches. The girl was in the skimpiest of bikinis, and Nacho was shirtless in a pair of jeans and flip flops. It was only sixty degrees outside. I knew they all had to be drunk, and it was barely noon.

"We need some more beer!" yelled Goose and then stopped dead in his tracks when he saw the deputy sheriff.

The deputy stood up with his mouth open in surprise, but he wasn't looking at Goose. He was staring at Nacho's scantily clad girlfriend. It suddenly dawned on me why the deputy had looked vaguely familiar.

"LeToya?" he exclaimed. "Now what the hell are you doing here?"

The black girl shrieked and tried to hide behind Nacho.

"LeToya?" I asked. "I thought you were from the Dominican Republic."

"The Dominican Republic?" responded the deputy. "Bullshit! She's from Dominican Street, and she's my little sister!"

"Wassup, DeAndre?" she asked, laughing and covering her mouth with her free hand. The other held a half-empty bottle of beer.

"LeToya," said the deputy. "Now you get yourself right home, you little bitch, understand? Your momma's been worried sick about you."

"You kiss my ass, DeAndre," said LeToya. She emerged from behind Nacho and stood proudly in her bikini, flaunting her taut little boobs and lithe body. I couldn't take my eyes off her. I hoped Goose had not defiled that luscious-looking specimen.

"And don't give me that sheriff act," she said. "I'm eighteen years old and can do whatever I want!"

"Jesus Christ!" exclaimed the deputy. "Have you been banging these 'Messicans'?"

Goose had been staring at the deputy sheriff, moonstruck, ever since he caught sight of his uniform and badge. I doubted he understood everything of that insane exchange, but he gradually came to understand that this deputy sheriff did not represent a threat to his freedom. Goose looked at me and pointed at LeToya.

"She's not from Santo Domingo?" he asked me.

I shook my head.

"No wonder her Spanish was so bad," he said. Then he turned to the DeAndre, the deputy. "What's wrong with banging Mexicans? Are you a racist or something?"

Chapter 15

"It's time to get back to work!" announced DeAndre.

The deputy sheriff put down his empty beer bottle and got up from the easy chair in the living room where he had been sitting for the last ninety minutes brazenly depleting my supply of Dos Equis. To tell the truth, I didn't mind him guzzling my beer. I was relieved he hadn't slapped a pair of handcuffs on me when I opened the door. The image of that police helicopter was still fresh in my mind and was giving me the jitters.

"Ya'll are alright for a bunch of white motherfuckers," he said. "Thanks for the beer."

"White, hell!" said Goose. "We're Mexicans. Except for him." Goose pointed at me like I was some sort of racial freak whose presence embarrassed him.

"Whatever," said DeAndre. "Just keep your hands off my sister."

"Shut up, DeAndre," said LeToya. "You're drunk."

The deputy staggered out the front door arm in arm with Goose and Nacho, singing an off pitch version of "La Bamba" and slid into the driver's seat of his official Sheriff Department's SUV.

"I'll drop by to pick you guys up after I get off work," he said. "We'll go to Johnson's Baby Grand and I'll introduce you around."

"What's Johnson's Baby Grand?" asked Goose. "They sell pianos there, or what?"

"Ha, ha, ha!" laughed LeToya. "This I got to see."

"What's so funny?" asked Goose.

"Not a thing," said DeAndre and turned to his sister. "Shut up you little whore."

He slammed the SUV in reverse and skidded backwards across the yard until he faced the driveway that led back to Sea Island Yacht Club Road. Then he mashed on the accelerator and the SUV lurched forward, fishtailing and spinning its wheels with the 6.0 liter engine redlining and shrieking like a horse being butchered.

I closed my eyes, wondering whether the deputy sheriff would be able to navigate the narrow gate without clipping one side or the other or knocking down the centuries-old oak tree that stood outside the property. It would be a close call, but I figured the Charleston County Sheriff's Department would be good for the damage in a worst case scenario although DeAndre might be out of a job.

"*Muy simpático* [19] ," said Goose as he waved goodbye.

I couldn't agree, but I didn't say anything. I hoped I had seen the last of our deputy sheriff. I don't like cops under the best of circumstances and saw no reason to make an exception just because DeAndre was black and Goose had probably porked his little sister earlier in the day. No affirmative action program in Rockville, South Carolina to my knowledge.

"I'm glad he's gone," said LeToya. "He was hot as fried fish, wasn't he?" She laughed and slapped Goose on the back of his boxers.

"I love South Carolina!" shouted Goose. He tried to kiss LeToya but she slipped out of his clutches and ran back into the house giggling.

Ten minutes later Goose, Nacho, and LeToya each took an armful of beer bottles next door to continue their mid-afternoon bacchanal. They were raging and unstoppable, and I envied them. Music blared and LeToya's occasional laughter carried over to the house on the cool breeze that blew in from the northwest. I wondered what Preacher John and the rest of the Aiken

---

[19] Nice guy

Second Baptist Church would think of their new convert now.

Meanwhile, I had an idea for the next episode of my serial novel and sat down at the computer to write. I tapped the screen on my Ipod for the classical play list and selected Wagner's "Ride of the Valkyries" for some inspirational accompaniment. I no longer thought of the music as opera. How could I? Pop culture had quashed any images I might have had of the eight Valkyrie sisters of Brünnhilde singing their battle cry on the way to Valhalla. All I could see was the Air Cavalry rocketing a Viet Cong village and Robert Duvall with his pearl-handled Colt .45 making his men surf under a mortar barrage. But that was just the kind of realism I was striving for in my novel. Just a hodgepodge of provocative images and hyperbolic innuendo that would validate the fantasies of any of my readers who thought they knew how the world really worked. It would be a parody of reality; an unrecognizable extrapolation from one or two kernels of truth.

Yeah, that was more my style. I turned up the volume and went into the kitchen to refill my glass. I poured three fingers of straight rum into a brandy snifter and returned to my desk.

It was time to jump-start the action in the plot. I wanted to drop a bombshell. Something so unexpected and yet seemingly believable, that my readers would stay glued to their Kindles and Nooks and their copies of *The Ganja Times*. I sat at my desk till midnight, the words flying off the tips of my fingers. I sipped the rum cautiously. Alcohol helped to dull my innate Anglo-Saxon intolerance and cultural biases. Without the booze I might spit out a gush of genetically programmed hate prose like a Pat Buchanan or Rush Limbaugh and not even recognize my transformation.

I had to be careful, though, not to cross the line and let the demon rum fuck with my creativity. Under the influence, my writing could lose its prickly elegance, and I would just be one more literary hack.

I always liked to think of myself as an edgy John Steinbeck or a pot-smoking Ernest Hemingway or maybe a twenty-first century Alexander Dumas, except white and not as fat. All modesty aside, I knew my time was coming, and I didn't want to compromise my art. I pushed the brandy snifter aside when the rum buzz threatened to escalate into a twisted state of sloppy drunkenness.

In the wee hours of the morning, I quit typing. I knew I had written something significant that would last and withstand the scrutiny of future generations, not to mention the acerbic pen of those *New York Times* critics who pretended I didn't exist. Hell, I suspected some of them weren't even real Americans. They probably had last names like Gupta, Bhatnagar or some such shit. Christ, look at our president. What was happening to America?

A full moon hung over Bohicket Creek like a brilliant white orb of preternatural origins, reflecting off the water and challenging me to spout my usual irreverent swill about anything that threatened to touch my soul. I was speechless for once, and tears came to my eyes and burned fiercely. It was beautiful and I wondered how many more nights like this I would have the privilege to experience. I knew from my own history what the sky looked like from a prison cell. How much longer before the feds caught up with me, or some dickhead from the Sinaloa Cartel gunned me down in the fresh produce section of Piggly Wiggly and I made the *Post & Courier* obituaries?

I was nodding off at my desk when the loud clumping of Goose's footsteps staggering up the warped stairs to the back porch woke me. I looked up to see him struggling with a body thrown across his shoulders. It was LeToya. I hoped Goose hadn't killed her in a jealous rage. I suspected he was capable of such things when he got drunk enough. He staggered across the living room and laid her unconscious body down in the love seat in the TV room. He looked up at me and smiled.

"I'm going to marry this girl," he said.

I looked at him through bleary eyes and tried to focus my thoughts.

"What about Nacho?" I asked. "Isn't she his girlfriend?" I asked.

Goose covered LeToya with a light quilt and kissed her gently on the cheek. I had never seen anything like it.

"I bought her from Nacho," he said.

"What?" I asked. Goose had my full attention now. "You can't do that. Slavery ended in 1863."

"Really?" he laughed. "You should have told that to Nacho."

That tipped me over the edge, and I stumbled toward my bedroom. I needed to contemplate this development after a few hours of sleep.

"Wait!" called Goose. "Let's have a beer."

I ignored him and lay down in bed without bothering to undress. It had been a long day.

Chapter 16

I slept late the next morning. The sun streaming through the Venetian blinds finally woke me and bored through my closed eyelids with the subtlety of an old-fashioned eggbeater drill. Rigo was sitting up in his bed on the floor, glowering at me with resentment.

"Alright," I mumbled. "I can take a hint."

I walked unsteadily to the kitchen and poured some dog food for Rigo and filled his water bowl. I was still only half awake and didn't force the poor animal to humiliate himself by dancing for his food like I normally did. He wolfed down his breakfast and stood in front of me begging for more before I even had time to pop a packet of Earl Grey in the Keurig. Then I remembered last night's flurry of writing and rushed to my desk in the living room, wondering what I would find. That's what happens when you drink and write. I turned on the laptop and finished making tea while it booted-up.

Yeah, I was right for once. This wasn't my normal drivel, full of pompous, self-indulgent descriptions of nature and the heavy sarcasm of my plodding political commentary. No, this was good. I breathlessly read my new episode, becoming more enthused with each page. Where did I come up with this shit? Yeah, Joel was going to love it. The episode was full of action and death and mayhem. I even laid the foundation for a love story in the middle of all the chaos. Maybe I'd even do a sex scene for the next episode. I took a deep breath, moved the cursor over the "send" icon and clicked. It was gone and would be in Joel's email in-box when he woke up in Los Angeles about three hours from now. I had made the deadline with time to spare. I could relax, at least for a couple of hours.

"What'd you write last night?" I heard Goose's groggy voice from the TV room and looked around the corner and saw a sprawl of naked bodies on the floor only half covered with a quilt.

"Jesus, Goose!" I exclaimed. "Don't keep doing this to me. Put on some clothes and cover that girl." I let my eyes linger on LeToya's nakedness a little longer than necessary.

"Quit looking at my girlfriend's ass," said Goose. *"¿Está muy buena la prieta, qué no[20]?"*

Yeah, she was. But what eighteen-year old wasn't, I thought, and pried my eyes away from those long milk-chocolate legs. I tried to ignore the rest of what I saw. Some things were going to have to change around here, or I'd never get any writing done.

---

[20] The black girl's good-looking, isn't she?

Goose walked out of the TV room and headed for the kitchen. I heard him start up the Keurig, and a few minutes later he reappeared with a cup of coffee held up to his mouth, slurping and smacking his lips. LeToya still hadn't stirred. I hoped she was alive.

"So what's in your new episode?" Goose repeated his question.

"Some good action," I said. "The cartel submarine sinks a Coast Guard cutter in the Gulf of Mexico off Padre Island, and the president is furious because the CIA can't figure out who did it."

Goose sighed. "That sounds safe," he said.

Joel called later in the afternoon. He was almost giddy.

"Clabe, I think you've hit the mother lode. This is a page-turner, and I don't even like the genre," he added.

"Just keep the cash coming to my PayPal account," I said.

"No problem," he answered. "You're earning it. But what about the FBI? Will they be calling me about this episode?"

I laughed and glanced over at Goose who sat in the living room in his boxers, drinking coffee and listening to the conversation. He rolled his eyes.

"Don't think so, Joel," I said. "Not this time."

The rest of the day was quiet. LeToya and the Mexicans were unusually subdued, nursing monstrous hangovers and popping ibuprofen by the handful. Rigo followed me around jealously, snarling at Nacho and Goose but not pressing the attack. He ignored LeToya completely. Maybe he was getting used to Latinos, and he just wasn't sure about her.

I took advantage of the silence and wrote, every now and then glancing across Bohicket Creek when the noise of a large outboard motor or the screeching of seagulls diving in the wake of a shrimp boat distracted me. Finally, though, I gave up on the story. I was just too sober to write.

That could be remedied, I thought, and walked into the kitchen. I waded through empty bottles and cans strewn across the floor and opened the refrigerator door. I stared dumbfounded at the empty shelves inside and the plastic six-pack yokes lying on the kitchen cabinets. It looked like the carnage left in the aftermath of a major battle. The casualties of that conflict happened to be sitting like zombies in the next room, and I had become collateral damage. My beer stash had been decimated. A lonely green bottle of Dos Equis lay forlornly on its side in the vegetable crisper. I cursed and retrieved the last beer in the house.

Five minutes later the four of us plus Rigo piled into Goose's truck with me at the wheel and headed up Maybank Highway towards Main Road and Piggly Wiggly. We were twelve miles from the nearest supermarket or liquor store.

"I wish there was a closer store," I said. "I don't like the idea of driving twelve miles every time we run out of beer."

"Yeah," agreed Goose. "We could be making that trip twice a day."

If yesterday was any gauge, Goose could be right.

"We don't have to go all the way to the Pig," volunteered LeToya.

"You know something closer?" I asked.

"Yeah," she replied. "The place DeAndre was going to take us yesterday, only he was too drunk."

I thought I heard the sound of a helicopter overhead and leaned forward and looked up through the windshield. Nothing but Spanish moss and flashes of sunlight and blue sky. I was getting paranoid. They couldn't have found us already, I kept telling myself. Surely yesterday was a coincidence or a case of mistaken identity, but I really wasn't so sure.

"Did you hear me?" LeToya asked. She followed my gaze and also looked up through the windshield at the sky. "Watcha looking at?" she asked.

"Thought I heard a helicopter," I replied.

"They fly over all the time," she said. "Looking for drug dealers. Lots of weed and coke comes up the North Edisto and Bohicket Creek. At first the police thought Nacho was one of the drug dealers."

I looked back at Nacho who seemed happy as a lark. Maybe pawning his girlfriend off on Goose was a relief, or maybe he was just too stoned to care. I wished I could believe LeToya. But what did an eighteen year old local girl know about the feds flying helicopters over Rockville, South Carolina?

"So you wanna to go to Johnson Baby Grand or not?" she asked.

"They sell beer at a piano store?"

"That ain't no piano store. It's a bar. For black folks," she explained.

"What do you mean a bar for black folks?" I asked. "You still have segregation in South Carolina?"

"Judge for yourself," laughed LeToya. "Slow down, here it is on the right."

I remembered seeing Johnson Baby Grand on our first trip down Maybank Highway. At the time I thought it was a damned odd place to peddle pianos.

"Look, there's DeAndre's car," said Goose.

"My brother is gonna get himself fired if he doesn't stop drinking during the day," said LeToya.

I turned off the highway and parked in the small gravel parking lot in front of the run-down wooden shack. A faded painted sign on the side of the building proclaimed "Johnson Baby Grand". I wondered if it was a good idea for me to go inside. I knew damned well there were neighborhoods in south Dallas I wouldn't even drive through, much less walk blithely into an all-black bar. Maybe it was different here. If worse came to worse, I reasoned, DeAndre would stand up for me.

We all climbed out of Goose's pickup, and I heard an old Motown tune from within. It was either the Temptations or the Four Tops, I thought. I never could tell them apart. There were two other cars in front of the ramshackle dive besides DeAndre's official SUV; a huge, low-slung, 1980s-vintage Oldsmobile, and an old 300 Series Chrysler sedan with an elaborate front grill and sweeping rear fins. Now that was an old car. I was pretty sure Detroit quit making those monstrosities in the mid-60s.

I followed LeToya through the front door into a smoky, dimly lit room. The furnishings were Spartan. The bar was on the left, and an old-fashioned radio cassette player perched on one of the shelves behind the bartender screeched a tinny version of an old song I vaguely recognized.

"Is that the Temptations?" I asked the middle-aged bartender.

"The Temptations? Hmmmph!" he scoffed. "That there's Smokey Robinson & the Miracles." He looked as surprised to see me as I was to have asked the question.

I wondered what had possessed me to walk into an all-black bar in rural South Carolina and then ask a stupid-ass question about Motown music that I knew nothing about. I tried not to look around the room, but I felt every pair of eyes in the place on me.

I don't think I'd had a single social conversation with a black person since I did my brief stint in the feds more than a decade ago. Back then I had played a lot of basketball and chess with the brothers, and was on at least a "wassup" basis with several of them. One day on the basketball court, one of them had even called me "niggah". I never did figure out what that was about.

"Here're my white friends!" shouted DeAndre. He got up from a picnic table that stood right inside the front door and gave me a bear hug. "These are the people I told you about who are renting Mr. Rivers' house on Bohicket Creek." He turned to the five or six people inside and gestured to us.

"I told you we're not white," insisted Goose. "We're Mexicans. There's a difference."

"DeAndre, are you drunk again?" asked LeToya.

"None of your business, little sister," replied DeAndre almost politely.

I assumed the only reason for DeAndre's chivalry was that he didn't want the rest of the Johnson Baby Grand clientele to know LeToya was likely making the two-backed beast with my two Mexican friends. Did that make it a three-backed beast, I wondered?

LeToya, Nacho, and Goose lined up at the bar and started where they had left off the day before.

"What kind of beer you got here?" asked Goose.

"Today we got Colt 45 malt liquor and Old English," said the bartender still staring at us like we were crazy. He was probably right.

"How about Dos Equis?" asked Goose.

"You fucked-up or something?" The bartender shook his head and laughed.

"Clabe, come over here. We need to talk," said DeAndre.

I sat down with DeAndre at his picnic table. It was covered with a plastic table cloth with a flowery design that reeked of industrial chemicals and stale beer.

Goose obligingly brought me a can of Colt 45 and set it in front of me.

"This is lousy beer," he said and walked back to the bar.

I looked at the can suspiciously and realized we were going to make that trip to the Pig anyway.

"What can I do for you, DeAndre?" I asked. I didn't like his sudden interest in me.

DeAndre was drunk, and he leaned forward and put his forehead against mine and held it there with the palm of his hand on the back of my head.

"I'm a deputy sheriff, Clabe" he said. "Wadmalaw Island is my beat."

I didn't like the way this was going but had no choice but to stay and listen.

"Yeah," I said. "So?"

"So tell me, white boy," he began. "Why is the FBI looking for you?"

Chapter 17

I glanced around the bar, wondering how many of the bleary-eyed drunks staring at me were DeAndre's snitches. My eyes shifted towards the front door where I expected a black S.W.A.T. team shouting "Go, Go, Go!" to burst into Johnson Baby Grand. They would cuff me, read me my Miranda rights, and take the long, silent ride with me to the county jail. But nothing happened. It was eerie, and some generic rap shit had replaced Smokey Robinson's tight Motown vibe. It was giving me a headache.

De Andre hadn't moved an inch, and his dark, expressionless eyes were less than an inch from mine and just stared. I noticed the whites of his eyes were dull and faded, almost yellow. Maybe from drinking, or maybe from long-time drug use. But what was this forehead to forehead crap? A South Carolina male bonding ritual? Rigo and I did something like this in the morning when he put his front paws on my bed and begged to be fed, but I was tiring quickly of DeAndre's caress or whatever the hell it was.

"You're hurting my forehead, DeAndre," I said.

He removed his enormous paw from the back of my head and sat back in his chair. My forehead left an imprint on his. I guess that made us some kind of temporary kin. Like blood brothers or something.

"Sorry," he said.

We stared at each other, but I wasn't about to break the silence.

"They're after you, aren't they?" he asked. His loud, conspiratorial whisper had attracted the attention of everyone in Johnson Baby Grand including the bartender. We might as well have been on stage, reciting our lines at the top of our lungs. Othello meets Hamlet or maybe Huckleberry Finn having a heart-to-heart with Jim.

"I don't know what you're talking about," I said.

"The hell you don't," he said. "Don't you lie to me, Clabe Taylor. I ran those Texas license plates, and then I did an NCIC check on both you and your Mexican friend."

He paused like he expected me to congratulate him and pat him on the back. This is what I hated about the police. The bastards obviously weren't above coming into your house, partaking of your hospitality, drinking a six-pack of your Mexican beer, and then running your name through a fucking computer afterwards. And then they bragged about it.

"I know Goose is an ex-con, and I know you're a writer. And what's this about you and the CIA?" he asked.

"You've got me confused with somebody else," I said lamely. At least he hadn't come across my conviction, I thought.

DeAndre took a long pull off his can of Colt 45.

"I don't think so," he said. "But don't worry; this stays between us."

"Oh yeah?" I asked sarcastically. "Like what happens on Wadmalaw Island stays on Wadmalaw Island?"

"Something like that," he answered and flashed those teeth at me in a drunken grin.

I didn't need to hear any more, and I wasn't about to admit to DeAndre that he was right, no matter how silly it was to keep denying it.

"Sorry, DeAndre," I said. "We've got to get moving. Got to get to the Pig before dark and replace all that beer you drank the other day."

"Relax, I'm not saying a word to anyone," said DeAndre in the same conspiratorial voice. "And thanks for the beer."

Goose and Nacho were happy to leave. They didn't like the malt liquor or the music. LeToya was just along for the ride. She didn't care one way or the other.

"DeAndre, you're gonna lose your job, fool," she said walking out the door. "Everybody around knows you're here drinking at Johnson Baby Grand when you're supposed to be out working."

"Shut up, LeToya. I'm working a case....it's confidential."

"Your ass is confidential," she replied.

We drove straight to the Pig and loaded five grocery carts with enough beer to cause Bohicket Creek to flood at high tide. Of course the beer wouldn't be the direct cause of the flood surge. It would just be Goose and Nacho pissing a river of diluted Mexican alcohol off the dock into that brackish water.

As we checked out, most of the Piggly Wiggly employees gathered in a knot around our cashier and watched wide-eyed as she rang up case after case of Dos Equis, Tecate, Pacífco, Carta Blanca, Modelo Especial, and whatever other kind of Mexican beer happened to be on the shelves that day. We bought it all. They stared at us when we left as if we were some kind of Bohemian reprobates. Goose had donned a beret he found under the driver's seat in his truck and was strutting his "Brown Power" retro look. Maybe that's what prompted the self-righteous condemnation that I read in the eyes of the Pig cashiers and bag boys. It was getting difficult to keep a low profile on Wadmalaw Island.

Things returned to normal for a couple of weeks. Of course, normal is a relative concept when you consider the company I keep. Worries about the helicopter fly-over faded to the back of my mind, and I spent my days writing and drinking straight rum with a twist of lime. I didn't even want to imagine how LeToya and the Mexicans spent their time. I saw them occasionally as they emerged from their den of iniquity to skinny dip in Bohicket Creek. I imagine Miss Myrtle was getting an eye full, but we didn't hear anything else from DeAndre, so maybe the old Southern lady was enjoying her neighbors' libertine behavior after all.

The bucolic serenity ended with an exclamation point a few days later about an hour before dawn. Rigo's whining and growling woke me with a start. Periodic flashes of piercing light illuminated the bedroom, and I heard the unmistakable thumping sounds of rapidly approaching helicopters. I ran to the living room and peered out the floor-to-ceiling window overlooking the water. By this time several helicopters were hovering just over the docks and had turned the impenetrable predawn blackness into the blinding sunlight of a South Carolina summer's day with their spotlights. Only it was the beginning of November and still six o'clock in the morning.

I looked out the kitchen window and saw four black SUVs wheel into Nacho's yard with their headlights off and disgorge a dozen uniformed SWAT team commandos. With unintelligible shouts and melodramatic hysteria, they kicked in Nacho's front door and poured into his tiny shack like small round turds spiraling down a toilet bowl.

I looked up at the three helicopters hovering between the houses and Bohicket Creek and saw men rappelling down ropes with weapons strapped to their backs. Rigo stood with his front paws on the kitchen sink and growled menacingly. He couldn't see what was happening, but he heard the shouting and saw the erratic illumination from the helicopter spot lights. He might have even picked up the scent of fresh shit from next door.

I'm not sure what there was in Nacho's rundown shack that warranted a raid by almost twenty heavily armed and uniformed "peace" officers, four SUVs, and three helicopters. I was half convinced they simply had the wrong house, and that Goose and I were the real targets. I suspected it was only a matter of minutes before the SWAT teams discovered the cockup and redeployed in our direction. But before that thought had time to register in my sleep-deprived brain, I heard banging on the front door. Rigo was beside himself. I looked at my faithful friend and wondered what would become of him.

I thought about making a run out the porch and down the back steps, but I knew it would be an exercise in futility. They would have the entire house surrounded with the muzzles of a dozen or more semi-automatic assault rifles trained on all the exits. It would be a macabre scene of butchery, like Butch Cassidy and the Sundance Kid being blown to bits in Bolivia; not the kind of death I had imagined for myself. No, I couldn't let it end like that. I took a deep breath, locked Rigo in the bathroom, and went downstairs to answer the pounding on the door that had not let up.

"Sir, we need to speak with you," declared a pot-bellied SWAT team member in a nasal twang, panting as if he had just finished the Charleston 10K Bridge Run.

"Sure, how can I help you?" I asked innocently, trying to keep my bladder under control.

"Sir, how well did you know your neighbor?" he asked.

"You mean Nacho, the gardener?" I answered his question with one of my own.

"Sir, he's no gardener, and his name's sure not Nacho," said the cop with a smirk.

"Well, who is he?" I asked. "Couldn't you have arrested him at a decent hour?" It always helps to play the irate, law-abiding taxpayer.

The conversation had just taken a promising turn, and I began to see a faint light at the end of the tunnel. Hope springs eternal even though I was sure it was going to be at the expense of Nacho's freedom. I noticed movement next door through the trees and glanced over just in time to see Nacho hustled to a waiting car surrounded by uniformed police commandos still wearing black balaclavas. The cops had put a towel over Nacho's head, something I guess they had seen on television, but I recognized their prisoner from his flip-flops and skinny legs. I recited a silent prayer for him because I knew the boy's life was over. He should never have crossed the Rio Grande.

The cop followed my eyes with his own and smiled broadly.

"You'll read about it tomorrow in the *Post & Courier*," he said. "Let's just say the supply of cocaine to Charleston County has just petered out."

"Really?" I tried to sound impressed.

"I hope you don't mind if I come back tomorrow to interview you?" he asked.

"Certainly not," I answered, with much more eagerness than I actually felt. I watched the cop as he waddled after his colleagues and got into the passenger seat of one of the SUVs.

My thoughts turned to Goose. I knew he was doomed too and would be facing a catch-all conspiracy charge at the very least. The feds would have no evidence against Goose, but they'd hammer him with vague counts of racketeering, which were far more likely to stick. When they learned Goose was an ex-con, they'd up the ante, and my sidekick would be facing a long, all-expense paid vacation in the Big House; all for getting laid in the wrong place and at the wrong time.

I kept my eyes peeled on the door to the shack, and one last figure finally came out. It was LeToya, but not the one I knew. This one was packing heat and wearing a bullet-proof vest with the letters "DEA" emblazoned on the front in large gold letters. A spare pair of handcuffs hung from her waist. She held her shoulders back and walked with a self-satisfied strut I hadn't seen before.

The truth hit me like a sledgehammer. LeToya wasn't some eighteen-year old local girl looking for fun and free dope with a couple of Mexican potheads like I thought. She was an undercover narcotics agent who obviously wasn't averse to fucking her way to an arrest. I watched as she slid into a waiting SUV. The driver of the lead vehicle slapped a flashing police light on the roof of the car, turned it on, and led the procession out of what had been Nacho's back yard.

Chapter 18

But where the hell was Goose? I walked down the back steps from the porch just as the first rays of sunlight glinted above the horizon just over Bohicket Creek to the east.

"Find Goose," I told Rigo.

He growled at the name and started running in circles with his nose to the ground, trying to pick up Goose's scent. Rigo ran out to the dock in front of the neighbor's house and started to bark. I saw something move in the water and then recognized Goose as he raised his body clumsily onto the dock and lay there motionless. I grabbed a couple of towels from the porch and ran to the dock where Rigo continued to bark. Goose was shivering uncontrollably, and I wrapped him in the towels the best I could and massaged his body to get his blood circulating.

After a few minutes Goose was able to stand up. I took his left arm and slung it over my shoulder and helped him limp back to our house. He mumbled incoherently and tears streamed down his cheeks, but I didn't understand a word of what he was trying to say.

"It's not what you think," said Goose, once he stopped convulsing from the cold. His lips were blue, and his teeth still chattered, but he could finally talk.

"Oh, and what am I thinking?" I asked. Most of the time I thought Goose's company was a definite handicap, and now I had concluded he was a liability I just didn't need. From the baptism with toilet water at an interstate rest stop on the South Carolina border to his frenzied fornication with an undercover DEA agent, Goose attracted the unhealthy attention of both plain folks and the authorities wherever he went. I regretted the Faustian bargain I had made in return for the use of his pickup truck.

"You think LeToya double-crossed us and just pretended to like Nacho and me so she could bust him," he declared.

I nodded my head. "Yeah, the thought had crossed my mind."

"But it wasn't like that at all," Goose insisted. "Well maybe for Nacho, but not for me."

"Oh?" I asked.

I carefully placed a small oak log on top of the blazing kindling in the fireplace. A few seconds later I laid another one alongside the first and then a third, perpendicular to the first two. Within a few minutes the logs caught, and heat began to emanate from the recessed fireplace. Nacho gratefully wrapped himself in a blanket I brought and sat down as close he could get to the flames.

"*No, para nada*[21]," he continued. "She woke me up this morning and told me about the raid just before the *chotas*[22] got here. She told me to get in the river and hide under the dock."

"And what about Nacho?" I asked. "You didn't warn him?"

"No, it was either him or me. LeToya said if I warned Nacho, she'd have to arrest me too."

Not quite Judas and not quite the Apostle Peter, I guess, but I couldn't blame Goose for ditching his friend. At the end of the day, Nacho had brought the heat down on himself.

"So Nacho really was a big drug dealer?" I asked.

"He was a *chingón*[23]. The biggest around. He was working for the Sinaloa Cartel."

"The cartel?" I was incredulous. "Thanks for letting me know."

---

[21] No way
[22] police
[23] big shot

Out of the frying pan and into the fire. That's how our flight from Texas was beginning to look to me. Of the hundreds of places we could have picked to lie low, we had to pick a place where our only friends were feds and drug dealers. The way our luck was going, the damned Russians would be pulling into our front yard soon and wanting to drink vodka with us right before they poisoned us with polonium.

"I didn't want to tell you. Figured you'd panic and want to move. I was having too much fun to leave," Goose confessed.

Well, that explained the helicopters on our boat ride, I thought. But it didn't tell me anything about what kind of a risk DeAndre represented after he ran our names through his law enforcement data base. My plan had been to remain in relative obscurity here on the South Carolina coast. Instead, my partner was unknowingly galloping a DEA agent, and her deputy sheriff brother was undoubtedly in on the ruse and conducting his own private investigation of his sister's contacts. The whole story had an unhealthy incestuous ring to it. I didn't like the glare of the limelight even on a dim local level here in rural South Carolina, and I toyed with the idea of hitting the road that afternoon. I was sure that Rivers Pickney wouldn't mind pocketing our six months of rent that I had so impetuously flung on the table only a few weeks before.

"I think I broke her heart," said Goose.

"You what?" I asked. Maybe the prolonged exposure to the 60 degree water in Bohicket Creek had resulted in a massive kill-off of active neurons in Goose's brain, or maybe he was just hidebound by an unshakable belief in his own Latin lover irresistibility. But I knew I had to be gentle with his sensitive ego. I thought of his mother in Alabama, and I suddenly felt sorry for my sidekick and wanted nothing more than to shield him from reality.

"She loved me, but she had a job to do," said Goose.

Goose was normally about as sexually discriminating as a stoat. Usually, though, his amorous conquests were nothing to write home about. This time was different. LeToya's inexplicable and misplaced attraction towards this societal misfit had messed with Goose's mind. He hadn't had to pay for sex; his partner wasn't a prostitute, and she had intervened and helped him avoid imminent arrest. Goose had rarely experienced human warmth in his life, and he responded with a predictable conditioned reflex just like one of Pavlov's dogs. He fell in love for the first time since he married a

16-year old prostitute in Durango, Mexico several decades before.

I heard the *ring-ding-ding* of the newspaper delivery boy's dirt bike and the slap of the morning edition of the Post & Courier as it struck a glancing blow against the front door. I trotted down the stairs with Rigo at my side barking. I opened the door just in time to see the departing dirt bike and a bluish-gray cloud of exhaust that slowly dissipated in the thick humidity of early morning.

I picked up the paper and glanced casually at the headlines. I felt a tingling that started in back of my testicles and then emanated like an electric shock into my lower intestine and kept moving north with the subtlety of a colonoscopy. I felt queasy, and bile rose to my throat. I looked again, and there it was in black and white. Gut-wrenching déjà vu.

"COAST GUARD CUTTER SINKS OFF TEXAS COAST".

I didn't even want to look at the article. I knew the story by heart. Hell, I had written it, and *The Ganja Times* published it over a week ago.

"What the hell's going on? It was fiction....just fiction," I kept mumbling under my breath.

When the *Washington Post* reported that the Sinaloa Cartel and the Russians were working together, it looked like speculation on the part of an overeager journalist. He had presented no evidence and only spoke in vague generalities. It was good guesswork, but there was no proof, no smoking gun. Granted, that was the story line in my novel, but the appearance of the article in the *Post* a few weeks after I published my episode could have been pure happenstance.

But this was different.

There was no coincidence here; no unlikely confluence of fact and fiction. We were no longer talking in abstract or academic terms about drug cartel *modus operandi* like in the first article. People were dying now; en masse. And I had written about it before it happened.

"Pack your bag," I said to Goose as I walked back into the living room. He was still sitting in front of the fire. "We're leaving in thirty minutes."

"Are you crazy?" he asked. "We're cool here."

"No, we're not," I answered. "It's bad enough that a SWAT team raided our next door neighbor, and you almost got arrested. It's worse that DeAndre ran our names through a computer and knows the feds are looking for us. But this breaks the camel's back." I tossed the newspaper in his direction and went to gather my things.

From the bedroom I heard Goose curse viciously in Spanish, again and again. I heard the floorboards creak and the plodding sounds of his footsteps in the hallway getting closer. I looked up and Goose was staring at me.

"Who ARE you?" he asked, his voice barely audible over the rasp of the ancient central heating unit that had just kicked in with a jolting rumble. I glanced up at Goose. He was disheveled, his hair still wet from the creek and plastered down over his eyes. The blanket was still wrapped tightly around his naked body. Rigo stood uncharacteristically at his side watching me too, maybe sensing that the newfound peace and serenity of our lives had been eviscerated.

"A week after your episode about the Coast Guard cutter gets published, and then it really happens?" Goose waved the newspaper over his head as if it were a grand jury indictment.

"Who ARE you?" he repeated.

I didn't have time to answer Goose's questions. Especially since I had no answers myself. Frankly, I could only think of two possibilities, each of them equally absurd and about as likely as there being an honest politician in Washington. In my mind it boiled down to this: either the Sinaloa Cartel was using my novel as an instruction manual, or I was subconsciously and supernaturally clairvoyant, or maybe both. I finished packing and took my things out to Goose's truck, mulling a variety of mad scenarios. Eventually I rejected my two hypotheses and accepted the one stark reality that would not be denied. The noose was tightening around our necks, and the longer we diddled around here in Rockville, the more likely we would be the targets of the next raid. I calculated that we had no more than a few hours to make our move. But where could we go?

Chapter 19

I had barely finished packing our things in the back of Goose's truck when my cell phone rang. I glanced at the caller ID before answering. It was Joel from *The Ganja Times*. I didn't feel like talking to anyone after the morning I'd had but thought Joel might have some information that could come in handy if Goose and I were to make good our escape from Wadmalaw Island. I was feeling cornered, and there was only one way off the island. We were sitting ducks for the feds if we didn't make our move soon.

"Clabe, is there something you're not telling me?" Joel asked without preamble and without even saying hello. His voice was strained.

"Sounds like you already read today's paper," I answered.

"READ TODAY'S PAPER?" he shouted. "That would be the least of my worries."

I heard Goose swearing in the bedroom and Rigo growling his pre-Banzai attack warning. Hopefully, Goose knew enough not to move, but I couldn't get off the phone right now to help.

"Look, I don't know any more than you. I had nothing to do with what happened in the Gulf of Mexico," I said. "All I did was predict it. Unintentionally, I might add."

"Well, let's see," he began sarcastically. "Two goons from the FBI interviewed me in my office this morning while a sleaze ball from the Russian consulate waited in the reception room. A half hour later some greaser comes in wearing a $1,500 pair of Ferragamos and enough gold jewelry to sink the Titanic and speaking English with a heavy Mexican accent. But they all had something in common, Clabe. Know what it was, goddammit?"

Joel was getting more and more worked up by the minute, and I had to hold the cell phone a foot away from my ear to avoid permanent damage to my tympanic membrane. I could tell his morning had been stressful. At least we had that in common. I could empathize with him, but I needed more of a hug than a tongue lashing at the moment.

"What?" I asked lamely.

"They all wanted to know where that asshole Clabe Taylor was!" Joel shouted.

I let him yell, hoping he would get it out of his system so we could have a civil conversation and I could find out something useful.

"I told 'em you were in Cabo, so if you are, get the fuck out of there right now. You're about to have visitors, and none of them looked particularly friendly," Joel shouted.

He was starting to get hoarse, and I patiently waited for an opening to ask some questions. Goose was shouting for help in the other room, but I was tired of bailing my sidekick out of trouble. He knew the rules of etiquette around Rigo. If he had violated them, he would just have to pay the price.

"Stay where you are!" I shouted. "Just don't move and you'll be fine!"

"*¡Tu madre!*" Goose shouted. "*¡Ayudame[24]!*"

"What are you talking about?" asked Joel. "Who's that yelling?"

"It's nothing," I said. "These damn Mexicans in Cabo are just afraid of dogs."

"Well, I happen to be afraid of those damn Mexicans, and they didn't start coming around my office until I started publishing your novel. That wasn't part of our agreement." said Joel.

I knew I had to calm Joel down, and there was no better way to do that than to steer the conversation

---

[24] Help me!

towards money. Joel would do anything for a buck, and I just needed to remind him that the minor harassment from his visitors today was a small price to pay for the financial harvest he was reaping. If Joel's readership had mushroomed over something as innocuous as the "Russian-Cartel alliance" episode from the previous week, think what it would do now. Imagine the increase in advertising revenues.

"So tell me, Joel, how's the magazine doing now? Financially, I mean."

I heard a sigh on the other end of the line. You could almost hear the dollar signs going *"ching-ching"* in Joel's mind, and I knew he was weighing the slight inconvenience of a few unwanted visitors this morning against his burgeoning Bank of America operating account.

"Christ, Clabe, it's unbelievable," he admitted. "I had to hire two more advertising salesmen this morning just to handle the incoming calls. Another episode or two like this and I'll be able to buy that villa north of Palma de Mallorca I told you about. Unless they shut me down before," he said.

"Shut you down?" I asked.

"Yeah, the FBI is saying if I keep publishing, I'll be a person of interest in a terrorism case," Joel said, his voice cracking. "They say they could start freezing my assets, including the magazine."

"You're as much a terrorist as my Blue Heeler," I said and immediately regretted the comparison.

"If he's anything like that dog in your book, he's a vicious sonofabitch," said Joel. "Plus he's a racist. That's not very reassuring."

"Listen, let me call you back in a couple of hours. I don't want the feds to trace this call if they haven't already," I suggested.

"Make sure you give me a ring. I've got some other news too," Joel said and hung up.

Meanwhile, Goose continued to roar like a newly emasculated bull calf in the other room, and Rigo was barking now and then to punctuate his incessant growling. The din was deafening. I walked around the corner and stopped in my tracks. Goose had managed to clamber on top of the dresser and now stood engaged in a desperate contest of tug of war with Rigo over the blanket he had been wearing. There was something prehistoric about the scene. It was a primordial battle for survival. I would have liked to have seen how it played out. I hated to separate the two, but we had bigger fish to fry. I called Rigo to my side and handed Goose back his blanket.

"You've got five minutes to get dressed, and then we're leaving with or without you," I warned.

"But it's my truck," Goose argued.

"Then I'd hurry if I were you," I said.

I think Goose's brush with the law and the realization that he barely avoided a lengthy sentence in the joint had, to a certain degree, humbled the man. I don't know how else to explain his about-face and sudden willingness to assume a subordinate role in our relationship. Maybe, it was the newspaper article and the riddle that surrounded it. He probably did wonder "who I really was". Maybe he even suspected I was somehow complicit in the sinking of the Coast Guard cutter off Padre Island, which would make me a super badass *cabrón*[25] in his eyes. Whatever it was, I welcomed his sudden smarmy deference. When Rigo and I made our way to the truck, we found Goose already in the shotgun seat. He handed me a cold beer when I slid behind the wheel.

"Clabe," said Goose and paused.

"What?"

"Remember when I asked you who you really were?" said Goose.

"Yeah."

---

[25] In this context – a badass

"Never mind. I don't want to know," he said.

As we eased the old pickup down Sea Island Yacht Club Road for the last time, I had mixed feelings. It had been a wonderful month. I had been able to forget, at least to some degree, that we were wanted men. The boat rides, sunrises, dolphin pods, fresh shrimp, and the screeching water birds had distracted me, at least temporarily, from the desperate plight we were in. But now I had to decide what we were going to do. Two things came to mind immediately. First, we needed more beer for the cooler. Secondly, we had to ditch Goose's truck and buy a different vehicle. DeAndre had jotted down the license when he first came to visit, and I didn't doubt that he would rat us out once he realized we were gone.

We probably shouldn't have risked a beer run to Piggly Wiggly, but for once luck was on our side. I made Goose stay in the truck where he and Rigo had established an uneasy truce. Rigo growled, but as long as Goose didn't move, the uneasy truce held. I bought several cases of Mexican beer, and the Pig employees didn't seem to recognize me without Goose or LeToya. Back in the truck, Goose and I discussed strategy while we drained the better half of the first six-pack.

I was in an introspective mood. It probably was the effect of mixing beer with the adrenaline residue still in my system from the morning's close escape from the law. I looked at Goose and those reptilian eyes and realized how much better suited he was for life in the 21st century than I was. He was honest to a fault and completely elemental. He didn't intellectualize a decision to death and then agonize over its possible consequences. He felt, and then he acted. I envied the man.

We retraced our route in reverse, south down I-95, draining bottle after bottle of Dos Equis. I knew I should quit drinking, but I had no wife to nag and harangue me about making better life choices. In fact, I had nobody but this Neanderthal throwback sitting next to me and that stinking dog in the back seat, and both were as much liabilities as they were assets. In their company I was unlikely ever to change my socially unacceptable habits. I suddenly realized I was becoming a social misfit, much like my two companions already were. Maybe it was time to get a tattoo and a piercing and join the crowd.

"We need to trade in this truck," I said, trying to rid myself of my uncharacteristic melancholy. I tried to talk myself back into the swashbuckling persona that I assumed when I wrote.

"I bet we can find a used-car lot in one of these little towns," said Goose. "Maybe even one that caters to Mexicans. They won't ask any questions."

Two hours later Goose's old truck stood parked in the used car lot of El Barrio Automotive Sales in Ridgedale, South Carolina with a FOR SALE sign on its windshield. The proprietor, a devious, hard-nosed case from East L.A., who also owned the "Happy Endings" rent-by-the-hour motel across the street, was pleased with the transaction. Goose had wanted to trade his truck in for a 1986 Chevrolet Impala lowrider, but at my insistence he settled for a late model Ford 150 pickup, and we paid the owner an extra $2500 in cash for the upgrade. Goose pouted for an hour after we left. In the end, the extent of his lowriding was a blue checkered bandana around his head and a pair of baggy Dickies khakis I bought him at a Super Walmart off I-95. He was happy with his new look, and we had a car that couldn't be traced to either of us.

"Where are we going?" Goose asked.

"Back to Texas," I answered. "I understand the people there better."

"*Hórale,*" he said and twisted the cap off another bottle of beer.

Chapter 20

If anyone had suggested that I would have sex with a former Miss Universe later that evening in a Macon, Georgia hotel room, I would have said they were mad. Absolutely bonkers. But I also didn't anticipate the furor over this morning's newspaper article about the loss of the Coast Guard cutter in the Gulf of Mexico. I certainly didn't think the national media would make the connection between the news and the episode of my serial novel published in *The Ganja Times*. So who am I to predict the future?

Joel had concealed that bit of heart-stopping news until I returned his phone call later in the afternoon. As he put it, Clabe Taylor had gone viral, and celebrity news anchors were besieging him with phone calls and were clamoring to meet the "renegade author". That's what they were calling me now, Joel said.

"Do you trust me, Clabe?" he asked.

"No," I answered truthfully.

"How about if I told you that a certain news network will pay you $50,000 for a ten-minute interview to be taped tonight at a location of your choice," he asked. "They just need a couple hours advance warning to get a crew to wherever you'll be."

Damn, that was a tough one. To tell the truth, I didn't trust anyone right now, but I sure needed the money. We had burned through a considerable sum in the last few weeks. Our beer bill alone was likely equal to the GNP of most third-world countries.

"Cash?" I asked.

"I'm sure that can be arranged," Joel answered.

"What do you want out of it?"

"Nothing. Your notoriety pays off handsomely in advertising revenues," said Joel.

Sex was still was the farthest thing from my mind as we raced down the interstate, trying to put as much distance as possible between us and Bohicket Creek. Goose was riding shotgun and reading out loud from a Spanish copy of the New Testament. He was fascinated with the Book of Revelation and descriptions of the Apocalypse. I thought that particularly fitting, given our own situation. My own thoughts were lofty and pure, even though I would probably blow three times the legal alcohol limit if tested. That alone should have spoken volumes about the likelihood of my involvement in a tryst later that evening. Carmen was right about the deleterious effect alcohol had on my sex drive.

The whole thing only took a few phone calls to arrange. Macon, Georgia was the next major population center in our path, and I dialed Joel's cell number and gave him the name of a high-dollar hotel right off the interstate as you entered the city.

"I thought you were in Cabo," he said and laughed. "I never did buy that, you know."

"Whatever. I can be at the hotel in two hours."

Five minutes later Joel called back. It was all arranged, he said, and he gave me the hotel room number. I imagined that a news crew would be hauling ass from Atlanta to make it on time. If they were late, I didn't plan to stick around waiting. I assumed I'd be talking to Wolf and the CNN team. I was wrong.

When I knocked on the hotel room door, a camera technician greeted me and said that Gretel would be with me in just a minute.

"Gretel?" I said. "What show is this?"

"Fox & Friends, of course," said the cameraman and continued to set up his equipment.

I look around the suite, dumbfounded. These guys traveled in style. In just a few minutes the crew had transformed the suite into a television studio. Technicians were working with the lighting, reflective umbrellas, background screens, and video cameras. A make-up artist grabbed me, called me "darling", and started powdering my cheeks before I even sat down. Someone thrust a glass of cold champagne in my hand, and a waiter walked around in a black vest and bow-tie carrying a tray of sandwich hors d'oeuvres and cantaloupe balls impaled by red, white, and blue toothpicks.

When Gretel made her appearance, trailed by two personal assistants who fussed over her dress, alternately brushing off stray pieces of lint and straightening out wrinkles, my jaw dropped. She was radiant. A former Miss Universe, Gretel's bedazzling beauty made everything else in the room recede into bland nothingness. Despite her All-American cheerleader looks, which I don't normally find appealing, there was something about her that aroused me and caused my loins to percolate despite my blood alcohol level. No, it wasn't the cleavage, which I had noticed during the Dallas studio interview. Nor was it her finely toned and tanned calves which led to a pair of perfect thighs and delightfully sized buttocks. It was more than that. Behind all the peaches and cream of her wholesome look, Gretel had that dirty-girl look in her eyes; something which I hadn't noticed in Dallas.

The interview itself was desultory, almost perfunctory. Sure, she asked all the right questions about the uncanny prescience of my serial novel and speculated whether I was associated with the Sinaloa Federation or the Russian Foreign Intelligence Service. She even touted her own courage at defying the FBI by meeting with me, something I didn't begrudge her, not at $50,000 a pop. But her heart wasn't in it, and she seemed to be in a hurry to end the interview, as if she had something else on her mind. That "something else" became obvious when the interview ended, and she unceremoniously shooed the entire crew and supporting cast out of her suite.

"Clabe, are you a Republican?" she asked as she poured me another glass of champagne and joined me on the sofa.

"A Republican?" I repeated. "Why do you ask?"

Gretel moved closer to me on the sofa and took another sip of champagne while she studied me at close range. Her face had become oddly flushed, and her breathing was shallow and rapid.

"Because I don't think you are," she said and leaned forward and brushed her lips across my ear. I felt my own face flush, and I began to throb in all the right places.

"Would it matter?"

"Maybe," she said. "Republicans are so predictable. They bore me." Her lips met mine, and her tongue shot out like the probing forked instrument of a Gila Monster in the Chihuahuan Desert. She began to unbuckle my jeans, and I didn't resist. She performed like a virtuoso, an experienced courtesan, or a well-trained Geisha girl. When she finally came up for air, she stood up and executed the most exquisite strip-tease I have ever witnessed. She was magnificent, everything you might expect of a naked former Miss Universe. If I were to fault Gretel's performance, and I admit it would be ungrateful and nitpicking to complain about anything, I might have silenced her incessant chatter. In between pants and moans and delicious sighs, she talked partisan politics and provided the most intimate descriptions imaginable of her trysts with the Republican leadership of both houses of Congress. She stressed that she only slept with Republicans, as if partisan fidelity justified her wanton behavior.

"But I don't think you're one of us," she repeated over and over.

I was craning my neck to get a glimpse of us in the mirror that hung over the bed and wishing the cameras were still whirring.

"No, of course I'm not," I finally admitted. "I was beginning to tire and wished she would climax so I could have another drink and catch my breath.

"Don't tell me you're a liberal!" she exclaimed and she began to writhe under me as if in agony.

"Say it!" she commanded.

"Say what? Liberal?"

"Ohhhh!" she cried out. I thought that had brought her over the edge, but she continued grinding away like an insatiable succubus.

"I'm more of an anarchist, really," I said and tried to keep myself under control for a few more minutes.

"Say you're a Democrat!" she demanded.

"Say what?"

"Just say it, Goddamn you to Hell!" she screamed. "I'm dying!"

I began to feel a bit uneasy about the noise level and hoped the rooms next to us were vacant.

"Just say you're a Democrat!" she howled and I felt like I was sixteen years old again, riding a wild saddle bronc at a weekend rodeo in Lockhart, Texas.

"Okay, I'm a Democrat!" I finally bawled, on the verge of physical exhaustion.

"Ohhhhh, my God! I knew it, you BASTARD!" She shrieked as a shattering orgasm distorted her features and froze her mouth in a scream that lasted a good thirty seconds. I shouted as well, but more from pain as she raked her sharp nails across my back. The pain was like a fiery razor.

We lay naked in each other's arms trying to recover from the wild wrestling match and didn't hear at first the persistent knocking on the door. Gretel was the first to notice and quickly threw on a white bath robe and walked to the door as if nothing out of the ordinary had just occurred.

"Ma'am, is everything alright? We've had some complaints about noise."

I looked out from the bathroom where I had sought refuge and saw a uniformed policeman standing in the doorway. He was well over six feet tall, rugged and handsome. I saw Gretel let her bathrobe fall open and she sipped her champagne provocatively, running her tongue over the lip of the glass. I knew I had better intervene before the situation got out of hand.

I came out of the bathroom wrestling a pair of jeans over my hips and threw a t-shirt on.

"Thank you, officer. We're fine. We got a little loud watching *The John Stewart Show* and laughing. Appreciate your checking on us," I added.

"John Stewart?" asked Gretel. "He's a Democrat, isn't he?"

I realized Gretel was more than a little drunk, and I led her back into the suite as the policeman smiled knowingly and shut the door. The champagne had gone to her head, and she staggered slightly as I supported her weight. I led her into bed, took off her robe, and tucked her in before leaving.

"Let's do this again soon," Gretel said, slurring her words. I nodded my head and kissed her goodbye on the forehead. I finished dressing, picked up the manila envelope with the cash, and grabbed some of the leftover hors d'oeuvres for Goose. Five minutes later we were back on the road, flush with cash and barreling towards Texas and whatever fate had in store for us.

Chapter 21

We drove through the night towards Mobile, Alabama, stopping every few hours at interstate rest areas to catch a few winks of sleep and to let Rigo out to pee. We felt safe in our new truck since it wasn't registered in either of our names yet. Goose was talkative and full of questions. It wasn't just the beer. He couldn't believe I had just earned fifty grand for a few minutes of television air time. Frankly, I couldn't either, but then Goose counted the hundred dollar bills in the manila envelope and rendered the verdict.

"*¡Cincuenta mil!*" he announced gleefully.

"That should last us for a while," I said.

I hadn't mentioned the wild tryst with Gretel. Goose was still coping with the discovery that his hot Low Country lover was an undercover DEA agent. He didn't need to hear about my sexual encounter with a former Miss Universe. Besides, somewhere in my southern DNA was an ironclad prohibition against a man talking about his sexual conquests. And to tell the truth, what kind of a conquest was it anyway when Gretel had been the one to ravish and use me to her own wicked purposes? I wondered if she was bragging to anyone about seducing an infamous writer on the lam.

"I wanna read your book," suddenly announced Goose.

"Really?" I laughed to myself.

Goose was an educated man despite outward appearances to the contrary. He had been an attorney in Mexico and had an enviable knowledge of Latin American literature and history. But in those days he had spoken only Spanish. When he came to Texas, it was in the company of U.S. Marshals, and he had been handcuffed and wore leg irons. He sucked up English like a thirsty sponge at El Reno, but by definition his vocabulary had some rough edges. When he spoke English, he projected more of a Latino "gangsta" persona than the smooth, debonair exterior he might have once presented in Mexico City high society. Goose was linguistically schizophrenic.

"Yeah, so what's the book about?" he asked. "Is there a badass hero who whacks everyone at the end?"

"Well, there's a hero. Haven't got to the end yet. But sometimes the hero doesn't win, you know?" I answered. In this particular case, I didn't think the hero would win, but maybe I was thinking more of myself than about any character in the book.

"Not in Mexico. That's for sure," Goose answered.

"Besides, your definition of a "hero" probably differs from mine."

"True," Goose said in English.

I was getting sleepy but knew we had to keep driving. Telling Goose about the plot of the serialized novel might be a good idea. It'd keep me awake and also might give me some ideas about where the plot should go from here. I had another episode edited and almost ready to email to Joel, but I needed inspiration and some new ideas for future chapters.

From what Joel said, there were at least three different organizations from three different countries looking for us. None of them had a reputation for charity or philanthropy, so I didn't know how any of this was going to end. When I thought of our dim prospects for the future, a lump rose in my throat and sat there stubbornly, almost choking me when I tried to swallow. A gulp of cold beer finally washed it away.

"Well, you know the beginning of the story. The Sinaloa drug cartel forms an alliance with the Russians and pays cash for an attack submarine."

I barely got the first sentence out when Goose interrupted.

"That never made sense to me even though I heard Salcido himself talk about it."

"Sure it does," I answered. "At least in my book. Salcido hates the United States because the Americans killed his brother. He already controls half of Mexico, but he wants even more power. He yearns to be a player in the international arena. Big ego, you know? The Russians, on the other hand, never change. They're always stepping on their own dicks and looking to regain superpower status. They think the alliance with the cartel is an opportunity to achieve that goal and hurt the United States at the same time."

"How do they plan to hurt the *gringos*?" Goose asked.

"Ahh, I can't tell you that. That's what the next episode is about."

"Yeah, and then it'll probably happen in real life a week later," replied Goose.

The smile on my face disappeared. That was the corpse at the Christening, of course. This was what gave me the heebegeebees at night. So far, everything I had written about had actually happened and made headlines a couple of weeks after being published by *The Ganja Times*. If the pattern repeated itself after the next episode hit the newsstands, the international economic system could very well collapse. The question was, if I didn't put my ideas to pen, would the world somehow avoid the doomsday scenario? I knew I had to be insane to even contemplate that possibility. How could I even think that something could actually happen just because I wrote a story about it? But I wasn't the only one thinking in those terms, was I? The whole world had gone bonkers.

"So who's the hero of the story?" asked Goose.

"They're a lot of characters in the book," I said. "One of the main ones is an ex-CIA officer named Mako Sloane. He's working for the governor of Texas trying to find out who sunk the Coast Guard cutter."

"Isn't that the FBI's or CIA's job?" asked Goose.

"Ha, ha! That's the big mystery in the book. The CIA itself might somehow be involved. But I can't tell you anymore. It might ruin the story."

Goose unscrewed the top from a bottle of beer and handed it to me. I hesitated. I knew our drinking was getting out of control and decided right then and there that we had to stop. We needed our wits about us as the dragnet tightened. Although beer fed my creativity, it dulled my judgment. Goose never had any judgment at all, of course, but the beer made him horny, and that was dangerous for both of us. I decided to quit....after my next beer.

"There're Mexicans in the book too," I said.

"Yeah, I bet. All criminals and drug traffickers, right?" asked Goose. "Or maybe they cut Mako Sloane's lawn and trim his shrubs."

No matter how much time I spent with Goose, he was still convinced I was a racist at heart. It didn't matter if I spoke Spanish with him all day or not. He had made up his mind, and nothing was going to change it.

"No, not all of them. Actually, the Mako Sloane character has a sidekick, a Mexican named Armando who used be the cartel's main attorney."

"You mean like me?" asked Goose after considering the idea.

"Yeah, that's what gave me the idea," I said.

The thought of being immortalized in a novel appealed to Goose. I hoped it wouldn't be the epitaph on his gravestone. I couldn't rid myself of the image of Goose and me guzzling beer and speeding along the interstate towards Kingdom Come with the truck radio tuned to a Mexican *norteña*[26] station.

An hour before dawn Joel called. It was two hours earlier on the West Coast. I figured Joel must have stayed up all night. His voice was gravelly and raspy, even more so than normal. I was sure he had been smoking cigarettes and drinking coffee for the last twelve hours. I knew he couldn't pass a piss test, but that was just an occupational hazard from working for *The Ganja Times.*

---

[26] a genre of Mexican music

He could claim it was second-hand smoke and probably beat the rap.

"Clabe, what an interview!" he said. "You've captured the imagination of the American people."

"What are you doing up at this hour, Joel?"

"My phone's been ringing off the hook all night," he replied. "More people watched your interview last night than the finals of American Idol. You're a beast."

Joel had something on his mind, I was sure. He never called unless he was working a new angle to make more money, or unless he was scared. Sometimes both. Fear had a way of distilling his remarkable ability to turn nothing into money. Sort of a Jewish Rumpelstiltskin with an L.A. twist.

"Make it quick, Joel," I suggested. "I'm sure the bad guys are listening."

"What'd you do to that woman, Clabe? She wants an exclusive series of interviews with you, and she's offering a lot of money for each one."

I considered the possibility that the FBI could use Gretel to find me, but then I thought of that pair of mammaries, fake though they might be. It was no contest. No weaning yet for this suckling pig. I was quite willing to risk my freedom for another shot at the former Miss Universe's private parts.

"Mobile, Alabama this evening," I said. "Call me with the hotel room." Then I hung up.

That became the pattern for our trip over the next few days. Each night in a new city, we rushed through a 10-minute interview, hashing out the latest announcements by the Federal Bureau of Investigation and the Central Intelligence Agency with me gnashing my teeth and beating my breast and proclaiming my innocence. I would give provocative hints of the action still to come in the novel, and then Gretel would hustle her crew out of the hotel room. She would pour two glasses of champagne and sit beside me on the sofa. It was the same script every night, but I never tired of it. The dialog always began with the same question.

"Clabe, are you a Republican?" she would ask.

Then she would insert that forked Gila Monster tongue halfway down my throat, and the festivities would begin in earnest. I never understood why she needed for me to finally confess, even in jest, that I was a Democrat, but it never failed to push her over the edge, and she would collapse on top of me in a seismic orgasm, all the while screaming and calling me a BASTARD. Gretel needed psychiatric help as did most of the crew at Fox News, but I hoped she never got it.

We crossed the Sabine River into Texas early in the morning. A dense fog had settled over the muddy water during the night, and traffic slowed as we drew near the bridge. I was rapidly approaching a state of complete physical exhaustion. The constant tension of being on the run combined with days of endless driving and the enervating romps with Gretel at night had taken their toll. My eyes were bloodshot and swollen, and my hands shook slightly from lack of sleep and depleted testosterone.

I had emailed my next episode to *The Ganja Times* the night before from a hotel suite on the outskirts of Baton Rouge. Gretel had already left, and I sat on the edge of the king-sized bed in my skivvies, drenched in sweat with claw marks fresh on my back and wondering whether I should hit the "send" button. The contents of the episode were explosive, at least in a fictional sense. If the FBI had linked me to the sinking of the Coast Guard cutter off Padre Island because I happened to write about it beforehand in an uncanny coincidence, imagine what they would do if this episode played out in similar fashion. Armed Predator drones would be buzzing the skies over Texas looking to take me out. What the fuck, I thought. I clicked on the mouse, and it was gone.

We passed through Houston and turned west on Hwy 290 without incident, and then the phone rang. I jumped and banged my head on the ceiling of the cab. Goose spilled his beer in his lap, and even Rigo woke up from his hypnotic stupor, wondering what had happened. I looked at the caller ID. It was Joel. I was sure he had just finished reading the new episode.

Chapter 22

"I don't know what to say," Joel said. "I loved it, but it scares the shit out of me. What if...?" He didn't finish the sentence.

"Don't say it," I responded. "I'll call you back in about two weeks when I send in the next episode. Let's wait and see what happens."

"What about Gretel?" Joel asked. "She's still calling."

"Sorry, no more publicity," I said. "It's gotten too risky."

I probably wouldn't have said that if my penis hadn't been in tatters and my body close to physical breakdown. Gretel was younger than I was, and she was killing me with her neoconservative kinky sex.

"Clabe, this is great fiction, but please tell me it's not going to come true."

"I don't see how it can, but I don't have a very good track record of predicting the future, do I?" I said.

"Actually, your track record is too damned good," said Joel.

"That's not what I meant," I said.

"I know," said Joel. "Look, this will hit the newsstands tomorrow. Find a good place to hide, but don't tell me where you are."

"*Adios,*" I said and signed off.

We turned north on Hwy 6 at Hempstead and then drove through College Station and on to Waco. When I turned towards Dallas and Fort Worth on I-35, Goose had a conniption fit.

"Where the hell are you going?" he shouted. "We can't go back home!"

"Relax. We're not," I replied. "I know a place where we can hide. Just trust me."

"Trust you?" he repeated, his spittle splattering the windshield. "I tried that and look where it got me."

He had a point, of course, and I didn't intend to argue with him. But I knew of a secluded piece of property about 30 miles west of Fort Worth where we might be able to rent a cabin in the woods. With my internet hotspot, we'd be in touch with the world but completely out of sight. When we arrived at the Hide-A-Way Cabins south of Weatherford, I had to do some smooth talking to convince the owner, a 78-year old ex-evangelical preacher from Tennessee, to rent to two grown men.

"Well, sir," he drawled, "we ain't that liberal in these parts, you know."

I caught his drift immediately. It was Rockville, South Carolina revisited. The old codger thought Goose and I were a gay couple, and I'm sure he wouldn't give a hoot about any threats of discrimination suits that Goose might make. Fortunately, Goose stayed in the car while I discussed terms with the old man. This redneck was a mite tougher than our South Carolina landlord. Preacher or not, this guy would just as soon shoot Goose as argue with him. He didn't like Mexicans out of principle. He glanced distastefully at Goose sitting in the car as if he were the spawn of the devil. A Mexican in his book was far worse than even a Yankee. A gay Mexican defied any gradation of evil he'd ever encountered. It was going to be an uphill battle to convince him to rent to us, but where there's a will there's a way. I turned up the charm, put on a drawl, and tried to look manly.

The owner's wife was a sharp-eyed harridan who stuck her head around the corner a couple of times and frowned fiercely, but I gathered the old coot kept her under wraps and made his own decisions. She likely harped at him and bitched and made his life miserable afterwards, but at least he stood his ground. I respected that. We talked for an hour, and I told him about the army and ranching, and he eventually came around. They all do when you thrust a fistful of cash in their face.

I paid for two months' rent in advance, and we moved into a two-bedroom wooden cabin that sat in a clearing in thick woods at the foot of a steep, rocky hill. Rigo loved it, and spent his days on the porch watching for squirrels or armadillos to chase. Even Goose found it peaceful. He sat in a plastic chair on the front porch all day listening to the birds and smoking one joint after another. I had sworn off reefer, at least for a while. One of us had to remain alert for any indication that the feds or the cartel was closing in. I didn't as yet take the threat from the Russians seriously. It would be difficult for them to operate in Texas. They'd stand out too much in Parker County where people from Kansas were considered foreigners.

In contrast to Rockville, we lived at the Hide-A-Way Cabins in perfect isolation. We didn't socialize with any of the locals, and they wouldn't have had it any other way. When we needed groceries and more beer, I took the car and drove alone into Weatherford, a burgeoning little country town full of gun stores and fast food restaurants with a picturesque courthouse on the main square. Behind a superficial, Potemkin-village show of hospitality, the locals were a closed and suspicious lot.

Weatherford society was about as welcoming as New York City despite their propaganda to the contrary. Oh yes, they would take your money willingly enough, but they looked askance at outsiders. Their English was quaint; full of verbs that didn't agree with subjects and a third-grade vocabulary that limited their range of conversation to the weather and the consistency of their pets' bowel movements.

Joel kept his word and didn't call. I refrained from sending emails to keep my cyber footprint as small as possible. I perused the national and international news websites every day and spent much of the day watching CNN on the small flat-screen television in the cabin. Each day I expected the axe to fall, along with the Dow Jones average.

"Are you waiting for something to happen?" asked Goose from the porch.

"I'm hoping it won't," I said. "So far so good."

Goose couldn't contain his curiosity any longer. He stood up from where he had been sunning himself, knocking over his plastic chair in the process. I heard him clumping around in his flip-flops, and then the screen door slammed. I looked up from the computer, and there he was swaying slightly from side to side with a bottle of beer in one hand and a smoldering joint in the other.

"Let me ask it another way. What is it you hope won't happen?"

"Step outside, Goose," I answered. "We can talk on the porch."

Yeah, there was more room outside to run in case Goose attacked me after hearing my answer. I always say if you don't want to hear the answer, don't ask the question. Or maybe "ignorance is bliss" was more appropriate. Goose, apparently, was not familiar with either saying.

"Now remember, this is just a story I've written. It's fiction. That means make-believe."

"Fuck you. I know what fiction means," Goose replied. "This is gonna be bad, isn't it?"

"Only if it really happens. Then it'll be worse than bad," I said.

"De Guatemala a Guatepeor?"[27] he asked.

"Yep, something like that."

Goose fell silent and sipped at his beer. Almost as if he were contemplating whether he really wanted to hear what was in the last episode. Hell, it had already been published. What was done was done. I doubted they sold *The Ganja Times* in Weatherford, but I'm sure it was

---

[27] Spanish equivalent of "from the frying pan into the fire"

available in Fort Worth or the Mid-Cities. Maybe I should pick up a copy for Goose's own edification.

"Tell me," he finally said.

"Remember you asked before how the Russians could hurt the *gringos*?"

"Sure."

"Well, in the book they use the cartel submarine to sink an oil tanker in the Houston Ship Channel."

"The Mexicans go along with that?" Goose asked.

"They don't have any choice," I replied. "The Russians are still training the cartel crew to operate the submarine. The Mexicans can't do anything on their own yet."

"So is sinking an oil tanker bad?" Goose asked.

"Yeah, it is. Nobody knows who did it, you see, so they don't know if and when it could happen again. The price of oil skyrockets, and the U.S. economy goes into a nosedive. The Russians kill two birds with one stone. They hurt the United States, and money pours into their own national treasury since their economy is so dependent on the price of fuel."

"That wouldn't affect the price of dope, would it?" asked Goose.

Goose looked at me with his uncomprehending eyes, cold as ice floes. I realized he was too high to really understand what I was talking about. I went back inside and continued writing. I was in a funk, and I didn't know whether I'd be able to finish the novel or not. The clouds seemed to be gathering, at least in my mind.

Three days later I turned on the early morning edition of Fox & Friends and saw "BREAKING NEWS" plastered across the bottom of the screen. There was Gretel looking fetching as always with her spit & polish mannequin good looks. Just ogling her, it was hard to imagine what a depraved soul lay beneath the thick layer of foundation makeup and mascara. Gradually, I pried my eyes away from Gretel's pouting lips, trying not to picture what those lips had been doing just two weeks ago, and began to notice other details on the screen; an aerial view from a helicopter showed the burning hulk of a large seagoing vessel on fire and listing heavily to starboard. A plume of black smoke rose skyward, and a flotilla of U.S. Coast Guard and Navy vessels had circled the doomed ship. I froze and saw the words "HOUSTON SHIP CHANNEL" flash across the scene.

My cell phone rang for the first time in two weeks.

"Are you watching this on CNN?" I recognized Joel's voice.

"I'm watching Fox & Friends, but I'm sure they're showing the same thing," I replied.

"This can't be happening," said Joel. His voice sounded strangely calm.   He was either beyond true emotion, or he had taken a heavy dose of Valium. Here in Weatherford, Texas my heart was jumping out my throat and my knees were wobbly. I was afraid I might soil my Wranglers.

"Clabe, I've sent you all the money I owe via PayPal in case the feds shut me down today or tomorrow. Listen, man, is there something you wanna tell me?" Joel asked. And then the line went dead.

I heard later that it had been a Russian oil tanker, and that two Exocet missiles had scored direct hits. But I knew all of that already. I had written the script two weeks before. The shit had hit the fan. Right on schedule.

Chapter 23

I watched dumbfounded as the price of oil doubled overnight and continued to rise precipitously. The stock market plunged. Retirement funds were decimated, and the personal savings of millions of American citizens were wiped out. The caterwauling from Washington was deafening. The administration howled and raged and threatened, but nobody had the foggiest idea who was responsible for the brazen attack. None of it came as a surprise to me, of course. I had laid it all out in Chapter 12 of my novel. But that was fiction, and this was stark reality. My head was reeling, and the world had gone stark-raving mad.

First Gretel at Fox News and then Wolf at CNN mentioned almost as a footnote that author Clabe Taylor's new serialized novel had predicted the attack with uncanny precision. My phone began to ring incessantly, and my electronic mailbox was soon overflowing with requests for interviews. I ignored them all. I was waiting for the other shoe to fall, and it wasn't long before it came crashing down.

It was our redneck landlord who ratted us out, of course. I made the mistake of dealing with the crusty old bastard in true name, an operational faux pas of such enormity that it pains me to admit to it. Goose and I were both sitting on the porch drinking beer when the landlord drove up the hill towards the cabin in an electric golf cart with half a dozen black SUVs behind him with lights flashing and sirens wailing. I knew what it meant as soon as I heard the piercing wail and saw the black vehicles with tinted windows. About the same time, I heard a crashing in the woods behind us as another team of intrepid FBI pukes came careening head over heels down the almost vertical cliff in back of the cabin. I quickly locked Rigo in the cabin for his own safety and stood on the porch serenely awaiting my fate. Unfortunately, the feds weren't quite as laid-back.

"Are you Clabe Taylor?" asked one of the agents.

"Who's wants to know?" I replied.

That wasn't the right answer, and I found myself in quick order lying in the gravel in front of the cabin, spread-eagle with my hands cuffed behind my back.

"Hey, don't forget my Miranda rights," I said.

"You've been watching too much cable television," the head agent said and tightened the handcuffs until they cut into my wrists. I saw out of the corner of my eye that Goose had met a similar fate.

"The fucking dog bit me," screamed one of the agents as he slammed the screen door and looked over his shoulder at a snarling Rigo. "Hand me the taser," he said.

"Don't kill the dog," admonished the head agent. "We'll have PETA and the media up our asses in no time."

I heard a yelp and a loud laugh from inside the cabin. "That'll teach the sonofabitch," came the same voice.

"You tasered my dog? Gutless bastard!"

That was the last thing I remember until I woke up on a cold concrete floor in a warehouse. I had no idea how long I had been unconscious, or where I was. It was freezing, and the feds had removed my clothes. I lay shivering on my side in fetal position dressed only in my Ralph Lauren boxer briefs, the baby blue ones with the red waistband. My teeth were chattering, and I had a splitting headache from the blow I received on the back of my head. As far as I could tell, neither Goose nor Rigo was with me.

The warehouse was full of people, most of them dressed in black fatigues and combat boots; all of them wearing ski masks except a short, rotund balding fellow with pink cheeks dressed in a pinstriped suit, baby-blue shirt, and tie. He stood off to the side with a clipboard and a pen, taking notes and looking like a half-witted cherub.

One of my captors walked up to me and took off his mask and glared. His head was shaved and he had a soul patch under his lower lip. He glanced over his shoulder at the cherub in the suit.

"Can we turn on the music now?" he asked.

"Just a second. Let me check to see if we have authorization for that," he replied.

He stepped away from us and took out a cell phone and dialed a number. I could hear him speaking in low tones but couldn't make out any words. I saw him turn around and approach me.

"Give me one minute, please," he said to the tough guy and kneeled down beside me with his clipboard.

"I've just received authorization from the director of the Central Intelligence Agency to soften you up for Enhanced Interrogation. Would you sign here, please."

"What is that?" I asked.

"It's just an acknowledgment that you have been briefed and that you agree to the Enhanced Interrogation protocol."

"Are you nuts? Who are you?" I asked. "Where are my clothes?"

"Sir, according to E.I. Memorandum No. 517, approved by the CIA Inspector General and the Office of Legal Counsel, I'm not required to identify myself or inform you of the location of the clothing that formerly belonged to you," said the suit.

"Are you out of your fucking mind?" I asked and tried to sit up.

The tough guy took two steps towards me and kicked me in the ribs. I collapsed to the floor in excruciating pain and tried to catch my breath. I gagged and almost vomited.

"Dusty, that's not authorized! I've told you about that kind of crap! Please step away while I speak to the detainee," said the suit in a firm voice.

"You're not supposed to mention my name!" shouted Dusty.

"Sorry, Dusty. I forgot," the suit confessed.

"You said it again, you dumb shit!" he screamed, his face turning beet red. I thought he was going to throttle the suit, but he restrained himself at the last moment.

The suit ignored Dusty and turned towards me again.

"What is this?" I asked. "Saturday Night Live?"

The suit had a pained expression on his face. He shuffled his feet and looked embarrassed. He glanced self-consciously at Dusty, who stood glaring at him.

"Try to understand. We're under a lot of pressure from Congress and the media. We're doing the best we can to avoid violating our constitutional principles and the ideals of the Founding Fathers," he explained.

"The Founding Fathers? Those motherfuckers owned slaves," I shouted. "What do you want from me?"

"That did it!" shouted Dusty. "I'm starting the music."

"Wait!" admonished the suit.

The suit knelt again beside me and whispered. "The CIA's Office of Legal Counsel has authorized the use of loud music at a decibel level that will not cause permanent hearing loss. Please sign here."

"*Besame el culo,*" I said and tried to spit in his face.

"That was rather unnecessary," the suit said and stood up.

"I know Spanish!" said Dusty. "He said to KISS HIS ASS!"

The suit shook his head sadly and scribbled something on the forms.

"Let's get started," said Dusty and turned to the suit. "What are you doing?"

"I'm forging the subject's signature on these disclosure forms. Congress won't let us continue until we get his agreement to be tortured."

"That's more like it!" shouted Dusty. "Let's ROCK N' ROLL! Turn on the fucking music."

I saw Dusty open a circuit box on the wall. He looked at me grinning and then threw a switch. The warehouse went pitch black and then he turned on the music. I don't know what I expected, but it certainly wasn't The Carpenters' 1970 hit *We've Only Just Begun* blasting at close to 100 decibels from massive surround-sound speakers suspended from the ceiling. In my worst nightmare I never expected to be tied up and bombarded with that sicky-sweet ditty from yesteryear. I would have preferred to have Megadeath's *Symphony of Destruction* forcing blood out of my inner ear than descend into the nethermost hell of EASY LISTENING MUSIC. I was sure the hooded CIA inquisitors would put on ABBA next. I had underestimated the depth of their degradation and sadism. After thirty minutes of the Carpenters, I was ready to sell out my own mother if only they would stop the music.

But nobody came, and at some point I lost consciousness and began to dream. Slobbering reptiles crawled over my naked body, and then morphed into

Gretel asking me in a throaty whisper whether I was a Republican or not. Just as she prepared to give me a blow job, she turned into Dick Cheney, and I kicked him away screaming and woke up. I moaned and gnashed my teeth until my gums bled, but I couldn't hear anything except the inane lyrics of that awful song and the hellish melody.

"We've only just begun to live
White lace and promises
A kiss for luck and we're on our way
We've only just begun"

I must have passed out again, and suddenly I realized the music had stopped although the insipid lyrics still echoed in my brain. I heard footsteps, and then there was a blinding flash of light as someone threw the breaker switch. I looked up at Dusty, and then I caught sight of the suit standing against the wall, still with the clipboard and pen in his hands. Dusty had a smirk on his face. He knew the hell I had just gone through.

"What's next?" Dusty asked the suit.

"Let's see." The suit rifled through the documents on his clipboard.

"It looks like waterboarding is next followed by ten minutes of threatening Mr. Taylor with snarling Rotweilers while he stands naked with his hands manacled to a chain suspended from the ceiling. Then sleep deprivation, of course."

"But I'll answer your questions now," I shouted in desperation. "I'll sing like a fucking canary!"

"I'm sorry, Mr. Taylor," replied the suit. "We have to strictly adhere to E.I. protocol. We've only just begun."

Chapter 24

The waterboarding was a bitch. I thought I was going to drown, and I retched until my guts ached, and I thought my head would burst from lack of oxygen. But give me waterboarding any day over hours of listening to the Carpenters at 100 decibels. When I complained that they were torturing me, both Dusty and the suit turned pale, and the suit stuttered.

"O-o-oh, n-n-n-o," he said. "It's not torture. Really."

He turned to three middle-age men who stood behind him taking notes and pointed at me.

"Are we torturing the detainee?" the suit asked.

The three men walked away from the rest of us to confer. When they returned, the most senior member of the group stepped forward and read from his own notebook.

"No," he read and looked up proudly. "According to the Department of Justice's definition, this is not torture."

"Then what the hell is torture?" I yelled almost incoherently.'

Dusty looked at me in disgust and answered for the group.

"Torture, is when the people fucking with you are slant-eyed little gooks or ragheads. We're Americans," he declared.

"Dusty, dammit. You know you can't use racial profiling or inappropriate stereotypical descriptions of ethnic minorities while you're on U.S. territory," admonished the suit.

"Stop using my name!" yelled Dusty. "Minorities, hell. There're more of them than us!"

"Shall we proceed?" asked the suit. "What's next?"

He referred again to the thick sheaf of documents on his clipboard.

"It's time for the Rotweilers," said Dusty and grinned at me.

"Wait! Were the Rotweilers trained on U.S. territory?" asked one of the three men standing in the background. I suspected that they were backup attorneys from the Department of Justice.

"No," replied the suit. "They were trained in Gdansk, Poland. We're in complete compliance."

"I'll talk," I suggested. "What do you want to know?"

"Sir, excuse me, but we've trained these dogs for years. We need to justify the taxpayers' money that we've spent." explained the suit. "Please allow us to do our duty." He handed me another form.

"Would you mind signing this release allowing us to intimidate you for ten minutes with three attack-trained Rotweilers that were whelped in the United States but reached sexual maturity and were trained outside of the country?"

I felt like I was acting in a particularly sick and sadistic scene from a Stanley Kubrick movie. They had broken my spirit. I took the clipboard and the pen and signed the form. I sobbed and my tears smeared my signature.

"Don't forget to date it, please," the suit reminded me as he beamed in my direction. "Bring in the dogs," he whispered to Dusty.

***

I'm not proud of how quickly I broke under torture. I always imagined I would be tougher. If they had started with the dogs, or with sleep deprivation, or even what they called "stress positions", I know I could have held out longer. It was that fucking Carpenters song that did it. That's the advantage our modern-day Grand Inquisitors have over the crude sadistic efforts of the Gestapo, the

KGB, or even the North Koreans and North Vietnamese. They had run my profile through a powerful computer software package, and the analysis spit out exquisitely tailored interrogation techniques that played on my phobias. At the end of the third day, I lay on the cold floor, a quivering mass of protoplasm incapable of further resistance or rational thought.

"That about wraps it up," declared the suit. "We can now proceed to the interrogation."

Dusty grabbed my arm and jerked me to my feet while one of his assistants unlocked the leg irons, belly chain, and handcuffs. They forced me to strip naked, and then they hosed me down with icy water. They tossed me a bar of soap and laughed as I bent down to pick it up. Afterwards they threw me a towel and an ill-fitting orange jump suit. Dusty, followed by the ubiquitous legal team dressed immaculately in their Brooks Brothers suits, led me into an adjacent room where a folding metal chair sat under the glare of spotlights.

"Sit down," Dusty ordered.

I looked around and bit my lip to keep from smiling through my tears. The whole scene was a parody of a Gestapo or KGB interrogation, but I knew that I invited more politically correct pain if I called attention to their lack of originality.

"You never told me what I'm accused of," I said.

Dusty and the team of lawyers exchanged nervous glances.

"Mr. Taylor, you have not been charged with a crime because you have been classified as an enemy combatant. We may keep you in custody and interrogate you indefinitely." The suit looked at me triumphantly and the lawyers glanced at each other and smiled.

"But I haven't fought anyone," I said. "How can I be a combatant? And I'm certainly not the enemy. I used to be in the CIA. I've risked my life for this country. Have you?"

Dusty stood up to slap me again, but the suit raised his hand and Dusty sat down, mumbling obscenities at me.

"We suspect you of complicity in the sinking of a United States Coast Guard cutter off Padre Island and the oil tanker in the Houston Ship channel. How else could you have described that in such detail in your novel EVEN BEFORE IT HAPPENED!" shouted the suit.

I started to answer and Dusty slapped me again.

"Bro, I'm not your friend," he said glancing down at a sheet of paper and reading his lines. "Every time you lie to me, I will hurt you."

I recognized that verbiage from the movie *Thirty Dark Zero*. Oscar Wilde would have been proud. This was an obvious case of life imitating art.

"Are you in contact with the Sinaloa Federation or the Russian Foreign Intelligence Service?" asked the suit.

Dusty had his hand poised to slap me again, but I could only tell them the truth.

"No," I answered and braced myself for the slap. I didn't have long to wait. My head started to ache, and blood trickled down from my lip.

"When's the last time you spoke with Mako Sloane?" asked the suit.

"Mako Sloane?" I asked incredulously. "Come on, he's a fictional character! I made him up."

"We know otherwise, Mr. Taylor," the suit said, raising his voice slightly. "You'll have to do better than that."

"Mako Sloane exists only in my imagination. Get serious!"

"You disappoint me, Mr. Taylor," said the suit. He nodded to Dusty, and he and the entire legal team turned on their heels and walked toward the exit. I felt like my life was walking out on me.

"Wait!" I shouted. "You've got to believe me!"

Dusty motioned to two of his assistants who had been standing against the wall. The three of them grabbed me and handcuffed me to the chair. I knew what they were going to do, and I knew it would drive me mad. A one-way ticket to insanity.

"Don't leave me with this moron," I shouted to the departing suits.

"Moron?" Dusty repeated and spat on the floor. "You'll wish you hadn't said that, bro. I warned you."

He was right. Even with his limited intellectual capacity, Dusty knew my weaknesses, and he played upon them with sadistic ingenuity. When he turned off the lights and switched on the loud music, I lost all hope. I wanted to die. Anything would have been preferable to what that sadistic bastard had in store for me. I looked in vain for something sharp to slit my wrists, but there was nothing. The room was deathly still, and then the sounds of *"Play That Funky Music, White Boy"* by Wild Cherry began to reverberate through the building. The walls shuddered and seem to expand and contract with the beat. I thought the roof would cave in and come crashing down on me. I lost count of how many times the song played, over and over in an endless loop of digital lunacy. I lost my bearings in space, and my sense of equilibrium played tricks on me. The chair toppled over, and my head hit hard on the unforgiving concrete. I mercifully lost consciousness.

***

I don't know how long I lay there. When I woke up, the music had stopped, but the lights were still out. It was pitch black and deathly still. I was lying on my side, still cuffed to the chair. I couldn't even see the outline of the walls, and my face lay in something moist and sticky on the concrete floor. I assumed it was my own blood.

I heard distant shouting; several faint shots rang out, and then it was silent again. I might have drifted in and out of consciousness, but it could have been an illusion. My mind was playing tricks on me at this point, and what felt like an hour was probably just a few minutes. Suddenly I heard the soft padding of running feet getting louder, and the door opened. A rectangle of light poured into the darkness, and two silhouettes moved quickly towards me. I cowered like a dog, expecting to be kicked or beaten.

"¿*Tienes las llaves*"?[28] I heard one voice whisper.

---

[28] Do you have the keys?

There was no response, but I heard the rattling of keys, and someone roughly grabbed my hands and unlocked the handcuffs. They fell to the floor with a loud clattering that seemed to echo throughout the room. The leg irons and the lock on the belly chain soon followed.

"Can you stand up, Clabe?" one of the men asked in perfect American English.

"I can if you've come to get me out of here," I answered.

"Then let's go," the voice said and I hobbled out of the room at a slow jog with my feet barely touching the floor, supported by two men I didn't know; or at least didn't recognize.

Whoever my rescuers were, they came prepared. As we exited the warehouse, the first thing I saw was a Texas National Guard UH-60 Blackhawk helicopter ringed with gunmen in civilian clothes. They opened a corridor for us as we approached the helicopter, and my two saviors lifted me up and practically threw me on my back into the chopper. A heavy weight immediately landed on my chest, and covered my face with slobbery, wet kisses.

"Rigo," I cried. "You're alive!"

Chapter 25

It was a homecoming of sorts, practically a family reunion. Minus the event planner and the embossed invitations, of course. There was no catering and no mariachi band either, and I hadn't had time to change out of my bright orange prison jump suit. Still, at that moment nothing could have made me happier than seeing the black patch over that Blue Heeler's right eye and even catching a whiff of the familiar reek that hovered over him like an invisible cloud.

Goose was there too. His face was bruised and swollen, but he was grinning like the village idiot. I probably was too. We embraced, and he looked at me with newfound respect. I guess he figured I had organized the rescue, and I didn't disabuse him of the thought. As the helicopter lifted off, I looked around at our rescuers, wondering who the hell they were and what organization they represented. Texas National Guard? That made no sense, but neither had anything else in the last twenty-four hours. I was ready to believe anything. Well, almost anything.

The civilian gunmen looked like hard cases, every one of them. Around thirty years old, they all wore jeans and khaki-colored Special Forces boots that looked like a cross between running shoes and combat boots. Tight black t-shirts accentuated their toned arms, making them look like caricatures of GI Joe action figures; probably veterans who had found a civilian employer with a need for their particular set of deadly skills. Each carried a small sub-machine gun I couldn't identify, and they all stared uneasily at Rigo. I guessed he hadn't been as eager to be rescued as Goose and I had been.

The two men who unchained and dragged me out of the warehouse were up front talking to the pilot as the chopper lifted off in a roar and a cloud of Texas dust. Then we were flying at treetop level over a bleak rural landscape with the rising sun on our left. I had time to look them over as I sat on a bench against the wall with my heart still pounding. They were dressed like the rest of the gunmen but had less of a military bearing. They were older too. The one who appeared to be in charge looked to be in his late fifties. He was Caucasian, tall and lean with a weather-beaten face and a long, blond ponytail streaked with gray. He had a piercing stare that made you feel guilty about something and want to look away. His partner was Hispanic and younger, but he shared the "don't fuck with me" bearing of the older man.

I was considering approaching the two when the older one turned and caught my eye. He motioned me forward with a nod of his head, and I undid my safety harness and walked toward the front of the helicopter, ducking my head instinctively even though there was plenty of head room.

"Clabe, how are you feeling?" he asked.

"Much better now," I said and tried to smile.

"I like your dog, by the way," he said. "A friend of mine has one just like him. An exact copy."

"I was afraid they'd killed him," I said and glanced at Rigo already asleep with his head on Goose's lap. Shared suffering has a way of bridging gaps, I guess. The two obviously had kissed and made up.

"I imagine you'd like to know who we are," he said. "And where we're going."

"The thought had occurred to me," I answered.

He stuck out his hand, and I took it in mine.

"I'm Mako Sloane," he said. "At your service."

I froze and my lower jaw dropped. I stared into his eyes and felt like I was falling down the rabbit hole, and there was nothing I could hold onto to stop my descent. I couldn't have been more surprised if he had introduced himself as the Mad Hatter, and I would have been more inclined to believe him.

"Something the matter?" he asked.

"Sorry, I didn't catch that name," I said.

"M-a-k-o," he said slowly. "Like the shark."

"And did you say 'Sloane'?" I asked.

"I guess you're not deaf after all," he said and grinned.

My thoughts were jumbled, and nothing seemed to make sense. I thought of stories I had read about parallel universes, or worlds existing in time warps, or invisible dimensions where our doubles lived out different trajectories of our own lives. Admittedly, things had really started to get weird when I began my series of clandestine trysts with Gretel. I hoped I hadn't been just imagining them, but I was beginning to lose track of the boundary between reality and fantasy.

"You can't be Mako Sloane," I said emphatically.

"And why the hell not?" he asked.

"Because I made Mako Sloane up," I said in exasperation. "He's a character in my novels. A product of my imagination!"

"Well, please don't tell that to my mother," he laughed. "The poor woman would be heartbroken."

"Armando, *ven acá*[29]," he called to his Hispanic companion.

---

[29] Come here.

"Armando?" I said, and I felt my temples begin to pound.

"Don't tell me you invented him too?" asked Mako. Armando joined us and stood with his arms crossed.

"¿Qué pasó?" he asked.

"Seems our friend here doesn't believe we exist," said the one who introduced himself as Mako Sloane.

"Really?" said Armando, switching into English. "And why not?"

"I suppose you're a lawyer from Mexico City?" I responded to his question with one of my own.

"How'd you know that?" asked Armando.

"And I guess you used to work for the Sinaloa Federation?"

"Mako, who the fuck is this guy?" asked Armando.

"That's what the CIA was trying to find out," said Mako and turned to Armando. "Clabe's writing a novel about the operation we've been working on. He seems to know everything that's going to happen; ahead of time. And he apparently knows everything about us."

"So that really was the CIA?" I asked. "Did you kill them all?"

I hoped that the suit and Dusty and their team of punctilious lawyers were indeed lying on some concrete floor riddled with bullets. I was just sorry that I couldn't hang them from the ceiling chains and have Rigo rip off their testicles.

"No, we just scared 'em a bit. They're tied up, waiting for their people to rescue them," said Mako. "We'll make a phone call to the FBI later and give them a citizen's tip."

I had to admit it. This was the way the Mako Sloane in my book might have done it, but the wild scenario seemed a little over-the-top even for him; if it was really happening, that is. Disarming and tying up CIA operatives and then freeing their prisoners? In the United States?

"Aren't you afraid of reprisals?" I asked. "I'd say you've committed a pretty serious crime."

"Are you kidding? We won't hear a peep out of them," Mako said. "Outside of the Congressional Record, the history of the CIA is the most shameful litany of lies, deceit, broken promises, and political cowardice you'll ever want to see. The governor's not going to be pleased to hear the CIA was operating a 'black interrogation site' on Texas soil and using it to torture American citizens. Can you imagine the media getting hold of that? No, the CIA doesn't need another scandal."

He paused and looked over at Goose, who was trying to catch bits and pieces of the conversation. I doubted if he could, though, over the roar of the engines.

"He IS an American citizen, isn't he?" Mako asked.

"He's got his green card," I replied.

I caught myself talking to his guy as if I really believed he was Mako Sloane. But what choice did I have? And what if he was Mako? Would that be any stranger that what had already happened? I stood like a Biblical pillar of salt, staring at Rigo and Goose without really seeing them. My mind was shifting through all the possible explanations for these outlandish coincidences, but each time I arrived at the same conclusion. There just weren't any explanations.

I don't know how long I would have stood there, but suddenly I caught a familiar pungent smell. Someone was smoking weed in the helicopter. I followed by nose and found myself looking towards the pilot's cabin where a column of smoke rose and wafted in a snaky plume towards the back. I saw a few of the gunmen glancing at each other and smiling. Maybe they were used to their helicopter pilot getting stoned in flight, but I wasn't. I stared at the pilot and saw him sucking on a huge blunt as he piloted the chopper at barely a hundred feet above the ground.

"Yeah, took me a while to get used to it too" said Mako as he followed my gaze. "He's the best there is, though. That's what flying thirty years for the most powerful drug cartel in Mexico does for you. It hones your skills at flying under the radar."

I had an uneasy feeling about this. Everything Mako said was way too familiar. I was overcome with a sinking feeling of déjà vu. My second novel had featured a former Vietnam fighter pilot, who found a more profitable application of his skills after the war flying loads of weed and coke into private landing strips in Arizona and New Mexico. In my book, he and Mako had rescued the daughter of the governor of Texas who had been kidnapped by the cartel. The way I described him, the pilot rarely saw a sober or straight moment. I began to wonder.

"Don't tell me that's Bronc Thornton?" I asked almost in jest. I should have remembered the Russian saying about there only being a little bit of a joke in every joke. If it WAS Bronc, I was the one that was going to take the next hit off that blunt.

"I thought you might recognize him," said Mako.

I didn't answer. What could I have said? Deny that he existed when he was flying the helicopter and sucking on that joint just like he would have been doing in one of my novels?

"I guess you're going to tell me you made him up too?" asked Mako.

I felt like a naughty schoolchild being chided for mischievous behavior, and Mako Sloane was my teacher.

"But h-h-how could it be?" I stuttered.

"That's what we want to find out," replied Mako.

"Oh, so you're going to interrogate and torture me too?" I asked, wondering if I had escaped the pot just to land in the fire.

"No, that's not my style," Mako answered. "But there ARE some people who'd like to talk with you. That's where we're going now."

"Let me guess," I said sarcastically. I felt myself getting angry although somewhere deep inside I knew I should be grateful to these people who had walked off the pages of my novels and hurtled themselves into my life. "We're going to Cotulla, Texas right?"

Cotulla, Texas was a small town on I-35 about an hour's drive north of Laredo. It had been the center of most of the action in my second novel. It was a real town, but some of the people and places I described were not. At least, I used to think that.

Mako laughed. He reached into a cooler and handed me a Shiner Blonde and pulled out a Dos Equis for Goose.

Christ, this guy even knew what we liked to drink! I couldn't assimilate any more astonishing revelations and just twisted off the cap to the beer bottle. I'd need more than just one of these.

"Now you're catching on," he said. "But first we're going to zip down to Laredo and meet up with James Brazzle. I think you know who he is. He's been looking forward to this conversation."

I breathed deeply and wished I had a mantra to repeat to calm myself. Of course, I knew who James Brazzle was. In my novels he was the head of the special People's Intelligence and Security Service (P.I.S.S.) that answered directly to the governor of Texas, but I had made him up. Just like Mako, Armando, and Bronc Thornton, all of whom were with me in the Texas National Guard helicopter and looking very much alive. I tilted my head back and drained the Shiner bottle.

Chapter 26

As we flew south towards Laredo, I tried to convince myself it was all a bad dream. I know a cliché ending when I hear one, but I wished someone could just wake me up from my afternoon nap and put a cup of tea and a plate of crumpets on my bedside table. It worked for Alice, I recalled. Or maybe I could click my heels three times, whisper, "there's no place like home", and wake up in my bed surrounded by worried relatives and friends.

I read once that hope is the last thing to die in men. But it turns out a Frenchman coined that phrase, so I don't believe a word of it. Besides, I had already passed beyond hope into the wishful thinking phase. Utter despair was next.

The only positive thing in the whole horrifying scenario was the smell of righteous chronic wafting back to the flight deck from the pilot's cabin. Goose's nostrils were twitching like a bloodhound, and I swear even Rigo looked interested. But I motioned for both of them to stay put. The old renegade pothead looked at the armed men sitting around him, and for once he didn't argue.

If it hadn't been for the painful chaffing on my wrists and ankles, I could have bought the line that this was nothing more than a nightmare. Logic alone told me that none of this was really happening. Could God really be sadistic enough to place us in this twisted scenario? I always suspected He spent more time watching the Dallas Cowboys or attending Miss Texas beauty pageants than He did showing mercy or saving souls. But now I was convinced. As it was, my aching joints and Goose's bruised face told me once and for all this was no dream.

I think Mako himself sensed my existential dilemma. I caught him looking at me several times with what I interpreted as sympathy, but maybe it was just pity. If the real Mako was anything like his fictional Doppelganger, he would be difficult to read and not the kind of man you'd want to cross. I decided it was better to keep my thoughts under wraps.

We touched down on a private air strip in the middle of a South Texas cattle ranch. A few skinny white-faced cows stared dumbly at us as they stood next to a moldy round bale and chewed their cud. The blades of a rusty Aeromotor windmill screeched as they turned slowly in the cool humid breeze, pumping a thin drool of water into a scum-covered trough. Half a dozen pickup trucks were waiting for us, and I was glad Mako hadn't stooped to using black SUVs with darkly tinted windows for his team of commandos. His men didn't even wear sunglasses to make themselves look badass like the U.S. Marshals and FBI agents did. From the look of them, these guys didn't require the affectation.

"Clabe, I'd normally put a hood over your head at this point to keep our destination a secret, but I think it would be superfluous. I'm sure you know exactly where we're headed," Mako said as he got into a pickup truck driven by a young Mexican wearing a straw cowboy hat despite the cool temperatures. I climbed into the back seat with Goose and Rigo.

He was right. I DID know where we were going. Unless I was sadly mistaken, we were on our way to P.I.S.S. headquarters, located on the top floor of the Hamilton Hotel in Laredo. If you had asked me yesterday, I would have insisted that James Brazzle, together with the People's Intelligence & Security Service, were both products of my fertile imagination. I said as much to Mako, but he begged to differ and insisted Brazzle was as real as he was. I continued swilling Shiner Blonde as we drove towards Laredo and soon no longer cared what was real and what was bullshit. In Texas there's a fine line separating the two, and it's hard to tell them apart.

Mako was as good as his word. There was no torture and no threat of enhanced interrogation once we arrived at P.I.S.S. headquarters. Quite the contrary; a secretary brought Goose and me cups of coffee and a plate of pralines and was classy enough to ignore Goose's lecherous stares down her blouse. Shortly afterwards, James Brazzle himself came into the conference room where we sat in luxurious overstuffed leather chairs nervously awaiting his arrival. He looked just as I had described him in my novel; tall, lean, and sunburned, wearing a beat-up Stetson. His fingertips were stained with tobacco, and his huge gnarly hands looked like he'd been stringing barbed-wire fence his whole life. In my novels, he was a retired CIA officer who had come back to Texas to live on his family's ranch south of Cotulla. I was beyond surprise at this stage and shook his hand without comment when Mako introduced him. I was vaguely pleased that my description of him had been so accurate.

"Clabe, I understand you've had a rough time of it," began Brazzle.

"Yeah, it seems I've fallen out of favor with the feds," I replied and saw just a trace of a smile on Brazzle's lips.

"You're lucky they didn't fly you straight up to Leavenworth," he said. "We couldn't have helped you there, but Texas is ours. Nobody tells us what to do down here. They were stupid."

"As usual," Mako added.

"Clabe, let's get right to the point," Brazzle said, and I stiffened a little in anticipation.

"I can't claim to be a fan of your books. I find them simplistic, cynical, and crude for the most part. At best they make the CIA look like a bunch of bumbling fuckups..."

"Which is accurate," Mako interrupted. "You know it as well as anybody, James."

"That doesn't mean I like it thrown in my face," Brazzle snapped back. "Clabe here was only in for a few years. I spent my whole career there, and I don't like to think it was in vain."

I just sat back and watched as these two Cold War veterans traded barbs just like they would have in one of my books.

"Now, where was I?" asked Brazzle.

"You don't like my books," I reminded him.

"Oh yeah. You're a glib smart ass," he continued. "But we want to get to the bottom of the latest crap you've been writing. The world is imploding, and you're writing about it like it was teenage vampire fiction. By the way, the governor's not pleased about the sex scenes with his daughter either."

Brazzle took a pack of Zig-Zag cigarette papers out of his shirt pocket, and for a second I thought the old CIA veteran was going to roll a joint. Then I saw him take a plastic pouch of tobacco from his desk drawer and sprinkle it thickly onto the cigarette paper he held carefully between his thumb and forefinger. I should have remembered that Brazzle was old-school. He wouldn't think of firing up a joint. He lit the foul-smelling cigarette and inhaled deeply. My lungs burned in sympathy as I watched him.

"Now that would be fine in and of itself," he continued, pausing to blow a series of smoke rings above his head. "A lot of authors write about imagined national crises that never happened and never will. But Clabe, you're writing about them before they happen…and then they do. So, do you want to tell me and Mako here what the hell is going on?"

I wanted to tell them, but what could I say? I had no answers, and the mystery had been driving me crazy ever since the interview with Fox & Friends in the Dallas television studio. I told them about the interview, blowing up the FBI surveillance vehicle, our headlong flight from Texas, and our close call in South Carolina when we narrowly avoided arrest for all the wrong reasons. They had seen my series of interviews with Gretel, and I saw no reason to enlighten them on Gretel's propensity to combine politics and sex. They were particularly interested in my experiences with enhanced interrogation, and Mako raised his eyebrows when I told him his name had been mentioned during the questioning.

Later that day, Mako moved our little contingent to the same ranch north of Laredo where Bronc Thornton had flown us after our rescue. We moved into a sprawling one-story wooden farmhouse with rough-hewn floorboards that left splinters in your feet if you weren't wearing shoes. Knowing our particular needs, Mako kept the refrigerator overflowing with beer and mixers. The liquor cabinet was well stocked too. Bronc Thornton joined us, and he, Goose, and Armando lit up the moment they woke up each morning and were stoned and singing narcocorridos[30] by breakfast. Rigo explored and hunted, occasionally bringing in dead varmints that he killed at night, depositing them on the front porch for our inspection.

After the meeting with Brazzle, there were three days of interviews with psychiatrists and specialists in extrasensory perception and parapsychology. I even consented to hypnotism although that ended badly when the hypnotist tried to fondle me when I dozed off during the procedure. The psychiatrists and ESP quacks soon left

---

[30] Songs about the lives and adventures of Mexican drug traffickers

without coming to an intelligible conclusion regarding the origin of what everyone had begun to refer to as Unexplained Precognitive Phenomena (UPP). Sure, they had their theories. One psychiatrist, in particular, theorized that tachyon particles, which were able to travel at speeds faster than light, had returned from the future and entered my cerebral cortex, thus giving me knowledge of what was going to happen. He never mentioned that the existence of tachyon particles was hypothetical at best. Frankly, I thought it was a crock.

"Well, it looks like you're back in business," said Mako one morning before breakfast. He had been supervising a remodeling crew ever since we arrived, and the crew was finishing up an office in one corner of the farmhouse.

"I've been talking to Joel," he said.

"From *The Ganja Times?*" I asked.

"Yeah, the FBI questioned and released him, and now he's back in L.A. at work. He's clamoring for more material from you."

"The FBI is going to let him publish?" I asked.

"They've got no choice," Mako said. "Unauthorized disclosure of classified information is a hard charge to prove. Being clairvoyant is not a crime last time I checked, and what was classified in what you wrote?

They'd have to prove that, you see, and then show the judge the classified material. Someone would promptly leak it all to the press, and the legal wonks don't want that. Besides, the FBI isn't looking to prosecute you. That's an empty threat, at least for now. They want information; only they don't know what we've already learned: namely, that you don't have it. But their immediate goal is to lure you out of wherever you're hiding. They think you'll resurface when you submit your next episode. I can make sure they don't find you."

"What's in it for you guys?" I asked.

This was a tough business, I knew. Nobody was going to defy the FBI and the rest of the federal government if there wasn't something to be gained; something big.

"Listen, the world economy is going down the tubes, and the U.S. may be about to start a war with the wrong people. Texas is right in the middle of it all. You and I can't just sit by and let it happen. If you're able to somehow influence events or are causing them, we've got to know."

"That doesn't really answer my question," I responded.

"Clabe, we've got a theory on who's masterminding the attacks in the Gulf of Mexico, but there're some blanks we need to fill in," said Mako. "We want you to keep writing your novel."

"How's that going to help?" I asked.

"Isn't it obvious?" he asked.

"Not yet,"

"You're going to tell us the future," said Mako.

Chapter 27

So that was it. Mako and Armando had rescued me from the feds and brought me down to the Laredo safe house to help them figure out who was the asshole trying to destroy the world's economy. Mako suspected Washington was hiding its own nefarious role in the crisis, and he knew Texas would have to depend on its own resources if it wanted any answers. For me the change in locations was more like a lateral job transfer or maybe like jumping out of the frying pan into the fire. It sounded like they wanted me to act as some kind of mentalist or a gypsy fortune teller. And some of my critics say I'M crazy.

Neither Mako nor Brazzle could bring himself to believe that I could really see into the future, much less that I might be creating it. They weren't wired that way, but the uncanny coincidences between my writing and the calamitous events of the last month had driven them to desperation. They were ready to try anything.

I thought about escaping and trying to make my way to Terlingua, a desolate old mining town in the Chihuahuan Desert near the Rio Grande. Nobody would look for me there. I could rent a rickety one-room shack built into the side of a mountain like a mine shaft or maybe find a single-wide trailer to share with scorpions, lizards, and a few rattlesnakes. When Terlingua cooled down to about 95 degrees in the evening, I could sit on the porch in the old Ghost Town and swill Lone Star beer with old derelict hippies, UFO-ologists, end-of-world escapists, and maybe even a disgraced Louisiana politician or two. Then I thought of Mako and realized I wouldn't get as far as the windmill before I felt those powerful hands on my shoulders. I had created my own jailer.

I was being selfish in wanting to leave. I knew that. Goose and Rigo were perfectly content where we were. Maybe I needed to think of their happiness for a change. Goose had a free supply of beer and *mota*[31], and I suspected that he and Bronc Thornton were punishing the psilocybin mushrooms as well. Rigo was rapidly killing off the possum and skunk population of South Texas and wouldn't have made a pleasant traveling companion in a truck anyway. More importantly, we didn't even HAVE a truck anymore.

In Mako's company, I alternated between feelings of paternal possessiveness and childlike awe. Part of me insisted that he was nothing more than a figment of my imagination, the physical embodiment of my literary vision. He was my creation. But then I would catch sight

---

[31] Mexican slang for marijuana

of him, and I knew that he had either outgrown my descriptive powers or had always existed in a parallel universe.

Of course, the hero of my novels was bound to be a force of nature, who dictated his own terms to the world. I never felt threatened in his presence or thought he would harm me, though. Wouldn't that be like Count Dracula feeding on the blood of Bram Stoker or the "fallen angel" harming Victor Frankenstein?

"It's time, Clabe," he said to me one morning when the workers had finished the office remodeling.

"Time for what?" I asked.

"Here's your new office," Mako said, pointing at the new work space in the corner of the living room with a 180-degree view of the cactus and mesquite wasteland beyond the window.

"It's beautiful," I said sarcastically.

"Here's your new laptop, and here's a cooler of ice-cold Shiner Blonde. Now sit down and write."

Now that, I didn't mind. I was full of ideas for the next episode and sat down and started typing almost immediately. Conspiracies, backstabbing betrayals, and scenes of hideous, blood-soaked death swirled through my mind and found their way to my fingertips, which pounded out the next episode of my serial novel. I remembered what Brazzle had said about the governor not liking the sex scenes with his daughter in my previous book, so I added an especially graphic description of her romp in the hay with two Mexican ranch hands. I wondered if it would really happen. If it did, I'd have to pencil myself into some similar scenarios. I was amused at the level of my own degradation. Two days later I handed a travel drive to Mako.

"Here it is. Send it to Joel with my regards," I said.

"Mind if I read it first?" he asked.

"Go ahead," I replied. "Just what I need; another critic."

"Thanks," said Mako. "Now keep writing."

I watched Mako out of the corner of my eye as he plugged the travel drive into his own laptop and began to read. I saw him smile and shake his head a few times. Then he exclaimed and snapped his fingers as if he had discovered something that had eluded him his whole life. He even took notes. Then he stood up abruptly and took out his cell phone. He glanced at me with a wild look in his eyes as he feverishly punched in a number and walked out of the house.

I froze as I considered the implications of what I had written. I hoped nobody would die as a result, but it wouldn't be my fault, would it? People were dying on the pages of my novel, you see, and I was worried. I had just fed a DEA agent to the sharks off the coast of Mazatlan. Well, I hadn't really done it, but I wrote about it. Would that make me a murderer or somehow an accomplice? Shit, I didn't know, and the hellacious quantities of Shiner I was consuming didn't help me solve the riddle. I was rapidly pickling my brain.

I began to wish I had written about normal people rather than the raffish crew I had described in my novels. Yeah, normal people like WalMart greeters and proctologists. At least they were predictable. Hanging out with this crowd was a definite liability. Bronc had a synergistic effect on Goose and exaggerated the already sociopathic side to him. And knowing Mako's innate ability conjure up mayhem from bucolic serenity, there was no telling what might happen with him around. I snapped out of my daydream in time to see Mako stride purposefully into the room with an armful of manila folders full of photographs and 201 files.

"We've got some work to do," he announced.

Mako was looking for a missing piece of the intelligence puzzle, but what he didn't know was that if it wasn't in what I wrote, I didn't know about it. He was barking up the wrong tree. I shook my head "no" for about an hour as he flashed photos of the usual suspects in front of me. Finally he gave up and commanded me to sit down again at my laptop and write.

That's when it hit me. I was a prisoner here in South Texas every bit as much as I had been in the clutches of the FBI and CIA. Only here my plight was even more diabolical. Here I was a prisoner of the very fictional characters I had created. I was in a hellish Alice in Wonderland nightmare of my own invention.

I could handle the possibility that I had the gift of future sight. It was a stretch, but I had seen convincing evidence regarding extra sensory perception and had always believed in the untapped capabilities of the human brain. After all, animals can sometimes sense a change in the weather and have been known to seek safer ground before an earthquake or a tsunami. Maybe I was that one in ten million who somehow is able to sense what's going to happen. But what about the possibility that I could create the future just by inserting it into my story? If that was true, at what point did my writing become reality? Was it as soon as the ink dried on the paper? Or was it only when Joel published a new episode?

Armando soon confirmed that the Sinaloa Cartel had executed a high-ranking DEA official precisely in the gruesome manner I described in my book. Apparently, I even had the name of Antonio Salcido's yacht right; *High*

Jinks. I was stunned and sat at my desk for several days staring at the scrubby vegetation outside the window. I was unable to make intelligible conversation, and my mind began to wander hopelessly. I was lucid enough to know I was drifting towards the razor's edge of sanity, but I had no control over my thoughts. I indulged myself in extravagant fantasies of bringing down corrupt political leaders with the power of my pen and fighting for truth, justice, and the American way. Mostly, though, I passed the time in erotic daydreams of luring Gretel into a recumbent position and plowing away while she blithered about the comparative sexual prowess of Democrats and Republicans. You can see which direction my brain went under stress.

My mind was in a free fall. Would the DEA official have lived if I hadn't executed him on the pages of my novel? That was what I kept asking myself over and over. Even the tingling in my loins at the thought of another interview with Gretel subsided when I considered the possibility that I was a serial killer.

The news from Mexico didn't seem to bother Mako Sloane and James Brazzle as much as the other intelligence bombshell I dropped in my latest bit of scribbling. P.I.S.S. was all up in arms over my hint that a high-ranking administrative official in Washington was a

Russian agent. They figured if everything else was coming true, this revelation might be on the money as well. Mako thought Washington was up to its ears in the scandal and possibly even calling the shots. He wanted to know who the traitor was and urged me to write more. Frankly, I had lost interest in the story. When it finally dawned on me that I might have been the cause of unimaginable chaos in the world's financial markets and the deaths of a dozen people, the last thing I wanted to do was to sit down at the computer and conjure up more of the same.

In the meantime, the rumor mill out of Washington had Mako worried. He said that both the U.S. and Russian governments had decided it was time to shut me up; permanently. Quite apart from my revealing the dirty secrets about their covert operations, the political wallahs in both countries feared I might have the power to bring the international economic system crashing into an abyss, from which there would be no return. Mako said the Russians were prepared to work alongside the Americans to prevent that from happening. He told me to keep my suitcase packed. I told him to keep my glass of Flor de Caña full.

"Clabe, get a grip on yourself," Mako said to me. "The world needs your help."

I peeled my gaze away from the almost featureless landscape and looked at Mako. He was wearing his ubiquitous tight black t-shirt, Wranglers, and an old pair of scruffy cowboy boots that had seen better days.

"Oh?" I inquired casually.

"That's right. You've indulged yourself for long enough. This doesn't get us any closer to finding out who's behind all this shit."

"You know who's behind it. It's the Russians and the most powerful drug cartel in Mexico. What more do you want?" I asked.

"I want to know whether Washington's in bed with the Russians on this. Or at least whether some high-ranking American official is freelancing."

"Well, I want to know whether I can create the future."

"And then what?" asked Mako.

"How the fuck do I know?" I barked and immediately regretted my remark. I knew Mako was right. I HAD been indulging myself; feeling sorry for my lot in life. It was pathetic. Mako, I think, had lost patience with me. He stood up and put on his cowboy hat.

"I'm going to meet with James," he said quietly and left. I was beyond caring if I had offended the man. I had myself to think of, and at the moment my thoughts were not good and getting worse.

Chapter 28

I never understood where they could have been hiding. There just aren't that many hills in South Texas high enough to conceal a Sinaloa Cartel war party riding to battle in four Land Rover SUVs and a Ford Taurus sedan. But they were skulking around out there somewhere and obviously had the ranch staked out. No sooner had the sound of Mako's pickup receded into the monotonous expanse of mesquite and cactus, than I heard them coming. The roar of multiple diesel engines descending on my residence-of-the-moment had become an unfortunate cliché. I wished my life were as easy to edit as my novels. There'd be a lot of red ink in my diary.

This was my first live, close-up look at the infamous *sicario* killers of drug cartel infamy, and, as you might have expected, the descriptions of them in my serial novel were spot-on.

Four paunchy thugs wearing backwards baseball caps, baggy jeans and ill-fitting t-shirts poured out of each SUV like Three Stooges clones. It would have been comical except for the assault rifles and Uzi submachine guns they carried. Half of them swarmed through the front door, and the other half kicked in the back door a moment later as I stood mesmerized, watching them. I took mental notes of their clothes, height and weight, facial features, moustaches, tattoos, and the weapons they carried. It was a writer's habit, I suppose. I was absorbing the local color for my next fiction project. The seriousness of my predicament had yet to sink in, and I still hadn't focused on the most likely outcome of this latest plot twist; there wouldn't be a next fiction project. Antonio Salcido and his über-bloodthirsty drug cartel were going to kill me. The only question was when.

"*¿Gordo, eres tú?*"[32] I heard Goose shout to a corpulent narco he obviously recognized. Goose smiled broadly and held out his arms ready to embrace his erstwhile friend. Instead, the scowling brute slammed the butt of his AK-47 into Goose's jaw. I saw my sidekick collapse to the ground with blood pouring from a gash on his chin. Then two of the cartel goons grabbed me by the elbows and marched me outside to the Taurus. I was wondering what had become of Bronc and Rigo when I spotted the Ford sedan. My heart sank. I knew from my research that the cartel favored the Taurus because of its large trunk space. I also knew why they needed the extra room.

---

[32] Fatso, is that you?

Two of the thugs held my arms behind my back while another blindfolded me with a sweaty handkerchief that smelled of human sweat and something much worse. Then they snapped a pair of plasticuffs on my wrists, and I felt myself lifted and thrown into the trunk of the Ford Taurus. My head banged painfully on a tire tool left unsecured in the trunk. The last thing I heard before the trunk slammed shut was Rigo growling and snarling like an enraged feral beast.

As the Taurus sped away, a solitary shot rang out, and I was sure Rigo was the target. The car careened erratically around potholes in the long gravel driveway, and my body bounced off the sides of the trunk like a corpse in a loose-fitting coffin. Tears of helpless fury stung my eyes as I envisioned Rigo halted in mid-air charge by a 7.62 mm bullet slamming into his chest; gunned down trying to protect me. I tried to block thoughts of my four-legged shadow from my mind and concentrate on my own dire circumstances. There would be time enough to mourn my loyal friend later. At least he died for something, I thought. He had followed his genetic programming to the bitter end. My death, on the other hand, would be the culmination of the misguided decisions and choices of a middle-aged wastrel. It would be a mere footnote in the annals of the War on Drugs. Nobody would mourn my passing, except maybe Carmen. Morbid thinking, I realized, but I just didn't want to die. A few hours later I had changed my mind and was ready to welcome the Grim Reaper with open arms.

Thirty minutes after my abduction the caravan stopped and I heard shouting and sporadic gunfire. I surmised we had crossed the U.S. – Mexico border, and that my cartel kidnappers were celebrating their successful mission. The trunk opened, and I heard the fizzy explosions of bottles being opened. A half dozen voices bid each other, *"Salud, compañero[33]"*, and I heard the familiar glug-glug of liquid gurgling out of bottles. My kidnappers were guzzling beer, I realized. My throat was parched, and I asked for a drink, but the sons o' bitches just laughed at me. I heard men grunting as if they were lifting a heavy object, and then a massive weight fell painfully on top of me. It cursed in Spanish, and I recognized Goose's voice.

So much for the roominess of the Ford Taurus trunk, I thought to myself. The trunk slammed closed again, and a sudden feeling of claustrophobic panic sent my bowels into seizures, and my hamstrings began to cramp. I felt a nostalgic longing for Dusty and the CIA's

---

[33] To your health, comrade.

Enhanced Interrogation procedures. I knew the CIA's attempts at torture would seem like adolescent shenanigans compared to what the Sinaloa Cartel had in store for me. Plus, I doubted there would be any cartel attorneys taking notes on clipboards and monitoring the legality of the torture.

Despite my distinct unease at the prospects of some rough handling once we got to where we were going, I wasn't really afraid. As odd as it seems in retrospect, I was more pissed off than anything else. Things seemed ass-backwards and out of kilter. Here I was, precognition soothsayer extraordinaire, kidnapped in broad daylight and shanghaied across the border, and I hadn't seen it coming or written about it ahead of time. Things were actually happening unilaterally without me first giving the "Clabe Taylor" stamp of approval in the form of an episode of my serial novel. Had I suddenly become irrelevant?

I had a pretty clear idea of our final destination. We were likely headed for Culiacán, Sinaloa; deep in Mexican drug country controlled by Antonio Salcido's cartel. I calculated it would take about 15 hours to get there unless Goose and I ran out of oxygen before that and suffocated. If I was still alive when we arrived, my hosts would haul my senseless body out of the trunk and toss me on the ground in the gravel courtyard in front of Antonio Salcido's ranch headquarters. Only then would the true horror begin.

I could already imagine the *ring-ding-ding* of a chainsaw's two-cycle engine as one of Salcido's minions fired up the infernal machine and prepared to decapitate me. Another assistant would be aiming his smart phone at me to video the ritualistic execution. It would be posted on *Blog del Narco* the next day. Or maybe they would rip out my fingernails, inject Tehuacán carbonated mineral water up my nostrils, or sodomize me with a broom stick. That would be before the decapitation, of course.

In the meantime, though, the air in the trunk was stale and infused with car exhaust. Within a few minutes, my head had begun to ache, and Goose's full-sized figure was pressing on my hip and cutting off the blood supply to my left leg.

"Goose, move over a little bit," I asked. "My leg's numb."

"I can't, you bony motherfucker," he answered. "Jesus, I feel like I'm lying on a sack of firewood or something. Get your elbow out of my ribs, *gringo*."

It was miserable, but I won't bore you with the details of our ordeal. Suffice it to say that five hours into the journey, Goose and I both pissed ourselves, and soon afterwards the trunk began to reek of dried urine. I'm not sure how Goose felt, but my joints were on fire, and I had a migraine headache that made me sick to my stomach, again and again. That too did wonders for the air we had to breathe. I'll hand it to Goose, though. He bore his misery with grace and in silence, much the way I imagined he had done his time in the feds.

In the back of my mind I kept hoping that Mako had discovered our abduction. In a previous novel I described how Mako and Bronc Thornton had rescued the daughter of the governor of Texas from the clutches of the cartel. Maybe he could do the same for Goose and me. That was likely our only chance at freedom, slight as it was.

My mind has always had a mathematical bent to it, and I spent my time in the trunk calculating the number of days I had left to live. In my most optimistic estimates I gave myself a week to ten days. That was at the beginning of the trip. As the hours passed, I grew progressively pessimistic and began to doubt whether even the great Mako Sloane was up to rescuing Goose and me from an actual cartel dungeon. It was one thing to have my characters commit their heroic acts on the pages of sensationalist novels. It would be quite another for Mako to traipse blithely into cartel headquarters in real life and save us from near certain execution. I figured if the Sinaloa Cartel had decided to put the kibosh on me, well, I probably better get used to the idea.

At some point during the trip I resigned myself to death and began to even welcome its prospects. I just hoped it would be quick and painless. I wondered if this was how a long-suffering dog would view euthanasia as the veterinarian inserted the needle.

Given my desperate state of mind, what actually happened upon our arrival in Culiacán was all the more mind boggling. I woke from a fitful sleep many hours later to the sound of the car finally rolling to a stop followed by angry shouting.

"You did what?" I heard a voice scream in Spanish. Two shots rang out in quick succession, and someone opened the trunk. The midday tropical sun blinded me even though the handkerchief was still tied around my head and covered my eyes. The piercing light jumpstarted my migraine, and I thought my head would explode.

"¡Cretinos!" [34] shouted the same voice. Another shot roared in the thick humid air, and this time I heard the distinct hollow thump of a body falling on pavement. At least that's what I always imagined it would sound like.

---

[34] Morons!

I rubbed my head on the side of the tire tool, trying to loosen my blindfold. I still couldn't see a thing.

"Untie them and get them both cleaned up," the voice commanded. I heard receding footsteps, and then I felt the luxurious relief of Goose's body being dragged off mine, and then hands were grabbing at my arms and legs and lifting me out of the car. Someone ripped my blindfold off, and I collapsed to the ground, unable to stand on my own legs. A body lay three feet away from me, the bullet-sized hole in the man's forehead still oozing blood. His vacant pig eyes seem to stare directly at me, and I thought I recognized his face.

These cartel types could use some fashion consultants, I decided. Maybe Joel could interest his Hollywood producer buddies in a new reality show with glamour gurus coming to Culiacán and giving these cartel assassins extreme makeovers. It might improve the bad press they always got. They looked like such dumbasses in police lineups. That was the cynical side of me coming out, though, and I knew I should be more respectful of the dead. After all, a bullet between the eyes was not how this man expected to be rewarded for driving brazenly into Texas and abducting one of the most-wanted men in America. Some things just weren't fair.

That was Mexico for you; cruel and unpredictable. The same game of Russian roulette likely awaited both Goose and me, our lives in the hands of a madman. Two men on either side of me half-carried and half-dragged me in the direction of a rustic white stucco house with a faded red ceramic tile roof. The last thing I remember before I mercifully lost consciousness was the sound of a flamenco guitar and clapping hands coming from within the house.

Chapter 29

Antonio Salcido was insane, of course. It didn't take long to come to that conclusion. Maybe the stress of being cartel capo *Número Uno* and one of the most wanted men in the world had finally pushed him over the edge. Think about it. The man had a very full plate to deal with. First of all, there was the never-ending internecine strife with the other cartels: the Zetas, Gulf Cartel, Knights Templar, La Familia Michoacana, and a dozen others. The Sinaloa Cartel had to stay on its toes 24/7 to maintain its top ranking. It was sort of like the competition between Hertz and Avis back in the 1960s, except the car rental executives didn't hang each other from bridges in Nuevo Laredo like the drug capos did. The Zetas were only #2, but they were trying harder.

Then there were the gun battles with the Mexican military and police, and when the government wasn't pretending to fight Salcido and his army of foot soldiers, Antonio had to pay them off. The greedy bastards were always demanding more and more. There were dozens of Mexican generals, police chiefs, and politicians who had amassed vast personal fortunes on their government salaries thanks to Antonio. Sprawling villas overlooking the Pacific Ocean outside of San Diego, credit cards with Nieman Marcus, and bank accounts with Wells Fargo didn't attract much attention in Mexico any more. Everyone had them; at least everybody who was anybody.

The occasional sacrificial lamb arrested during a brief anti-corruption campaign was usually enough to keep the critics and the media happy, but nobody wanted the drug money faucet to run dry. On the U.S. side of the border there were corrupt DEA, Border Patrol, and U.S. Customs officials, along with local sheriffs and mayors in Texas, New Mexico, and Arizona. They all stood in line with their hands out, and it was Salcido's job to keep everyone happy. It was damned stressful.

On top of everything else there was Antonio's day job: exporting weed, cocaine, and methamphetamines to the drug-crazed *gringos*. Salcido's organization was vertically integrated, and he operated a vast international conglomerate with branches in numerous countries in Latin America and Europe. His business boasted a sophisticated corporate structure involving large-scale growing projects, the transshipment of cocaine from South America, the importation of precursor drugs from Asia, and the operation of heroin and methamphetamine laboratories in Mexico itself. He even had a special department that maintained a working relationship with urban Latino gangs in the United States. The Aztecas and the Mexican Mafia in El Paso, San Antonio, and Chicago always appreciated the extra work he threw their way. Antonio outsourced his murders and kidnappings in the United States to the gangbangers, but it all required management and oversight. Who had the time? It was hard to find good help these days. I didn't blame the man for losing his mind.

I knew all this about Antonio Salcido, but had no idea he was a "Clabe Taylor fan" on top of everything else. But after he shot three of my abductors presumably for their abominable treatment of me, I began to hope I might emerge from the kidnapping scenario with nothing more than soiled trousers and aching joints. It took me a while to put two and two together, but I had an excuse. Being kidnapped and brutalized in the trunk of a car in Mexico has a way of muddling one's mind.

I stepped out of the bathroom thirty minutes later with a towel wrapped around me. A petite Philippine beauty clad in only a thong met me with a bottle of Eucalyptus oil and motioned for me to remove my towel and lie down on the massage table. A recording of ocean noises played softly in the dimly lit room, and I smelled incense and scented candles. From the trunk of the car to the massage table in thirty minutes! That must have been some kind of a record. I glanced at those taut little bouncers, and knew I was going to get along well with the head of the Sinaloa Cartel. I liked his style. Antonio met me after the massage with an *abrazo*[35] and a copy of *The Ganja Times* that contained the first episode of my serial novel.

"Clabe," he said to me in excellent English with only a trace of an accent. "Would you do me the honor?"

He handed me the magazine along with a Mont Blanc Meisterstück fountain pen. This was surreal. Instead of meeting me with a chainsaw and threatening me with 2-cycle death, the head of the Sinaloa Cartel was asking me to autograph his copy of *The Ganja Times.* I looked at Antonio and grinned for the first time since the attack on our safehouse ranch.

"You're the last person on earth I'd expect to be a fan of mine," I said.

"Are you kidding?" Salcido guffawed. "Our exports to the United States this year are up 11.8%. I attribute the increase to your insight, Clabe. You're a visionary. You're my Dalai Lama."

What was this? Salcido was comparing me to the Dalai Lama? I was flattered. Was His Holiness into drug

---

[35] manly embrace

trafficking too? I waved my hand dismissively and shook my head. I didn't want to take responsibility for increasing the flow of drugs across the border. No good could come of that.

"Alright," Antonio continued. "I'll take some of the credit if you insist. The submarine WAS my idea. The Russians were eager to help us, but you showed us how to exploit it most effectively and how to manage the *gringos.* And then your idea about the sharks and the DEA agent; that was brilliant!"

Shit, that's one of the things I didn't want to hear. So, Salcido HAD been using my writing as an instruction manual. My head spun with the implications. But wait! Did that mean that I didn't really have the gift of precognition?

"You mean....?" I started to ask.

"Sure. I can't tell you how excited we are each time our copies of the magazine arrive. I send my private jet to Los Angeles, and it comes back with a dozen copies. Each member of our Board of Directors reads the latest episode, and then we meet to discuss options.

"You have a Board of Directors?" I asked.

"Of course, what did you think?" he responded.

"Oh, I don't know....I guess I thought you made all the decisions and murdered anyone who disagreed with you," I said, hoping the cartel capo had a sense of humor to match his ego.

Antonio roared with laughter and clapped me on the shoulder.

"You're fucking hilarious, Clabe," he said. "Listen, the Sinaloa Federation is a Fortune 500 company. Well, at least we should be based on our annual earnings. We have to follow the pharmaceutical industry's Best Practices procedures. We answer to our stockholders like any other corporation."

I didn't dare call Antonio's attention to the illicit nature of his business and the fact that he was a wanted man despite his entrepreneurial success. He seemed oblivious to that reality.

"I'd like to apologize for the unfortunate way my invitation was delivered," he said. "My men were NOT supposed to mistreat you. It won't happen again, I promise you."

No, I didn't think so either, recalling those lifeless eyes staring at me. That was Best Practices? I would have thought a written reprimand and a counseling session with HR would have been more appropriate. A bullet in the forehead puts a rather large exclamation point at the end of performance evaluation report and a resume.

"I hope this won't affect our relationship?" Antonio asked.

I knew the right answer to that question.

"Not in the least, Antonio. I understand. Where's my friend, by the way?"

"You mean Goose?" he asked. "He used to be my lawyer, you know. The damned *gringos* took away five years of his life, but you know what? He never gave those *pendejos* what they were looking for. He never whined like a little bitch, and he never ratted out his *camaradas*."

"Yeah, Goose is as tough as they come, but where is he?" I asked.

Antonio laughed and gestured with his thumb back towards the spa.

"Where do you think? He's probably chasing one of the Philippine masseuses around the table right about now. He's a good man, but he's hornier than a billy goat."

"And what about my dog and Bronc Thornton?" I asked. Now that I knew Antonio was not planning to kill me, I thought it would be a good time to clear the air.

"I understand one of my men shot and killed Bronc. The bastard unfortunately betrayed me a few years ago. He dishonored me and my organization, and I just couldn't let the precedent stand. I'm sorry."

A chill ran down my back. That wouldn't sit well with Mako, I knew. If it was true, I was going to miss the old stoner. After all, he had piloted the chopper that rescued us from the feds.

"And the dog?" I asked.

"Your vicious dog mauled several of my men, but they know better than to kill an innocent animal," answered Salcido. "Can you imagine what that would do to our image?"

So, the shot I heard had been for Bronc. Dogs were off limits, but people weren't? That was just one of many examples of Antonio's twisted logic. Maybe one's personal value system had to be a little out of whack if you were the head of the most powerful drug cartel in Mexico. But who was I to argue with success?

"Clabe, let me introduce you to some of my friends," Antonio continued as he led me down a long hallway with salmon-colored Saltillo tile on the floor and rustic hand-carved wooden benches placed strategically along the wall. Oil paintings depicting Mexican victories in armed conflicts decorated the wall. Admittedly, there weren't many of those. As we approached a mission-style arched door at the end of the hallway, the flamenco music I heard earlier became louder, and I heard rhythmic clapping and shouting from what sounded like a crowd of people.

"Are you having a party?" I asked.

"You might say that. We're finishing up a stockholders' meeting, and we're just beginning the entertainment portion of the program.

Salcido flung open the arched wooden doors, and I caught my breath. A wall-to-wall mass of humanity greeted us with a cheer as we walked into the spacious room. My jaw dropped as I gazed around the crowd, picking out a familiar face here and there that I had seen before in newspapers, on Mexican television, or in music videos. I felt as if I had barged into a modern-day version of the 1930's beautiful people scene in Mexico City with clones of Diego Rivera, Frida Kahlo, and Leon Trostky smoking cigarettes in elegant ivory cigarette holders and holding court for groveling sycophants. Scantily clad starlets of the Mexican soap opera industry preened and strutted through the all-star assembly, showing off the latest advances in North American cosmetic surgery. Businessmen in $5,000 Italian suits raised their vodka martinis in toasts to us as we slowly entered the hall, grasping extended hands, kissing cheeks, and mumbling incoherent greetings. Cattle ranchers in full Charro regalia with ornamented trousers and vests waved their huge *sombreros* and shouted the traditional Mexican *grito*.

Antonio joined the multitude in a rousing ovation, and everyone began to chant, "Clabe, Clabe, Clabe." I was flabbergasted, but my amazement was nothing compared to what I felt when I looked up and saw a banner that hung from the rafters above and stretched from one side of the hall to the other.

"BIENVENIDO[36], CLABE TAYLOR", read the banner extending a formal welcome to the headquarters of the Sinaloa Cartel.

---

[36] WELCOME

Chapter 30

The next day the Salcido ranch resembled a morgue until early afternoon when the last of the bedraggled revelers from the night before staggered out to their waiting chauffeur-driven Land Rovers. Bell helicopters from the Ministry of Defense and the Office of the Attorney General shuttled a few of Antonio's highest-ranking guests directly to private jets parked at the Culiacán airport, but by midday everyone had departed.

"Clabe, how's your head?" Antonio asked as he stuck his head in the guest bedroom where I lay dozing, trying not to throw up.

"I feel like death warmed over," I confessed.

"We all do," he replied. "It was quite a party. Get dressed and come out for some *menudo*".

I cringed at the mention of *menudo,* a traditional Mexican soup made from tripe that is a popular folk cure for a hangover. The broth is delicious, but the texture of the tripe always made me nauseous even if I hadn't been drinking the night before. When I walked into the kitchen, I saw Antonio, Goose, and several of Antonio's bodyguards sitting at a long wooden table, looking forlorn and eating steaming *menudo* from large ceramic crocks. Goose was in far worse shape than I was, and even the bodyguards apparently had let down their hair the previous night. Nobody greeted me, and nobody spoke. The bloodshot eyes, the occasional moans, and the nonstop slurping of the hot soup told the whole story.

Had it really been just twenty-four hours ago that I sat moping at my desk on the ranch outside of Laredo, swilling beer and tearfully lamenting my possible role in the murder of a dozen people and the near collapse of the international financial system? Since then I had been kidnapped, thrown into the trunk of a car and taken to Mexico. I had pissed my pants, witnessed three execution-style murders, and received a rejuvenating massage complete with a happy ending. Later I had autographed Antonio Salcido's copy of *The Ganja Times* and basked in the adulation of a crowd of avid "Clabe Taylor fans" at a party held in my honor at the headquarters of the Sinaloa drug cartel. It was a lot to process. Plus, I was having trouble keeping the *menudo* down.

So much had happened over the past several weeks that I tried to put it all down on paper in the form of flow chart when I returned to my bedroom. I thought a graphic representation of the uncanny events might help me understand what had happened and where my life was headed. I was wrong. It just made me realize that I had a twisted sex life and that I needed to go to alcohol and drug rehab as soon as possible. It was a revelation. I had no idea I was such a mess.

I wadded up the flow chart and threw it in the trash can in my bedroom. Now what? What does Antonio want from me? I sat on the side of the bed and paged through a copy of the Bible in Spanish. I wondered if Antonio had found Jesus somewhere along the line and if so, how he reconciled his nonstop killing with Christianity? Of course, the Catholic Church hadn't had a problem with that, so why would he? He was a god in this part of the country anyway. Next time we drank together I would have to remember to ask him. I heard a knock on the door and Salcido's voice.

"Clabe, can I come in?" he asked.

I recognize a rhetorical question when I hear one. I toyed with the idea of telling him to bugger off, but then relented.

"*Adelante,* Antonio!" I called out, breathing deeply to settle my stomach.

I studied Salcido as he walked into my room. He affected a U.S. southern preppy look, complete with immaculately coiffured salt and pepper hair and a baby blue sweater draped over a pink Polo shirt. I wanted to remind him that it was a muggy 95° F. outside but held my tongue. It was obviously part of the persona he wanted to project.

"Clabe, let's talk turkey," he said. "Isn't that what you Americans say?"

"Well, not really," I answered. "At least not since Dwight Eisenhower was president. But what's on your mind?"

"Business, as always," Antonio answered. "I'm a businessman, Clabe. I make money and create jobs. My product makes people happy."

"Well, why don't you invent a drug that cures hangovers? That'd really make some people happy. Might even get you elected president of Mexico," I joked.

Antonio sat down with me on the bed and threw his arm around my shoulders. It made me feel uncomfortable, but I didn't want to abuse the man's hospitality by pulling away.

"Why would I want the hassle of political office?" he asked seriously. "They dance to my fiddle anyway. You know what they call me, don't you?"

"What?" I asked.

"They call me 'El Protegido', The Protected One," said Antonio in a conspiratorial whisper. "You know why?"

"Yeah, I know," I replied. I had heard the rumors of how the Mexican government protected Salcido himself while they went after his competitors and just busted the occasional low-ranking Sinaloa Cartel lieutenant for show.

"I drink tequila with the president," Antonio said. "Not to mention what I do with his wife when he's out of town. She once gave me a hand job under the table at a dinner for the Chinese ambassador. Actually, though, I prefer the attorney general's wife, but he keeps a close eye on her. He's an insecure, jealous bastard."

"Okay, I get the picture," I said. "Got any video of that, by the way?"

"Clabe, you've got a weird sense of humor, but don't piss me off,"

I realized I needed to learn some boundaries with the unpredictable head of the Sinaloa Cartel. I would have to be more careful with my off-the-cuff comments to avoid being on the receiving end of one of his legendary temper tantrums.

"Don't get me wrong, Clabe. I like you and respect your business savvy and strategic vision. That's what I want to talk about," he said.

"My business savvy?" I asked. "Strategic vision?" Uh-oh, I felt a job offer coming, one that I probably couldn't refuse, or, at least, one that wouldn't be healthy to refuse.

"Clabe, I want you to come work for me. I need an educated man, one that understands both business and politics and isn't afraid to think outside the corporate box. I think you're that man."

Oh, Christ, I thought. If I let Salcido hire me, I'd never get out of Mexico alive, and it would give the U.S. authorities a real reason to come after me with a cruise missile or a drone. I could be severely limiting my life expectancy and would become an international pariah in the meantime.

"How does 'Vice-President for Strategic Planning' sound?" he asked. "You'll report directly to me and have whatever staff and logistical support you need."

I had a feeling the script called for me to clap my hands and be overjoyed at this opportunity, but I hesitated. Listen, I'm no feckless mama's boy, and I've done things in my life I'm not proud of. In fact, sometimes when I think of the asinine capers I've pulled off in the past, it's downright embarrassing. But I knew I should draw the line at Salcido's offer and just say no to drugs. How in the world, though, do you turn down an offer from a man who decapitates and tortures his competition? I decided to stall and pretend to negotiate.

"What does this job pay, Antonio?" I asked.

"How much do you need?" he met my question with one of his own.

"What would you say to $10 million a year plus health insurance and a 401K plan?" I just spit out the first figure that came to mind. I knew he'd turn it down and make a counteroffer.

"Done," he said. "When can you start?" Damn! No wonder so many DEA and U.S. Customs officials are on the take, I thought.

That's how I became a senior vice-president of the Sinaloa Cartel, but I was guessing it wasn't a career-enhancing move and wouldn't do much to spice up my resume. Of course, at my age a resume really didn't mean much, so what the heck. Besides, I could always claim that I had been a consultant for the pharmaceutical industry.

Antonio set me up with an office, complete with a secretary, computer and internet, and he let me hire Goose as my corporate legal advisor. We had a luxury Toyota Land Cruiser and access to Antonio's private jet. He immediately tasked me with mapping out a strategy to deal with the Russian alliance and how to best utilize the attack submarine. I knew I had to talk him out of that one, but it was going to be tricky. The image of a scowling Mako Sloane was never far from my mind either. He might not understand my precipitous promotion to the top levels of the cartel hierarchy. Of course, at this point I didn't know whether I'd ever see him again.

Two days later I had my first business meeting with Antonio. He had insisted that I give a Power Point presentation. In fact, he even suggested the title: "Short & Long-term Prospects for a Strategic Alliance with Russia". That morning the maid hung a pin-striped business suit and baby blue dress shirt in the closet of my guest bedroom and placed a pair of wingtip tassle loafers on the floor in front of my bed. I dressed slowly and occasionally leafed through my Power Point slides, reviewing a point I wanted to emphasize. I wondered if Salcido was goofing on me with his impersonation of a Fortune 500 CEO. How far would he go with this comic opera? I got my answer a few minutes later when I entered a carpeted conference room with a long mahogany table in the middle, a laptop computer on one end and a coffeemaker with saucers and cups on the other end.

Pretty traditional, I thought, as a buxom beauty in a tight, low-cut red dress poured coffee into a half dozen Talavera cups. Her wanton show of cleavage would not be well-received by the P.C. and gender-equality storm troopers in the United States, but everything else was very Fortune 500. Well, almost.

Salcido departed slightly from the corporate script when he walked by his secretary in the red dress and slapped her soundly on a pair of buttocks that was straining to burst free from the confining red fabric. She shook her boobs saucily at Antonio, and I realized there might be a few extra perks in the arrangement that did not figure into my contract. I could see I probably wouldn't have to attend any sexual harassment classes and doubted sensitivity training would be high on Antonio's list either. Maybe this was my kind of company after all.

I looked around at the other cartel executives present for my briefing and didn't recognize anyone from the night before. Except for some heavy five o'clock shadow and a few shoulder holsters under expensive Italian silk sport coats, there was little to distinguish the gathering from any other corporate meeting I had ever attended. I took a deep breath and clicked the laptop's mouse to bring up the first slide. That was when all hell broke loose.

Chapter 31

It was a good thing the operator at the drone facility outside of Las Vegas, Nevada sneezed when he did. Otherwise, the Romeo Hellfire II missile launched from the Predator drone cruising off the Mexican coast would have obliterated the Sinaloa Cartel's corporate presentation room....with me in it. At least that's what Mako told me a few days later after we returned to Texas in an unmarked Blackhawk helicopter. Some things just aren't meant to be, I guess, and my career as a senior V.P. for Antonio Salcido and the Sinaloa Cartel was short-lived. It was a shame, too. Think what I could have done for their sales forecasting ability and their downstream supply chain performance.

When Mako Sloane came bursting into what was left of the Sinaloa Cartel conference room with a team of his heavily armed commandos, the plaster was still falling in chunks from the exposed beams overhead. Smoke and dust filled the air, and the few survivors were coughing and cursing as they tried to crawl out from under the piles of rubble.

"Clabe!" I heard a familiar voice shout.

"Over here," I yelled, choking on the smoke and crawling on my hands and knees across broken pieces of stone and glass towards the voice. I dragged my body past a headless torso, and before I turned my head away from the gore, I saw a baby blue sweater and a flash of pink. I looked at what was left of Antonio Salcido and marveled at the irony of poetic justice. What's good for the goose is good for the gander, I guess. I couldn't have written a better ending for the mad drug lord myself.

A few desultory shots rang out, but I didn't know who was shooting or why. My ears rang, and I was dizzy and disoriented.

"Can you walk?" someone asked.

"I can try," I responded.

I felt hands grab me under my armpits and my feet began to make occasional contact with the earth as my senses gradually recovered from the blast.

"Where's Mako?" I asked.

"He went to get your friend," I heard someone reply.

"Goose?" I asked.

"Yeah, the big hairy Mexican."

I limped out of the pile of rubble that used to be Antonio's house. By this time I was feeling better and starting to walk on my own. I saw the rest of Mako's team strategically positioned around the house. There was more shooting, but further away now. I heard sirens in the distance and wondered if the police were coming to the aid of their late benefactor. The location of Antonio Salcido's headquarters was no secret to the local police although the Mexican authorities always shrugged their shoulders and pleaded ignorance when pressed on the issue by their American counterparts.

A scant five minutes later we all were airborne and flying north in a hurry. I noticed the stub wings and external fuel tanks on the helicopter and knew we wouldn't have to stop to refuel. Mako knew his stuff alright. Just like I described him in my books. He made James Bond look like a prepubescent Cub Scout.

Goose was sitting across the aisle from me, his hair and face covered with dirt and grime from the explosion. He looked dazed, and for once I knew his confusion wasn't cannabis or alcohol-induced. I glanced towards the pilot's cabin and saw a familiar silhouette and recognized the pony-tail and tie-dye headband.

What the hell? Bronc's alive? I thought. I started to ask the question but saw that everybody was looking out of the helicopter windows at the remains of Salcido's house. The entire structure had been flattened except one room where half the roof and several uprights were still standing; the conference room.

"You lead a charmed life," said Mako pointing towards the rubble below.

Mako had an odd perspective on human existence, I thought. The last couple of months hadn't exactly been excerpted from a Lassie script or a Walt Disney movie. Charmed isn't quite the adjective that came to mind when talking about my life. Wherever I went I seemed to be a target for somebody.

"You were part of this?" I asked Mako, who had come to sit beside me on the bench that ran the length of the chopper. "Cut it a little close, didn't you? You almost killed me!"

"Relax, Clabe. We had nothing to do with the explosion. It was as much a surprise to us as it was to you," Mako answered. "Drone strike, by the looks of it. The shock wave almost brought down the chopper. If we had arrived a minute earlier, we'd have been collateral damage."

"He's not dead?" I asked pointing towards the pilot's cabin.

"Who, Bronc? What are you talking about?" Mako asked.

"Salcido told me his men killed Bronc," I said. "For revenge."

"Oh that," said Mako, brushing off Bronc's close call with the Angel of Death as if it were barely worthy of mention. "They missed. Cartel shooters are notoriously bad marksmen. They like to spray bullets around with automatic weapons without aiming. What are you doing wearing a suit in this heat, by the way?"

"I was giving a Power Point presentation," I started to explain.

Mako looked at me as if I was crazy, and I realized my dithering wasn't making any sense.

"It was part of my new job," I said, hoping that would clarify everything.

"Clabe, are you alright?" asked Mako. He rummaged through the ice in a cooler beside him and handed me a Dos Equis. "Sounds like you need one of these for the trip home."

I took the bottle of beer gratefully and saw Mako reach across the aisle and hand one to Goose as well.

"No, really," I insisted. "Salcido hired me. I was senior vice president for strategic planning. Had a 401K plan too."

"Strategic planning? Well, you did a piss-poor job, didn't you? Why didn't you see this drone attack coming?" asked Mako. He was laughing so hard he choked on the beer.

"And you did?" I asked.

"No, definitely not." said Mako. "Doesn't make any sense to me. Mexico's not exactly Pakistan, and Antonio Salcido is not Osama Bin Laden. Neither are you. A lot of risk for very little payoff, I'd say. There's going to be an international firestorm over this one, mark my words."

I listened to Mako with my jaw agape, amazed to find myself at the epicenter of a major U.S. foreign policy debacle. The narrowness of my escape was just sinking in, and I began to tremble in the realization of how close I had come to becoming a smudge of fried ectoplasm far from home at the back of Mexico's beyond.

"Using a drone to kill Antonio Salcido is a monumental foreign policy fuckup if you ask me. Trying to kill an American writer they don't like is going to be even harder to justify. They obviously weren't counting on anybody surviving."

"You mean you think they were trying to kill me?" I asked.

"I don't know yet, but I'm sure they knew you were there. Not that they'll admit it, of course. Think about it. Not knowing you were there is a great alibi. I can just hear it now. 'The death of author Clabe Taylor was unintended collateral damage.' But wait a minute, they'll say! 'What was Mr. Taylor doing at the headquarters of the Sinaloa Cartel?' At some point it'll all boil down to 'national security' and 'trust us' and then everybody'll have to shut up and march over the cliff like a bunch of fucking lemmings."

I saw Mako's point immediately, but there was nothing to do but wait for the fallout. It didn't take long. Less than twenty-four hours after our return to Texas, the Mexican press began to trumpet the news of the drone strike and the gross violation of its national sovereignty. An hour later the starved-for-scandal American media jackals were on to the story like flies on excrement. They were slabbering in anticipation of the feeding frenzy as they lined up their talking heads for an orgy of political analysis. The news that the United States had used an armed drone to assassinate Mexico's top cartel capo on Mexican soil was grabbing headlines all over the world, but the real bombshell was still to come.

"Look, that's the Mexican attorney general!" I exclaimed as we watched a live feed from a Mexico City television station on CNN. "I saw him at Salcido's party. Antonio was banging his wife on the sly, you know. Claimed she was a world-class bounce."

"Enlightening," commented Mako. "I'll have to remember that."

Mako motioned me to keep quiet, and I didn't argue with him. CNN patched in a simultaneous interpreter, who announced that the body of a Russian diplomat had been identified at the site of the American drone strike. The name didn't mean anything to me, but as I turned to Mako with the question on my lips, he already had his encrypted cell phone in his hand punching in a number.

"SVR[37] Rezident[38] in Mexico City," he whispered. "Looks like Washington was going for the trifecta. Salcido, you, and the Russian. No wonder they pulled the trigger."

The Russian must have been in Salcido's conference room for my Power Point presentation, I realized. He would have had almost a parental interest in what I was going to say. Was this really happening, or was this something from one of my serial novel episodes?

"It's over," said Mako into the phone. "They got the Russian too." He hung up the phone and sat back with a satisfied sigh.

"No, it's not over," I said feeling anger bubbling up from deep in my gut. I was feeling self-righteous. It must

---

[37] SVR – Sluzhba Vneshney Razvedki (Russian Foreign Intelligence Service)
[38] Rezident – equivalent to CIA Chief of Station (COS)

have been the Dos Equis. I'm usually not that sanctimonious.

"What about a high-ranking U.S. official collaborating with the cartel and the Russians? What about the U.S. government torturing me and then trying to kill me? No way it's over. I want to tell the world all about this. Haven't you ever heard of human rights? How about Amnesty International or the American Civil Liberties Union?"

"Clabe, don't be an ass," said Mako. He was a shrewd judge of character.

"First of all, there's probably no U.S. spy involved," he continued. "That was just your imagination running wild. You wrote a novel, remember? You don't have the gift of future sight or precognition. There's no such thing. You made a couple of lucky guesses, and then Salcido implemented a few of your crazy ideas."

"And secondly?" I asked.

"Secondly, don't try to fight the U.S. government, or you'll end up at the Florence Super Max wearing see-through plastic shoes and doing consecutive life sentences. You can't win. Take the royalties from your book and disappear with one of your groupies to a deserted beach in Central America. When she starts to bore you, trade her in for a local surf bunny. That's my advice to you."

"Mako, I appreciate you saving my life again, but you are one cynical sonofabitch. That may be how it works in your slimy cloak and dagger world, but I like to think that the truth matters for something in America," I said. "Besides, I'm still not sure you're real."

I didn't know what had come over me, but for the moment I was filled with outrage over the government's cavalier treatment of Goose and me. Deep down inside I knew I was crying crocodile tears, and that I had no real emotion left. The world of international intrigue had sucked me dry. There was one question, though, that still lingered in my mind, unanswered.

"No such thing as future sight, you say? No precognition?" I asked. "Then how'd I know all about you and Armando and James Brazzle?"

"Oh that," Mako answered. "Well, I haven't quite figured that one out yet."

Chapter 32

So where did this all leave me? That's what I wanted to know. The U.S. government had pursued me halfway across the country, captured and tortured me, and then blatantly tried to kill me in Mexico after my abduction at the hands of the Sinaloa Cartel. And now Mako expected me to sit on my ass in Laredo and wait till he figured out what to do next? Well, I was tired of being on the receiving end of politically correct sadism and high-tech assassination attempts. One thing I knew for certain; I sure didn't want to give them a second chance. Maybe next time the drone operator wouldn't sneeze. I knew what I had to do.

No, it's not what you think. It wasn't the image of Gretel on her knees in front of me or the promise of more kinky partisan politics that made me call Joel. Well, maybe that was part of it, but it wasn't the deciding factor. I knew that publicity, and lots of it, was the only chance I had to force the feds to leave me alone, and Joel was synonymous with publicity. I wanted my life back. All of it; complete with a bottle of Shiner Blonde at breakfast and long walks with Rigo, who, by the way, had survived my Mexican ordeal in fine style.

As soon as Mako left me alone for a minute, I dialed Joel's number.

"Joel, it's me," I whispered. I was hoping that prospects for cashing in on my infamy would outweigh his leeriness at talking to me on the phone.

"Clabe, you're alive? Be careful. You know they're collecting metadata on all our calls. I read it in the news."

"Metadata?" I responded. "That's the least of your worries. They probably concealed micro transceivers in those suppositories you stick up your ass every morning. They could be listening to every word you say."

"You really think so?"

"Jesus, Joel! Listen, just call my 'Friend' and set up a meeting in San Antonio. Use a different phone," I suggested and hung up. I hoped he would understand the not-so-subtle reference to Fox & Friends, but I needn't have worried. Joel was as sharp as they come when the smell of money was in the air. He called back within thirty minutes.

"Three hours," he said cryptically and gave me the name of a hotel on the River Walk.

It was like old times, and I felt a stirring in my loins that made me optimistic about the future of nuclear disarmament, democracy in the Middle East, and single sex marriage. Now I just had to figure out how to get to

San Antonio. I waited until Mako went out to the barn to saddle his buckskin gelding for his daily horseback ride into the brush country. He was usually gone for at least two hours, plenty of time for me to make it halfway to San Antonio without detection unless they came after me in the damn helicopter. When I saw Mako trot his gelding down the path towards the windmill, I scooped his keys and Browning 9 mm off the dining room table, left a note promising to return the pickup truck and handgun, and scampered out the door like a school kid stealing a dollar from his mother's purse.

On the drive up I-35 to San Antonio I thought about what had happened since my last tryst with Gretel outside Baton Rouge. Had it really been that long ago? I knew I was taking a risk meeting Gretel. By this time, the FBI could have interviewed her numerous times, and who knows whether she had caved under the pressure or not. I hoped she hadn't been as craven as Carmen. Ambitious news anchors like Gretel could be tough as nails, though, and she could defy the federal government if she wanted. Besides, she obviously had a thing for me and was inordinately horny for a middle-aged white woman. She wouldn't rat me out, would she?

The hotel was an elegant Old World palazzo that made me forget that I could probably order a take-out

Whopper and some fries right around the corner in a fast food restaurant with plastic tables and chairs. A Mexican cameraman holding a reflective umbrella opened the door to the hotel room when I knocked, and I subconsciously cringed, thinking of the interview in Dallas and of Rigo latching on to the studio technician's Achilles tendon. My eyes took in the suite, and I saw Gretel sitting on the sofa receiving the final ministrations of two makeup artists, who hovered and fussed over her as if she were a priceless sculpture they were restoring. When she caught sight of me, she smiled and her upper lip began to twitch lustfully, or so I imagined. My first impulse was to snatch her into my arms and confess that I was a liberal pro-choice Democrat. I'll say anything for a B.J. But then my pragmatic side took over, and a voice inside urged me to play it cool. Debonair is definitely not my style; I have to work at it. However, I was able to put all thoughts of sex on the back burner and concentrate on the task at hand. Gretel was going to help me send a shock wave throughout America.

"Clabe, it's good to see you again," Gretel began the interview.

I nodded my head in acknowledgment and took a deep breath, trying to calm my nerves.

"Over the past few days there have been some earthshattering revelations coming out of Mexico about alleged conspiracies involving the Sinaloa drug cartel, the Russian Foreign Intelligence Service, and our own government. You know, when I read the reports of our foreign correspondents lately, I feel like I'm reading the latest installment of your serial novel. I have a feeling that you can enlighten us and perhaps fill in some of the gaps on what's going on down there."

I did more than that. I told her everything; the enhanced interrogation techniques at the hands of the CIA, the dramatic rescue by the heretofore fictitious characters from my novels, my abduction by Mexican drug traffickers, the drone strike, and my second rescue and flight back to Texas. I decided to omit my recruitment as a senior vice president for the Sinaloa Cartel and my Power Point presentation. That might be considered a conflict of interest, and I saw no reason to muddy the waters with superfluous details. Besides, you never know who might be listening to Fox News.

"That's quite a story, Clabe," said Gretel. I immediately knew something was wrong. Where were her lascivious leer and the rush to boot her studio crew out of the room so we could begin thrashing out our political differences?

"You don't expect me to broadcast this for a national audience, do you?" she asked signaling to her cameraman that the interview was over.

"Gretel, what are you talking about?" I asked. "This is the biggest U.S. government conspiracy and attempted cover up since Watergate. Maybe bigger. There's probably a high-ranking administration official working with the Mexican drug traffickers and the Russians!"

Gretel just shook her head and motioned for her crew to begin packing up. I stood up and watched them. I couldn't believe my eyes.

"You can't be serious," I said.

"Oh, you better believe I'm serious," she replied. "I'm a professional journalist, and I can't take the word of some yahoo off the street, who comes into my studio with alcohol on his breath, making the wildest allegations I've ever heard in my entire career with no proof whatsoever to back it up."

"Yahoo off the street?" I asked, feeling my face flush with anger. I wasn't going to challenge the "alcohol on his breath" statement. Admittedly, I'd thrown back an entire six-pack of Shiner Bock on the drive up I-35.

"Have you forgotten Macon, Mobile, and Baton Rouge? All those cities where you interviewed me, Gretel?" I asked. "What about us?"

Gretel just shook her head. Christ! I felt used. I hate it when women objectify men and just use us for their own sexual gratification. I thought there was something real between us. I was so flabbergasted my vocal chords failed me, and the burgeoning signs of renewal in my much neglected package disappeared in a shriveled recollection of happier days.

"So you say you were tortured by the CIA and forced to listen to 'We've Only Just Begun' by the Carpenters? That happens to be my favorite song, you insensitive bastard!" Gretel said indignantly. "Let's see. What else was there? Oh yeah, you can't tell me where this all happened, and you claim you were rescued by a character from your novels named Mako Sloane and flown to a safehouse near Laredo in a Texas National Guard helicopter?" She shook her head in ridicule.

"Oh brother," she said. "Do you realize how that sounds?"

"Don't forget that after all that, the cartel kidnapped me and took me to Mexico. I was almost killed in the drone attack that everyone's talking about," I added.

"Dusty, I'm sorry. I shouldn't have doubted you," she said and looked over my shoulder.

The name rang a bell, and I turned around to see my former torture chamber inquisitor standing behind me smirking. Next to him was the pudgy CIA lawyer, who had been so concerned about the legalities of Enhanced Interrogation. The two looked smug and vindicated. Dusty took out a pair of handcuffs and walked towards me. The lawyer began to read me my Miranda rights, but his words struck me as nothing more than gibbering lunacy.

I looked at Gretel again. It was difficult to imagine this was the same wanton trollop that I galloped time and time again in hotel rooms across the country on the way back to Texas. She had turned into an iceberg of a government snitch.

"You insult my intelligence, Clabe," she shot one last barb at me.

"Well, you don't insult OURS!" shouted a vaguely familiar voice. The door to the hotel room burst open, and I saw the recognizable bearded phiz of the famous CNN news anchor followed by a half dozen other media types. One of them was the deliciously cute blonde, whom I had seen on one of the CNN morning news shows.

"We heard it all, and we want to tell the world!" announced the bearded CNN anchor. "We want an exclusive!" He was in a state of near hysteria.

"Wait, this man is in federal custody!" shouted Dusty.

"Who are you? Let me see some I.D.," shouted the bearded anchor.

Dusty took out a badge that looked like it came out of a box of Lucky Charms. The CIA's Office of Technical Services had gone downhill since my days as a spook. That was the worst forgery I'd ever seen.

"Dusty?" read the famous new anchor. "You're CIA?"

"Don't say my name out loud, dammit! I'm under cover!"

"Well, not anymore!" said the CNN news anchor. "The American people have a right to know. Make sure you get some film of this spook." He gestured to his camera crew, who were pushing their way into the now crowded hotel room and setting up their equipment.

"Hey, this is MY interview," yelled Gretel as she stepped defiantly forward.

"It's ours now you uptight paleolithic bitch," screamed the blonde and jumped on Gretel's back and started pulling her hair.

"We'll see about that, you subversive cunt!" shouted Gretel, and the two rolled on the floor kicking, scratching, pulling hair, and surprising me with some respectable Brazilian ju-jitsu moves.

"Wait, don't leave yet," said the CNN news anchor to Dusty and the CIA lawyer who were beating a hasty retreat and holding their hands over their faces to prevent the cameramen from recording their images for the evening news. "I want to interview you!"

"No interviews!" said the lawyer emphatically.

"We're monitoring your phone records, you know," added Dusty as he turned his back to the beard. "You better watch your step!"

"Shut up, Dusty," said the lawyer.

"Will you stop using my name!" said an exasperated Dusty as the two jogged down the hallway towards the bank of elevators with their suit coats now draped over their heads.

The bearded news anchor turned to me and nodded toward the retreating CIA officers. "A free press is the key to democracy, don't you think?" he asked rhetorically.

"And what do you call that?" I asked pointing to the two women wrestling on the floor, still locked in a roiling tangle of legs, arms, and torn clothing. I noticed the "subversive" journalist from CNN was freebuffing, a sight for sore eyes.

"Those are two professional journalists fighting for a story. Inspiring, in my opinion," he responded, nodding his head in the direction of his colleague whose tight skirt was now hiked up around her hips.

The blonde got up off the floor where Gretel still lay gasping for breath like a landed largemouth bass. Flushed with victory and straightening her hair, the blonde approached me, stood on her tiptoes, and brought her face close to mine.

"Let's get started," she said provocatively.

I wasn't sure what she had in mind, but my alcohol-inspired imagination began to run wild. I wondered what kind of sexual preferences liberal news anchors had. Would I have to confess to being a Republican?

"GO, GO, GO!!!!!" Suddenly I heard yelling and shouting and the sound of heavy footsteps. Before I had a chance to turn around and see who the latest additions to the party were, someone grabbed me roughly from behind and yanked a scratchy, opaque hood over my head. Everything went pitch black, and I was half-carried, half-dragged out of the room and down the corridor.

"Who was that? Did you get those guys on film?" I heard the CNN news anchor shout as the chaotic yammer from the hotel room faded, and my new captors hustled me down the emergency stairwell.

Chapter 33

I've been kidnapped by the best in the business. Maybe I should have been flattered by all the attention, but at the end of the day enough is enough, you'd have to agree. Why couldn't people just leave me alone? Once again it was the same old hackneyed scenario; abducted in broad daylight, tossed into the trunk of a get-away car, and bounced around for hours on end in a wild, panic-stricken ride to parts unknown. My bruises from the last kidnapping hadn't even healed yet, and here we were, at it again. I cursed fate and bad timing and the Star Spangled Banner, and wondered why Mako had let me escape. Didn't he care anymore?

I had been through the abduction scenario often enough to realize that there was something different about these guys. After a few hours the vehicle stopped, and I heard voices in southern-accented English. That was my first clue. The second unexpected development came when my captors opened the trunk and ripped off my hood. I fully expected the car to be standing in the middle of the desert or some other desolate location where I could be conveniently dispatched with a bullet in the back of the head or buried alive for the ants to devour. Instead, we were parked in an interstate rest area, and my abductors were wearing black balaclava masks, oblivious to the wide-eyed stares they were attracting from the families waddling back and forth from the rest rooms and vending machines.

They led me around the back of the car and pushed me roughly into the middle of the back seat. There were four of them. Two sat on either side of me, brandishing billy clubs, and the other two were in the front seat. One of them noticed me staring at his club.

"We're not authorized to carry firearms," he said in explanation, almost apologetically. "But these clubs can really hurt. Don't try anything."

"Mr. Taylor," said one of my masked adversaries, and he turned his head towards me from the front seat of the car. Bemused travelers continued to stare at us as they walked past, slurping soft drinks and eating candy bars on the way back to their Airstreams and Pierce Arrows.

"Yes?" I replied.

"We're special agents from the South Carolina Department of Natural Resources, and you're under arrest!" he said.

"You're special agents from WHERE? Are we on Candid Camera or something?" I asked. I was too flabbergasted for a more serious response.

"I'd heard you were a smart ass," the obvious leader of the group said and nodded his head knowingly. "You didn't think you were going to get away with it, did you?"

"Get away with what?" I asked. I was genuinely perplexed and had no idea what these clowns were talking about.

"Conspiracy to dynamite fish in Bohicket Creek, that's what!" he replied. "You sick sonofabitch. We know what you and that damn Mexican were planning."

I stared blankly at the special agent.

"You're facing hard time in the Charleston County Jail," he said. "Up to seven days and a $500 fine, motherfucker."

"Oh no! Not seven days in jail!" I exclaimed, trying not to smile. Over the past couple of months I had been through it all. The CIA and the Sinaloa Cartel had tortured, kidnapped, and tried to assassinate me, and now the state of South Carolina sent a bunch of undercover game wardens halfway across the country to fine me $500? Wait till I tell Mako. He probably needed a good laugh by now.

"Wait," I said. "You've got to extradite me first. I'm a resident of Texas."

"That's where you're wrong, bitch," replied the special agent to my right and he raised his billy club threateningly. "That's why we're here. We're from the Black Ops Section, and we're authorized to do whatever it takes to execute the mission and bring dangerous poachers to justice. We don't give two hoots about legal niceties."

"Two hoots, uh?" I repeated.

Something was poking me uncomfortably in the back, and I remembered I had grabbed Mako's Browning 9 mm on the way out of the house. I glanced again at the agents and their billy clubs and made my decision. I drew the handgun from the back of my jeans and thrust it in the arm pit of the agent to my left.

"Open the door, dickhead," I said with all the badass authority I could muster, still trying to suppress my laughter.

The agent squealed.

"Don't shoot," he said and began to snivel softly. "I've got a wife and kids...and our bowling league tournament is next week."

"Hey, our intelligence reports didn't say anything about him being armed," complained another agent.

"The South Carolina Department of Natural Resources has an intelligence service?" I asked.

"Sure, doesn't everyone?" he replied. "I heard even Dunkin' Doughnuts is getting into the Homeland Security business. Lots of government contracts. You don't even have to be qualified."

"Sounds like a great opportunity," I replied. "Now move it!"

I forced them all out of the car at gunpoint and left them standing on the sidewalk of the rest area looking forlorn in their black balaclavas and holding their billy clubs at their sides. The lead agent took off his balaclava, and I swear he had tears in his eyes. He was going to have a hard time explaining this flap to the department director. I felt guilty. They were well-meaning, upstanding citizens, just trying to do their job and earn a state pension, but I couldn't let them take me back to Charleston.

I blew out of the rest area at high speed, made a U-turn at the first exit, and headed back towards San Antonio. I didn't really have a plan. I was hoping I would evolve into something by the time I exchanged my stolen car for Mako's truck, which I hoped was still parked near the River Walk hotel. That's when it occurred to me that I had screwed up. I forgot to take cell phones away from those South Carolina buffoons! They might have already called the police to report the stolen vehicle. Maybe they were even contacting the FBI to report that Clabe Taylor had escaped their custody and was on the loose. Of course, in that case the special agents from the South Carolina Department of Natural Resources would have to come clean and admit they were mucking around, playing commando about 1,000 miles west of their jurisdiction. That might land them in even more hot water, so I wasn't sure what they'd do.

But as I approached Seguin an hour later heading west on I-10, I saw a roadblock ahead and all traffic appeared to be exiting. Police cars and a fire engine were blocking all westbound lanes, and there were at least a dozen uniformed men standing in a line across the interstate behind their cars. There were probably other state police and highway patrol officers checking the cars as they exited. All in all, the odds against me were mounting rapidly.

So, the game wardens had decided to call in the cavalry after all. I felt a tightening in my throat, and my heart began to pound. A wave of nausea doubled me over and my bowels cramped. This was all so unfair. I was innocent, a victim of circumstance and why? Just because I had made a couple of lucky guesses about the future and written a novel that the Sinaloa Cartel used as an instruction manual. Jesus, nobody in the federal government these days has a sense of humor.

I stomped on the accelerator, and the late model sedan leaped ahead like a 3-year old thoroughbred pounding down the dirt track on the home stretch at Churchill Downs. I'm not sure what I was thinking, or how I thought my decision to run the roadblock was going to make things any easier for me. Nonetheless, a few brief seconds later I was barreling down the interstate at 85 mph towards a police roadblock, all four windows down and screaming at the top of my lungs.

"*A la chingada*," I shouted, wild-eyed and desperate. I didn't know where "*La Chingada*" was, but I should have realized from the name, that it wasn't going to be a pretty place. Spittle flew from my mouth as I shouted obscenities in Spanish. I ripped out the 9 mm from the back of my jeans, pointed the handgun out the driver's window, and jerked the trigger again and again until the magazine was empty. That might have been a tad theatrical.

The police obviously didn't appreciate my sense of melodrama, and a dozen semi-automatic weapons and handguns opened fire from the roadblock in reply. My windshield disintegrated as I fired the last round from my 9 mm. Tiny shards of glass sprayed throughout the inside of the sedan in a prickly mist, and warm, sticky fluid poured down from my forehead in rivulets, clouding my vision. I felt a heavy blow to my right shoulder, and realized I was hit. I heard the *"ka-boom"* of the front tires exploding from the impact of bullets. The car swerved dangerously and careened sideways into the line of vehicles. It ricocheted off the back bumper of the fire engine, smashed into the front fender of a police cruiser, and hurtled over the roadblock, twisting and turning in the air. The car landed with the loud crunch of bending steel and shattering glass and began to roll. My head smashed against the steering wheel, and everything went black....again.

Chapter 34

I don't know how long I was unconscious. When I awoke, I had but a jumbled memory of the headlong dash down the interstate towards the police roadblock. I remember screaming in bowel-loosening terror and firing the Browning 9 mm in the general direction of the police. The thought of how it all must have looked on the local news that night made me cringe. The networks love police chase videos, and this inane caper must have been one for the ages. I hoped I looked better on camera than one of those meth-crazed, toothless rednecks running from the law and threatening to kill himself after murdering a girlfriend or mother-in-law.

Much of the incident was still hazy to me, but it was coming back. I remembered the police returning fire and my car hurtling through the air before everything went black. It had been insane and heroic, or so I imagined. My own rash assault on common sense reminded me of a solo version of the Charge of the Light Brigade at Balaclava. Maybe not worthy of an epic poem, but someone might dedicate an obscene limerick or two to the fiasco. I might even write one myself.

I felt tightness in my chest when I breathed, perhaps from a broken rib or two, and my head throbbed.

There was stiffness and a dull ache in my shoulder, and I remembered I had been shot when the police opened fire. I heard soft, soothing music, and everything around me seemed shrouded in white, fleecy, cumulus clouds. For a second I wondered if I had died and gone to my just rewards. If there was a heaven, I was sure that's where I'd be. Hell was for prison hacks, pedophiles, and IRS agents. In contrast, my own intentions had been pure, and I didn't mean to hurt anyone. Admittedly, somewhere along the line things had taken a turn towards the dark side, but I merely had been swept along by the evil current. My conscience was clear. Well, except for taking that job as senior vice president for the Sinaloa Cartel, but St. Peter wouldn't quibble over details, would he?

"Mr. Taylor, can you hear me?" I heard a male voice inquire.

I opened my eyes and saw a middle-aged man with a kindly face dressed in a white gown with a stethoscope around his neck. He was smiling and holding a small syringe.

"I'm Doctor O'Reilly," he said. "Welcome back. You had us worried for a while." He leaned over the bed, adjusted my arm, and gave me an injection directly into the vein. I jumped involuntarily at the pin prick but then felt a cottony relaxation slowly envelope me.

"Is that your real name?" I asked dreamily.

The doctor just winked in response.

"Where am I?" I asked. "And how long have I been here?"

Doctor O'Reilly's smile was benevolent, but on the mawkish and saccharine side, like an insincere evangelical minister or a Catholic priest trying to distract attention from his impure thoughts and hairy palms.

"You're in a hospital," he answered. "You've been in and out of consciousness for two weeks."

"What hospital?" I asked.

"I'm really not at liberty to say," answered the kindly doctor.

I had a gut-wrenching feeling of déjà vu. It seemed like every time I regained consciousness, I found myself in the clutches of the CIA. The doctor might as well have spelled out the initials. He wasn't hiding anything by being coy. I knew where I was.

"You mean this is a CIA facility?" I asked, pleasantly groggy from the injection. I tried to shift my body to a more comfortable position and realized that a series of parallel leather straps across my torso secured my body to the bed and prevented any movement.

"Let's just say I do my patriotic duty, Mr. Taylor. Could we leave it at that?" he replied.

"I was just doing mine too," I said with a weak smile.

"That's not exactly what I hear," mumbled the doctor. "Do you feel well enough to receive visitors?"

I didn't, but I needed to know what was happening. I clinched my jaws together and forced myself to sound chipper.

"Sure, bring on the fucking inquisition," I said boldly. "Free Angela Davis!"

"Mr. Taylor, your sarcasm won't be appreciated here," the doctor warned. "I've yet to encounter anyone in this organization with anything that even remotely resembles a sense of humor."

"Been working here long?" I asked.

"Five years. But they had to give me a special security clearance to attend to you."

"Have you read my serial novel?" I asked.

The doctor glanced around quickly to make sure we were alone. He lowered his voice to a conspiratorial whisper.

"Yes, I have. And just between you and me, I'm a big fan," he said. "How do you do it?"

"Do what?" I asked.

The doctor rolled his eyes. "Predict the future, of course," he said.

"Oh that," I replied. "Just lucky guesses, really."

"Well, it's great stuff. All my friends love it. But do yourself a favor, will you?"

"What's that?" I asked.

"You'll cooperate with these guys if you've got any sense. They're from a joint CIA/FBI/DEA task force that was formed last year to weed out domestic home-grown terrorists. They think they've discovered a link between medical marijuana and the jihadists."

"Then I'm really screwed, aren't I?" I asked, already losing hope.

"I'm afraid so. They've already discussing administering a lethal injection. I'd hate to euthanize you, Mr. Taylor."

"Wait, I know my rights. I haven't even been tried yet!" I objected.

"Rights?" asked the doctor. "Don't be naïve. You have no rights. These guys have extraordinary wartime powers, and their very existence is above the TOP SECRET clearance level."

That sounded like the guys who had been dealing with me alright. I expected they were waiting out in the corridor, ready to come in as soon as the doctor signed off on my medical clearance.

"Is one of them named Dusty?" I asked apprehensively.

"Yes, as a matter of fact. Dangerous brute, that one. A real knuckle-dragger. Do you know him?" asked the doctor.

"Yeah, we've spoken," I said vaguely.

"Well, are you ready?" he asked.

"I guess so," I responded. "Don't I need to sign some document authorizing them to interrogate me?"

The doctor scoffed.

"Not here," he said. He loosened the leather straps across my body and cranked the wheel at the foot of my bed to elevate my torso.

"Why not?" I asked. "What so special about this place?"

"Oh yes," he said. "I guess there'd be no way you could possibly know."

"Know what?" I asked. I was starting to think the doctor was playing games with me.

"Mr. Taylor, you are in the detention camp hospital in Guantanamo, Cuba. Welcome to Gitmo."

GITMO? I had a sinking feeling in my stomach, and my jaw must have dropped. Well, that made sense, I thought. After all I HAD been unconscious for two weeks. But how would Mako ever find me here? I was a dead man and I knew it. I steeled myself for whatever was coming and tried to act nonchalant. If there's one thing the Agency respects, it's coolness on the exterior, even if you're quaking on the inside and ready to soil your hospital skivvies.

"Shall we?" asked the doctor.

I nodded my head and Dr. O'Reilly, or whatever his real name was, opened the door to the corridor.

"Mr. Taylor is ready, gentlemen," he announced.

Yeah, here they came. Familiar faces every one of them. Dusty and the cherub lawyer led the way although I wasn't sure why his legal advice would be needed here at Gitmo. They were accompanied by several security types that I recognized from the Enhanced Interrogation. I guess Dusty wasn't taking any chances even here in the detention camp. I tried to smile and act superior, at least intellectually. I knew that would drive Dusty crazy.

"Checkmate, motherfucker," said Dusty to begin the conversation. It was less than an auspicious way to renew our acquaintance.

"Good move, Dusty. I didn't know you could play chess. Congratulations, you win. Now what?" I asked.

"Now what?" he hissed. "Now you die, that's what."

"You can't kill me," I said. "I haven't even been charged with a crime, and I'm entitled to a court-appointed attorney."

"Ha, that's a good one....a court-appointed attorney. I'll have to remember to tell that one to my grandkids," said Dusty.

"You were tried and sentenced to death in absentia," interjected the lawyer.

"You can't do that!" I shouted. "I'm an American."

"We're not so sure about that. We never could locate your birth certificate, and we have a witness who claims you were born in Mexico. I heard you speak Spanish. For all we know you don't even have a green card. At any rate, you were tried as a foreign enemy combatant."

"What?" I screamed. "Where's my attorney?"

"Sorry, he's unavailable," replied Dusty.

"This is a miscarriage of justice...a farce! Do I look like a Muslim extremist? How about some profiling around here, for Christ's sake! Use some common sense. I was born in Texas and baptized in the First United Methodist Church of Luling. I played Little League Baseball and was in the Cub Scouts. Come on, my great grandfather was in the Ku Klux Klan! I'm as American as sarsaparilla!"

I tried to get out of bed, but the leather straps virtually immobilized me. I moaned from the pain in my ribs and shoulder and lay down again. Dusty laughed.

"I'd like to stay and relish the moment a little longer, but we've got other terrorists to hunt down and execute," said Dusty. "Give him the paper and a pen and let's get out of here."

The lawyer opened his briefcase and extracted a tablet of lined writing paper and a BIC pen. He left it on one of the stainless steel tray tables at the head of my bed.

"Tell him," said Dusty.

"You are scheduled to die by lethal injection tomorrow morning at 0900. You are authorized to make out your last will and testament. Otherwise your property will be forfeited and seized by the U.S. government."

"Have a good life," said Dusty snickering under his breath, and the two disappeared through the swinging doors. The drone of the central air conditioning sounded loud in the quiet room.

The doctor reappeared and solicitously asked, "Is there anything I can get you to make your last night more comfortable, Mr. Taylor? Some morphine, perhaps?"

"No, thanks, doc," I said, trying to conceal my trembling hands. "Are you going to administer the lethal injection?"

"Unfortunately, I am," he said. "And it just makes me sick to have to euthanize my favorite author."

"Don't give it a second thought, Doc. Do what you have to do," I said. A tear formed in the corner of my eye, and the doctor wiped it away with a tissue.

Chapter 35

It was comforting to know that the man who would administer my lethal injection was a "Clabe Taylor fan". I would hate for a perfect stranger to euthanize me. It would seem so impersonal. That's just me talking, though. I also wouldn't want a preacher who hadn't known me in life to deliver a eulogy over an urn of my cold ashes, and that sort of thing happens all the time.

Before Dr. O'Reilly left for the evening, he placed pen and paper within easy reach and loosened the leather straps across my body, so I would at least have the freedom to write. I wished he had left one of those syringes close by as well. Whatever it contained packed a wallop, and I sure could have used another one. I don't like being sober in the best of times, and especially not when my life is hanging in the balance.

I had no intention of composing my Last Will and Testament, of course. I had no property to speak of, except cardboard boxes full of autographed copies of my unsold novels, whose value was certainly open to debate. Rigo was the only thing I owned that I cared about, and who am I to say whether he was really mine. He would probably object to being classified as property, and I think he'd have a point. I missed him, though, and his pugnacious Blue Heeler spirit was probably what gave me strength to play my ace in the hole. Still, it was a long shot. Sort of like putting your entire 401K retirement account on one number in a game of roulette. Maybe my odds were even worse, but I had no other choice.

A sober examination of the facts, without embellishment or blind faith in a warm fuzzy denouement, was not encouraging. Here I was in a virtual strait jacket, strapped in a hospital bed in the Guantanamo detention camp, slated for lethal injection in about twelve hours. Even if I managed to break loose from my bonds, where could I go? The room was sure to be heavily guarded, and the hospital itself was within the boundaries of a secure military base. Let's say I was able by miracle to get outside and crawl undetected through the razor wire surrounding the camp? Then what? Seek refuge in Castro's Cuba? *No, gracias.* I had no desire to sully the purity of my cause by defecting. That would destroy my credibility and cast aspersions on my integrity. I would rather die in the knowledge that my martyrdom stood for something. Of course, I had no idea what that might be, but it sounded morally uplifting, and that felt good. Besides, deep down inside I knew I wasn't going to die.

You can see where my thoughts were heading. At least for me, the elephant in the room was not whether or not I had preternatural powers of precognition or extrasensory perception. I knew I did, at least to some degree. How else would I have known about Mako Sloane, Armando, James Brazzle, and the People's Intelligence and Security Service (P.I.S.S.)? Even Mako had admitted he hadn't solved that riddle. No, my quandary was more complex. The real question for me was whether or not my writing had the power to create the future. Merely predicting the future was child's play. Well, maybe not for the CIA, but for me it was elementary; like a basic trick from a magician's repertoire. Like pulling a rabbit out of a top hat or eliciting an erection from a drooping, inert organ with a blue pill. Now that was magic! I was betting the farm that I could do more; that I could shape events and command the future to do my bidding. These were my thoughts as I lay strapped in that Gitmo hospital bed. Imagine what I would have been thinking with a few hits from Goose's bong under my belt!

As my thoughts crystallized into a plan of action, I reached over for the pen and paper on the stainless steel tray table, made myself as comfortable as possible, and began to write. From a literary point of view, it wasn't my best stuff, but I wasn't writing for my readers or the critics anymore. I didn't have time to develop any seamless transitions, edit for syntax, or correct my abominable spelling and punctuation. Action was what I needed, and I wove a tale that I hoped would save Clabe Taylor's ass from the ignoble fate the feds had prepared.

I finished the chapter about an hour after midnight and signed the last page with a flourish. I carefully folded the pages and lay them on the tray table. I fell asleep with the knowledge that I had done everything I could. If I died in a couple of hours, it would not be for lack of trying. We would see how mighty the pen really was.

I woke to the sound of a nurse walking into my room with my bedpan and breakfast on the same tray, an unappetizing combination that did nothing to improve my mood. Was this a subtle message from my jailers? A metaphor of sorts? Was I nothing more than a human sack of excrement? In one end and out the other? I looked at my corn flakes and sweet roll and then at my bedpan, and decided not to give my jailors the satisfaction of using either. I squeezed my butt cheeks together and listened to my stomach growl.

Dr. O'Reilly was next to come into my room, and he was as kindly and sympathetic as he was the night before, but perhaps a trifle too enthusiastic. I think deep down inside he was looking forward to euthanizing his favorite author. That would give him something to talk about for years to come.

"Good morning, Mr. Taylor," he said. "I hope you slept well."

"Sure," I replied. "Got to be well-rested to get executed."

"Now, now…." he said. "No need to be morbid. Could I offer you an injection to go with your breakfast? It will steel your nerves for what's to come later this morning."

"Yes," I replied. "By all means. Give me some of that, and keep 'em coming."

I was actually expecting all hell to break loose at any moment. I wanted to see Mako and his team of commandos burst through the door and cut down the good Dr. O'Reilly in a hail of bullets. One fewer reader of my novels wouldn't have much effect on my royalties, I figured. I wanted to hear explosions and the *wap-wap-wap* of that beautiful Texas National Guard helicopter, and somebody singing the Aggie War Hymn as they cut the leather straps across my torso and liberated me from these enemies of The Bill of Rights. But everything was deathly still. It was eerie. An enlisted man in starched fatigues entered the room and handed Dr. O'Reilly a form to sign.

"What's that, Doc?" I asked.

"I just certified that you're healthy enough to be executed," the doctor replied, clicking his ballpoint pen and inserting it back in his shirt pocket.

"That's fucked up, Doc," I said as the doctor leaned over my bed, probed my arm for a suitable vein and injected me with a "feel-good" drug that was obviously designed to keep me calm and facilitate a smooth execution. "Why didn't they just let me die in Texas? It would have been easier for everyone."

"Mr. Taylor, every citizen is entitled to due process of law," replied the doctor. "Legally, they couldn't deprive you of that."

"But they brought me to Gitmo just so they wouldn't have to bother with due process, right?" I said. "Besides, they claim I might not even be a citizen."

"That's all above my pay grade, Mr. Taylor. The Lord works in mysterious ways," said the doctor. "Are you ready for the final procedure?"

"You mean the Final Solution?" I asked.

"Mr. Taylor, please. You're making this more difficult than necessary."

If I had thought Dr. Reilly was really going to go through with the lethal injection, I'm sure our conversation would have been different. I would have been straining at the leather straps across my body, gnashing my teeth, bawling, and begging for mercy with spittle flying everywhere and drool running down my chin. As it was, I was almost nonchalant with the doctor as he spoke to me in a soothing voice that make me feel like I was in an episode of *Mister Rogers' Neighborhood*. I fully expected to be rescued in the heroic style I described in the chapter I had written last night and wasn't taking the bland doctor seriously.

Two stalwart lads, each over six feet tall and in prime physical condition, came into the room. They transferred me from my hospital bed to a steel gurney and immobilized me again with leather straps, but I still wasn't worried. The sedative was taking effect, and, if anything, it was more potent than last night's dose. As they wheeled me towards the execution chamber, I wished someone would turn on some music. I had a sudden urge to dance, maybe do a few Texas Two Step weaves to an old George Jones song. I looked around for a nurse to grab, but saw nothing except the solemn faces of my military escorts pushing my gurney down the corridors. I began to chuckle as I thought how surprised everyone was going to be when Mako Sloane made his dramatic entry, armed to the teeth and as pitiless as Nero playing the fiddle while Rome burned. Goose was probably going to be wearing a black beret and Che Guevara t-shirt, a Latino ninja in a frenzy of blood lust. I couldn't wait to see him. I loved those guys.

The gurney came to a gentle stop, and I looked up, my head buzzing from the sedative. I saw a group of military men in uniforms and civilians in suits and ties on the other side of a long bank of glass windows. Their faces swam in a blur of reflected glare from the fluorescent lights overhead. A waiter in a tuxedo vest and black bow tie walked among the observers, serving drinks and hors d'oeuvres. I saw the men clinking glasses, and they were shaking each other hands and talking animatedly. The room was spinning slightly now, and everything looked as if I was seeing it through murky water. I shook my head to clear my vision, but the haze only seemed to thicken.

I looked to my left and saw another gurney and another prisoner securely strapped down. His head turned towards me, and he gave me a guilty smile.

"*Hola*, Clabe," he said. "*¿Qué tál?*" I was shocked to recognize Goose's voice. A few seconds later the significance of his presence beside me in the death chamber broke through the fog of sedation that continued to sweep over me in waves.

"Goose! What the hell are you doing here? Where's Mako?" I asked, desperation slipping into my voice.

"Over here, Clabe," I heard a second voice and turned to my right. Holy Crap! It was Mako tied down to yet another gurney.

"What happened?" I asked.

"They were waiting for us," he said dolefully. "We got ambushed. Looks like this is it, *amigo*."

"It's over?" I asked, my voice breaking with emotion.

"Yeah," said Mako. "I guess you can't create the future after all."

No wonder the audience on the other side of the glass was celebrating with cocktails and slaps on the back and manly embraces. They had hit the jackpot. With one stroke they had decapitated the Hydra of Lerna. The thought crossed my mind that I had been set up; that someone had snatched up my last chapter while I slept, read it, and set a trap for my rescuers. Dusty had outsmarted me. That's what hurt the most.

A clergyman approached, holding the Bible in front of him. When he reached my gurney, I smelled alcohol on his breath.

"Got any more where that came from?" I asked.

He mumbled something about eternal life and called me "his son" and then staggered over to Mako's gurney and said something equally unintelligible. He attempted to perform his version of the last rites over Goose, but a torrent of Spanish obscenities sent him scurrying away. The doctor then walked slowly into the room carrying three large syringes. I wanted to scream, but the sedative short-circuited the neural impulses traveling from my brain to my vocal chords. I glanced over at Mako, and the sonofabitch was grinning at me.

"Guess you never thought the story would end like this, did you, Clabe?" he asked.

"Clabe, my mother loves you," yelled Goose. "She told me so. That makes us almost family."

The doctor wrapped an elastic band around my upper arm and began probing for a vein.

"Doc, don't do it," I pleaded.

He slid the needle painlessly into my vein, and before he depressed the plunger with his left hand, he made the sign of the cross with his right hand in the air above my body.

"In the name of the Father, the Son, and the Holy Spirit….."

I knew what came next, and I expected the doctor to punctuate the abrupt downward movement of his thumb on the syringe plunger with the word "Amen". I braced myself for the darkness that was sure to wash over me, but it never came.

EPILOGUE

Now wait just a minute! Surely you didn't think the doctor was going to depress the plunger and euthanize Clabe Taylor, Goose, and Mako Sloane, did you? What about Clabe's gift of precognition and his power to create the future? Did you think that was all make-believe? What about the legendary Mako Sloane, who makes the immortal James Bond look like a prepubescent Cub Scout? Did you think that he would be powerless in the end to pull Clabe's chestnuts out of the fire one last time? No, it was never going to end that way. Have a little faith.

It WAS a close call. There's no denying that. But at the last second the news crews from Fox & Friends and CNN, collaborating on a story for perhaps the first time ever, burst into the death chamber and began filming the execution. The horrified doctor abruptly removed the syringe from my arm, covered his face, and scampered out of the room like a kitchen cockroach when you turn the lights on. How the news crews ever got through all the armed checkpoints was a mystery. At least that's the way it seemed if you hadn't read the final installment of my serial novel that I wrote while awaiting lethal injection.

Mako told me later he was afraid the news crews had lost their way and would be late to our rescue.

Without FOX and CNN and their cameras, he admitted, it would have been a suicide mission. That had been the plan all along, you see. It was risky, but it worked.

The first reaction of the military command was to call in the troops, but with microphones thrust in their faces and video cameras whirring, they got cold feet. They tap-danced and backpedaled and tried to assure Gretel and the bearded CNN anchor that it had all been an unfortunate misunderstanding. That day we learned WHO REALLY runs the country, as if there had been any doubt.

What I didn't know when I wrote the final chapter of the novel from my Guantanamo hospital bed was that Gretel had had a change of heart back in San Antonio. When she saw the agents from the Black OPS section of the South Carolina Department of Natural Resources drag me out of the hotel room, she realized that I might actually have been telling the truth. She was aghast at her own perfidy and lack of faith. She broadcast my interview the same day, bless her heart. Come to think of it, the interview probably aired an hour or two after my spectacular crash through the police roadblock outside Seguin, Texas.

That same evening CNN publicized its own involvement in the affair and lambasted the alleged collaboration between FOX and the CIA. You see, collaborating with the spy agency is the worst possible sin in the eyes of the media wallahs. From that moment on, both networks were stumbling over each other to hype the story and find Clabe Taylor.

To make a very complicated and long story short, the response from the public to Gretel's interview and the shocking revelations about what had happened to me were overwhelming. Outraged "Clabe Taylor fans" deluged members of the House of Representatives and the Senate with emails and phone calls demanding justice for the author who had mysteriously disappeared.

During the two weeks the CIA held me in "protective custody", as they later termed it, Congress launched unprecedented investigations into the Agency and the administration. Impeachment proceedings against the president began almost immediately for "high crimes and misdemeanors". In other words, for systemic violations of the citizenry's constitutional rights. That meant mine.

When Mako Sloane contacted the CNN and Fox crews with an urgent proposal to film the operation to liberate me, they almost pissed themselves in their eagerness to scoop one another on the story. Both crews were waiting at the private airstrip in South Florida in designer camouflage fatigues, $75 t-shirts, and trendy combat boots even before Mako and his team arrived.

The rest is pretty much history. When we all returned to the United States after the rescue mission, the Gambrinius Company, owner of the Spoetzl Brewery where they make Shiner Beer, paid me a fortune to star in a series of beer commercials billing me as "The Most Interesting Man in Texas". With the money I was able to buy a 1,000 acre ranch in the Texas Hill Country near Bandera. Gretel comes to visit me regularly, and now my reputation as a "bad boy" excites her as much as my fabricated political confessions.

Goose attended the Southwestern Baptist Theological Seminary in Fort Worth. After graduation he became a minister and moved into the guest house on my ranch. Goose is a local celebrity and may soon have his own TV evangelical program. Personally, I think he abuses his position to ravish his young female parishioners. That's legal, however, and he is the envy of his Catholic peers.

Rigo, as always, can be found at my side. Unfortunately, even my fame and money were powerless in the face of his extraordinary -flatulence. Veterinary medicine could find no cure for his affliction, and he still farts in the most awkward of social settings.

Mako...well, Mako's another story altogether. He checks in now and then and we'll have a cold beer together and talk about old times. I gather he still rides his buckskin gelding every morning on that ranch outside of Laredo and tries to avoid the fame he earned as the most famous covert operative in the world. He still freelances for the state of Texas, and now that means he works for me. Oh yeah, I forgot to mention something. Six months ago a grassroots movement led by politically conscious "Clabe Taylor fans" put my name on the ballot in the Texas gubernatorial election. I won by a landslide without even campaigning. Well, it came as a surprise to me too.

I love the idea of having my own private intelligence agency, even though the "People's Intelligence and Security Service" (P.I.S.S.) is probably not the name I would have chosen. Anyway, Mako and James Brazzle are coming up from Laredo tomorrow. I have a few ideas I want to discuss with them. Things have been a little too quiet lately.

THE END

ABOUT THE AUTHOR

Clabe Taylor is a fifth-generation Texan and a former U.S. diplomat, who spent most of his career abroad in Europe and Latin America. He speaks Russian and Spanish in addition to his native English. You can read more about Clabe and his novels at www.clabetaylor.com, and you can follow him on Twitter and Facebook.

Creed Tucker is an old-school Texas cowboy who finds himself at the epicenter of a firestorm when a Mexican drug cartel moves its operations across the Rio Grande River. With the help of a team of retired CIA operatives, Creed learns of a bizarre conspiracy to seize political control of South Texas involving the drug cartel, the leading Mexican presidential candidate, and a high-ranking U.S. politician. Creed and his allies navigate their way through kidnappings, murders, and assassinations that threaten to unravel the very fabric of Texas society and destroy the Tucker family...only to discover that the real threat lies much closer to home.

Mako Sloane is a CIA legend, but his dizzying rise to stardom in Moscow is matched by his precipitous fall from grace after he discovers a secret that vested interests in both Russian and the U.S. want to keep quiet. Ten years after Mako's mysterious disappearance investigative reporter Max Crandall is writing Sloane's unauthorized biography. Max's research inadvertently dredges up ghosts from the past, and he finds himself the target of a manhunt as unidentified operatives try to derail his project. Max lures Mako out of self-imposed exile, and the two discover the truth behind a bizarre conspiracy that threatens to send the world spiraling into a superpower confrontation of unprecedented proportions.